The Dunn Deal

a novel

Catherine Leggitt

Ellechor Publishing House, LLC

Ellechor Publishing House
2431 NW Wessex Terrace,
Hillsboro, OR 97124

Copyright © 2012 by Catherine Leggitt
2012 Ellechor Publishing House Paperback Edition

The Dunn Deal/Leggitt, Catherine

ISBN: 978-1-937844-97-4

Library of Congress Control Number: 2011945175

Ellechor Publishing House,
2431 NW Wessex Terrace,
Hillsboro, OR 97124

Printed in the United States of America

www.ellechorpublishing.com

BOOKS BY CATHERINE LEGGITT

Hurray God! (Compilation)

CHRISTINE STERLING MYSTERY TRILOGY

Payne & Misery

The Dunn Deal

Parrish the Thought

To my husband, Bob with love.
Without your blessing and support,
writing would not only be impossible
but also no fun.

AUTHOR'S NOTE:

Although I used many actual street names and landmarks from scenic Nevada County, I took frequent liberties with their locations. Mixed with the real names, I also used names birthed solely in my imagination. I ask the readers' kind indulgence and understanding. THE DUNN DEAL is a work of fiction and in no way depicts any actual events or people living or dead. I found my Grass Valley neighbors to be considerate, helpful individuals, and my memories of living there are sweet.

Always choose truth.

"Then you will know the truth, and the truth will set you free."

~ John 8:32

"How many legs does a dog have if you call the tail a leg? Four; calling a tail a leg doesn't make it a leg."

~ Abraham Lincoln

"Post modernists believe that truth is myth, and myth, truth. This equation has its roots in pop psychology. The same people also believe that emotions are a form of reality. There used to be another name for this state of mind. It used to be called psychosis."

~ Brad Holland

Catherine Leggitt

1

CHAPTER ONE

The sketchy details of Baxter Dunn's death seeped into my brain while I struggled to organize them. A hideous image of his mangled body, strapped onto a stretcher and being dragged from a remote ravine, flashed through my mind. Shivers rocketed down my spine and blasted acid into my stomach. None of it made sense.

Shaking my head to clear the haze, I forced myself back to the present. Socially appropriate words passed my lips as I embraced Zora Jane Callahan, my best friend. "I'm so sorry." How inadequate they must sound. "So very, very sorry." I repeated, as if repetition made the words more effective.

Zora Jane blew her nose on a soggy tissue, honking a bit louder than normal for a classy woman. No one would hold that against her—not with her beloved son-in-law lying dead on a slab in the morgue.

Her words, with alternating sobs, rolled out like stormy waves. "What about the children? They need him. He's so good with them and they love him so much. What will they do without him?"

I'd never heard the name *Baxter Dunn* fall from Zora Jane's lips without words of praise or thanks to God attached. I mumbled another string of powerless expressions. "He was an extraordinary man." When I reached toward her, she dissolved into my arms.

As this latest wave of sorrow trickled away, she pulled back to grab another tissue. "I started praying for him when I rocked Kathleen to sleep as a baby. I asked God to prepare a man for my daughter. A God-fearing man to cherish her and bring out the best in her, to be the spiritual leader in their home, generous and compassionate. God answered every one of my prayers when he gave us Baxter."

I nodded, feeling older and more useless than my fifty-six years warranted.

Fresh tears flowed as she wailed, "What will Kathleen do now?"

I usually babble when stressed, but right now I could only wield a Kleenex box. *What words would be comforting?* I'd never be able to cope if this happened to one of my children. I held her and prayed she would soon remember God's sovereignty and ultimate goodness, although I couldn't see how even God could bring good from this tragedy.

As each new detail reached us, I wrestled anew with how to reconcile the reality. But how could anyone grasp the finality of such devastating news? The high-speed car chase. Falling off a high cliff and being impaled on a rusty spike. The terrible imagery of Baxter's untimely death lurked behind my eyelids, making me afraid to close my eyes. I might never sleep again.

Maybe it wasn't true. Maybe someone else's body had been discovered in that ravine. *Please, God. Make it all go away.*

Once I reached home, I pummeled my husband Jesse with my questions. "Where was God? What kind of God separates a father from his little children? From his family?"

Jesse held me, rocking from side to side. "These foothills should have been heaven on earth. That was the plan." Yet two murders had intruded on our lives in less than four short years. Who could have predicted such atrocities? Our nearest neighbor, Lila Payne, was murdered under bizarre circumstances and now the son-in-law of our best friends.

Assigning blame seemed imperative. It must be Jesse's fault. He convinced me that this quiet place in the country, fourteen wooded acres in California's Sierra Nevada foothills, would buffet us from the world's craziness. Retirement allowed us to leave the noise and pollution behind in Southern California but look what happened? We moved to a place where neighbors got murdered. Railing against Jesse, screaming and pounding my fists on his chest might make me feel better. But I knew it wasn't his fault. "Guess we wouldn't be safe anywhere these days."

Jesse answered with a slow shake of his head.

I scanned his face, noting that the sparkle had drained from his hazel eyes. This horrible event had aged him in mere hours. A solitary tear squeezed out the corner of one eye and trickled down his cheek. I reached up to wipe it away and my anger dissolved with the tear. *How could I be mad at such a tenderhearted man?*

The dreadful news of Baxter's death settled on our community like a dense, paralyzing fog. No one could conceive that such a thing could happen to this dedicated young deputy. Soft spoken, caring, productive; exactly the kind of man every mother hopes her son will become.

The Callahan's house in Grass Valley became the gathering place for the bereaved. We spent most of the next week there as family and friends came and went; the ebb and flow of tides riding out a storm. Baxter's mother and father, Ted and Ida Dunn, camped out in the spare room. His brother and sister slept on the couch and the living room floor. Kathleen Dunn clung to her in-laws, weeping most of the time.

Deep sorrow and grief blanketed the house, oddly punctuated by the chirping of children's laughter. Kathleen's sisters, Olivia and Jolie, did their best to keep the small brood under control, but it was a tough assignment. Children sense turmoil no matter how adults try to disguise it. Often the children acted out in ways that seemed counterproductive. Kathleen and Baxter's four, together with their combined nieces and nephews, gave new meaning to the term 'full house'.

To make myself useful, I took over keeping the coffeepot full and the dishes washed. I usually answered the door, giving the Callahan's uninterrupted time for receiving consolation from the steady stream of friends and coworkers who stopped by. Typical of Zora Jane's ultimate trust in God's goodness, after the initial shock wore off she did far more comforting than receiving comfort.

I opened their front door late Monday afternoon to find a group of visitors in crisply ironed, dark green deputy sheriff uniforms on the porch. Their smiles looked forced, their bodies rigid.

Hoping to ease their discomfort, I waved them in, producing a smile of my own. "Thank you for coming." Six officers from the Nevada County Sheriff's Office where Baxter worked for eleven years filed through the door.

The first deputy looked into my eyes. "How's the family holding up?"

"About as well as you'd expect. It's been a terrible shock. Helps to have so much support."

Just behind the group, a friend from church carried a covered casserole with both hands. "Hello, Christine." She grinned. "I'm glad you're here."

"Trying to be useful. Seems like precious little at a time like this. Can I take that for you?" I moved quickly to the kitchen and stuffed the casserole into Zora Jane's already bulging refrigerator, bumping the door closed with my hip. Mountains of bread and desserts covered the kitchen counters, with casseroles stacked in the freezer. There would be food for months.

The phone rang and Jesse beat me to it. His hearing had gotten so bad that I hovered nearby anyway in case he needed an interpreter.

"Callahan residence." He cupped one hand over the earpiece. "What? The newspaper, you say?"

I shook my head and sighed. Stubborn man. He wouldn't admit his hearing loss and refused to ask for help.

Jesse stared into the wall above the phone as if captions for the hearing impaired would appear. "No, I'm sorry. They're not available to make a statement. You probably know more about what's happening than we do."

He shifted the phone to his other ear. I stepped closer.

"Say again?" The furrows on his forehead deepened. "I suppose I could confirm what you already know." He rolled his eyes at me. "Correct. His wife spoke with him on Friday afternoon when he called from work to tell her he'd be home late. Baxter didn't come home Friday night. They found the body Saturday night."

Another round of listening. "Exactly. You know as much as we know." He bent toward the receiver as if he couldn't wait to hang up. "What's that?" He straightened, the vein in his neck bulging when he tightened his jaw. His voice sounded tense. "Naturally. An autopsy will be performed next week. The family can't schedule the funeral until that is completed." Jesse turned his back on the room. After thirty-nine years as his wife, I could tell when he neared the end of his patience. "Look, you idiot, I told you. We don't know anything else!"

Baxter's widow, Kathleen, lifted red-rimmed eyes when Jesse slammed the receiver into its cradle. "Thanks, Mr. Sterling. News people have been calling all day. The kids and I had to push our way out this morning through the crew camped outside our house."

The audacity! I wanted to stomp my foot. "You shouldn't have to deal with them right now. Why won't they leave you alone?"

Jesse's expression mirrored his frustration. "Vultures! That's what they are. Anything for a story."

Zora Jane's soft sigh fluttered out like a delicate bird. "I think we should pray for them."

Although surely most of the people in the room didn't feel any more like praying for the media than I did, we all hushed our talking and bowed our heads while Zora Jane led us.

"Dear Father, I pray blessings on these media people. Help them separate truth from rumor. Please give us patience to deal with them in kindness. Help us remember that we are your ambassadors here on earth. Even though we don't understand why this awful thing has happened, we know you can bring good out of it. Use our suffering to glorify your name. Please, dear Lord, help us stay out of your way while you work."

Pastor Gregg, the senior pastor from our church, continued the prayer. "Lord God, you know how injured this family is. The Bible says You care so much about our sorrow that You record each tear in Your book. Please, Lord, bind up these wounds tonight. Bring comfort and peace to this family."

When he finished, Zora Jane extended her hand. "Thank you for staying all afternoon, pastor. It means a lot to have you here."

Ed Callahan, Zora Jane's husband, clapped the minister on the shoulder. "Yes, we appreciate it. You bring a comforting presence wherever you go."

Not knowing how else to help, I picked up the coffeepot and wandered among the small groups gathered around the great room. Subdued discussion gradually resumed.

Kathleen's younger sister, Olivia, sat in one of two recliners, holding a small boy with curly red hair. The third sister, Jolie, perched on the thick upholstered arm beside her.

Olivia scowled at her mother. "Sometimes I don't understand how she can pray for evil people. They don't care about our pain. Why should we care about the media?"

"She's right, though," Jolie said. "Just because we're hurting doesn't mean we stop being witnesses. People are watching to see how we'll react. Jesus experienced unimaginable pain on the cross, but he never stopped thinking of others. Remember? He asked John to care for his mother and took time to comfort the thief."

Sounds like Jolie inherited her mother's heart.

I raised the coffeepot, but they shook their heads. I continued on my round through the house.

Baxter's parents reclined on the sofa, Ida's head leaning against Ted's shoulder. Their faces sagged as if weighted down by lead sinkers.

A woman I didn't know asked, "You have no idea why he went into those mountains?"

Ted shook his head. "No one knows."

Ida straightened and placed her delicate pale hand on Ted's arm. "Remember that abandoned mine shaft where the boys used to play when we visited the Williams family out in Cedar Ridge years ago? Do you suppose that's the same location where they found Baxter?"

"Could be." Ted sandwiched her hand tenderly between his. "But I thought they sealed those old tunnels long ago. They're dangerous. People get hurt there." Fresh tears surged into Ted's eyes.

Ida embraced him.

I moved towards Ed Callahan, who was wearing his typical plaid golf pants and colorful golf shirt. He leaned against the wall near the French doors, talking with two officers I didn't recognize. They appeared to be ten or fifteen years older than Baxter, so I assumed they weren't rookies. I took note of the three gold chevrons decorating the sleeve of the man closest to Ed. *Does that make him a captain?*

Ed was in the middle of a conversation. "…County. Is that standard procedure?"

The officer with the chevrons nodded. "Nevada County's a small office. We don't have morgue facilities or a forensic pathologist either. We contract with Placer County. Toxicology requests go all the way to Pennsylvania. Takes a long time to process them. It's probably quite different working in San Francisco."

"You bet." Ed Callahan had retired from the San Francisco police force. His sea blue eyes peered over his spectacles. "That's the good news as well as the bad."

Seeing me hovering nearby with the coffee pot, he held out his cup. I filled it.

The others declined.

Janet from church huddled near Zora Jane in the dining room. Another lady I didn't know bent close, compassion radiating from her face. Zora Jane swayed slightly while she talked, arms hugging her chest over the top of a brown sweater set with turquoise flowers cascading down one side.

Tsk. Such a shallow thing to notice her attire at this tragic time. Unfortunately, my fascination with Zora Jane's wardrobe plagued me constantly. Tall and willowy, Zora Jane could drape a gunnysack over herself and still look smashing. Instead, she always wore outfits that perfectly matched, right down to the shoes.

Amazed, I shook my head. Even in the midst of her grief she'd managed to throw together a stunningly coordinated outfit. Turquoise flowers like the ones on the sweater set, but smaller, danced around a flared brown skirt. Brown flats with floppy turquoise flowers completed the ensemble. *Did she attach the flowers herself?*

With a burst of resolve, I squelched the urge to race down the hall and peek into her closet. Instead, I pulled myself toward a group of law enforcement officers hunched in the hallway. One of them, Deputy Sam Colter, I'd met six months earlier during the investigation into the murder of my neighbor, Lila Payne. I didn't like Deputy Colter then, and time had not improved my opinion of him. He still had that air of superiority and disdain. The lone woman in the group, Deputy Laura Elliot, had filed our missing person's report on Lila. The other two were strangers.

I lifted the coffeepot toward them, but they appeared not to notice. I wasn't offended, since at roughly five-feet it would be easy to overlook me.

Deputy Elliot spoke in hushed tones. "You've been out there. Did he fall into that ravine or did someone push him?"

Push him? I inched closer.

Deputy Colter shook his head, speaking just above a whisper in an affected robotic cadence. "It appears that he slipped on loose rocks at the top. It is highly unlikely anyone caused his fall. The evidence supports that conclusion."

The expression of one of the strangers registered a flicker of surprise. The name tag on his uniform read *G. Rogers*. "You've concluded that the fall caused his death? Aren't you a bit premature?"

Deputy Colter peered into his coffee cup as if consulting tealeaves. "Placer County forensics will draw their own conclusions based on their investigation, of course. I merely state my personal theory based on twenty years' experience. Dunn slipped at the top where piles of loose rocks render footing unstable. At the bottom of that ravine is a dump site for rusty metal tools and machinery from the old mining operation. In the fall, he impaled his body on a metal spike. C-O-D appears to be obvious."

The initials threw me for a moment. *C-O-D? Cause of death?*

Perhaps I let out an involuntary, "Oh!" when I winced because they all stopped talking at once to stare at me.

I blinked from one to the other in turn. "Uh, w-would you like more coffee?"

They shook their heads in unison.

Deputy Elliot handed me her mug. "No, thanks. Gotta shove off." She scurried down the hall without a backwards glance.

Forgetting my waitress mission for the moment, I focused on Deputy Colter. "Why did he go out there in the first place? Was he chasing someone?"

Colter raised one eyebrow. His beady brown eyes peered around his rather substantial nose as if he'd just noticed an insect. I remembered how annoyed I'd been during our previous encounters. *Does he remember me, or is he just debating about whether to share information with a peon?*

Seconds passed while he tapped his forefinger on his mug. "Official findings have not been released, as I said. It is far too early in the investigation. I merely report preliminary facts I gathered from visual inspection of the scene."

"But why did he go out there?" I repeated.

Another deputy spoke. His name tag identified him as *E. Oliver.* "I was at the office when Baxter got a call. He left just after five."

Colter continued. "According to his last communication, Deputy Dunn had answered the call and started for home when he stopped a van."

There he goes again, that condescending tone. He must think I'm terribly stupid. I spoke slowly, enunciating each word in case Colter didn't understand English. "Where was he?"

Deputy Oliver answered. "Out on Highway 20. Just past Half-Moon House."

Deputy Colter sent him a glare.

Was that a breach of code? "Why?"

Colter's fingers drummed his coffee mug, perhaps stalling while he decided whether to answer or not. Almost everything they'd shared so far, except Deputy Colter's theory about how Baxter's death actually occurred, I'd already heard on the news or from the family.

No one answered, leaving my question hanging in the air. Maybe they didn't know what I was asking, so I clarified "Why did he stop the van?"

Deputy Colter heaved a dramatic sigh before answering, "His final radio communication came in at 21:25, that is 9:25 pm. At that time, he reported following a speeding black van. When dispatch ran the plates, they came up stolen."

I tried to locate Half-Moon House on my mental map. "Where did they find his body?"

When Colter paused, one of the others spoke. "In the ravine just west of the main entrance to the old Star Mine."

Deputy Rogers's forehead scrunched as if puzzling over how to fit the pieces together. "That's at least ten miles north of Half-Moon House."

I mimicked the frown. None of it made any sense to me. "Ten miles is pretty far to chase someone. How did he get way over there?"

In that instant, they all became mute again.

I searched each face. "Did he drive there?"

Blank stares.

"Where's his patrol car?"

Deputy Colter's eyes darted from face to face before he turned to me. "The patrol car has not been located yet."

I wanted to grab his shoulders and shake information out of him. "The morning news reported that he didn't have his weapon or his radio with him. Why would that be?"

The others observed Deputy Colter with eyebrows raised. Rogers crossed his arms over his chest. The tempo of Colter's thrumming increased.

Deputy Oliver stared at the carpet. "Maybe he removed them when he went off duty."

Deputy Colter stopped drumming. "Or they fell off when he went over the side of the cliff." He glowered down from his lofty position at least a foot above my head. "We cannot ascertain any of this with accuracy yet. There must be a thorough investigation."

A minute suspicion wriggled into my consciousness, fueled by Colter's evasiveness. More a feeling than a conscious thought, I couldn't identify exactly what troubled me. "What time did he fall?"

Deputy Colter answered a little too quickly, as if he had anticipated my question. "Around midnight. Of course, you understand they will pinpoint T-O-D when they do the autopsy."

Time of death?

His small eyes bored into mine with renewed fervor as if I'd become a person of interest. *Would that be a P-O-I?*

I focused on Colter's shiny shoes shifting on the carpet while suspicion tickled my brain. "Something just doesn't feel right." As soon as the words left my lips, I wished I'd censored that thought before I spoke. The *feeling* explanation never worked with men.

Deputy Colter snapped into a military at-ease position, feet spread, and arms akimbo. "You are Christine Sterling, are you not?"

I nodded, dreading his next words.

He glared pompously down at me, as if about to pull a dead cockroach from his soup. "I remember you from the Payne case. Look, Mrs. Sterling, an officer of the law has died under unexplained circumstances. The sheriff's office takes the death of its officers very seriously. This is no matter for amateur sleuths. We will handle the investigation in a thoroughly prudent manner. You will not interfere in any way. Is that clear?"

My frustration trailed out in a sigh. *Not a matter for amateur sleuths, eh?* He didn't know me very well.

Once that suspicious feeling surfaced, I simply couldn't let it go.

CHAPTER TWO

Thursday afternoon, I backed my Jeep out of Zora Jane's driveway and nearly ran over the Channel 11 news reporter who jumped out of his van to rush me with a microphone. A spry cameraman in a t-shirt followed behind with his camera pointed at my face.

The squeal of my brakes had barely subsided when the news guy shoved his microphone at my face through the window I'd opened to see whether I'd done them any serious damage.

"Has there been a break in the Deputy Dunn murder?"

I wanted to say, "Don't be an idiot!" But it didn't come out. Instead, I said, "Do you know I would have hit you both if I hadn't been able to stop? Why would you run behind a moving car like that?"

"Can you get me inside to interview the family?"

Might as well be talking to the television. I tried his tactic by answering a question with a completely unrelated question. "What do you mean murder?"

He leaned toward me. "The sheriff's office is currently investigating a suspicious meeting Deputy Dunn had on the night he died, a meeting with known drug dealers. Was Deputy Dunn a drug user?"

"Oh, for pity sakes! You're making me wish I had run over you! He was an officer of the law. They're supposed to round up the bad guys. That means they have to *talk* to bad guys sometimes. You'll grasp at anything to sensationalize this story, won't you?"

I shoved his microphone out of my way and started to roll up the window. "I've never understood why news pieces with no redeeming value grab the media's interest and won't go away while stories that benefit the public get no press at all. Can you explain that to me?"

The microphone moved toward me again. Since I considered my question rhetorical, I closed the window as fast as I could and accelerated.

The news guy ran alongside my car for a short distance, huffing and puffing. Through the window I heard, "Does the family wish to make a statement about Deputy Dunn's involvement in the drug trafficking industry?"

By Sunday, strange rumors concerning Baxter's death flooded the airwaves. Each day a new, scathing headline on the front page of the local newspaper detailed every minutiae of the investigation. Ed, Zora Jane, and Jesse agreed not to read or listen to the distorted news stories. I half-heartedly nodded along with their decision, wondering how much information I could accidentally overhear by pretending not to listen to the news.

Fifty miles away, Sacramento papers carried the story. I tried to ignore them at first, and then I'd read a few lines when Jesse wasn't looking, always sorry afterwards that I had indulged. The articles were riddled with misleading statements and contradictions. One headline proclaimed, "Botched Drug Deal Tied to Death of Deputy," asserting a conclusive connection between Baxter and drug dealing. "Late Night Tryst Contributes to Deputy's Death," implied that Baxter participated in an affair with an unnamed woman. "Search for Mystery Woman," requested information from the public concerning the woman in question.

Other articles contained plain bald lies. For example, that between his last communication and the time Baxter fell off the cliff, he had engaged in various questionable activities that included buying and selling illegal substances, consorting with known criminals, and accepting bribes. Supposedly this explained why he didn't radio headquarters during that time.

For some unknown reason, the media seemed to unanimously conspire to defame Baxter's reputation. By suggesting that the Nevada County Sheriff's Department investigated his illegal or immoral activity as well as his death, they planted the notion that his own guilty actions precipitated his death. That old lawyer trick of turning the victim into the perpetrator. I just couldn't understand the motive. *Why were they collaborating against Baxter?*

Friday morning, Zora Jane and I sat on the deck at the back of her grand yellow Victorian house enjoying the sunshine and steaming cups of decaf. Jesse left early to ride his horse. Ed had gone into town. The girls attempted to return to some semblance of normalcy. Of course, normal had forever been changed for Kathleen, but she was anxious to get back into her routine, mostly for the sake of the children.

Where Zora Jane and I sat, a view of the sloping pasture spread before us like a idyllic tableau. Several sheep, two Jerusalem donkeys, and Zora Jane's three-legged goat, Eileen, wandered among spring grasses, munching contentedly. Farther down, Mustang Hill Road cut through the little valley between the Callahan's hill and ours. I could see the driveway that trailed up to Lila Payne's former residence. Our small part in solving her murder and getting her killer sent to prison ended last fall, but the abandoned gray and white house still scarred the landscape, reminding us of inhumanity's painful consequences.

A little ways up the hill, I could barely make out the back of our three-story log house. Jesse's barn and fenced practice arena peeked through the hundred year old oaks; new lime-green leaves covering the branches. Verdant spring grasses sprouted on the hillsides with wildflowers popping up among them.

Zora Jane leaned back in her chair and sighed. A vision of spring in her baby blue running suit, she wore tennis shoes with blue accents. A matching headband held back her curly reddish hair. Underneath the jacket, a chartreuse shell with a scattering of baby blue polka dots peeked out.

"The Lord has created another beautiful day." She inhaled a long draught of fresh spring air. "How can evil exist on a day as perfect as today?"

Watching her pleasure, I couldn't help smiling. "Makes you feel as if you could tackle the world."

She tilted her chin back and closed her eyes. "It does, doesn't it?"

"Now's the perfect time to deal with those funeral details we still need to finish." I consulted the folder we'd filled with plans. "There's not much left." Most of the decisions had already been finalized through family consensus.

"A shame about his badge." Zora Jane frowned at the page where I'd written *Find badge* in bold letters at the top. "I wish we could've found it. Seems like he should be wearing it on his uniform at the funeral."

"I wish we had his badge."

Zora Jane straightened. "Did you hear something?"

I sat as still as death, straining to hear. At first, not a sound. Then, a rumbling like a buffalo stampede growing louder. We turned to see what caused such a racket.

Not buffalo. A herd of reporters came into sight, rounding the corner at a fast clip. Most were strangers, but in the center of the pack I recognized the Channel 11 news guy's pudgy face, jowls pinned back in the wind while he hurried along.

As each one scrambled for position, they jostled each other, grunting more like wild pigs than buffalo. Audio-visual gear dangled from their shoulders. Black microphones stuck out on all sides like porcupine quills.

Even before anyone spoke, three vehicles screeched into the driveway. Their logos advertised news stations in Sacramento.

"Oh, no! Something bad has happened."

Zora Jane turned toward the approaching throng. "Dear Lord, give us patience and kindness."

Out of the mishmash of voices that erupted when the herd surrounded us, I caught only two phrases: *patrol car* and *Rawlins Lake.*

Zora Jane held up one hand to plead for silence. "Slow down and speak one at a time. Please. We can't understand what you're saying."

Mr. Pudgy Cheeks panted. Hard to say if it was from over exertion or extreme excitement." The patrol car, Deputy Dunn's. They found it at Rawlins Lake. *In* the lake." He stuck his black padded microphone in Zora Jane's face. "Care to comment on the murder of Deputy Dunn? What about Dunn's involvement in the drug trafficking industry?"

Zora Jane blinked. "I'm sorry. We know nothing about this."

Murder? Who made that leap? I shot a look at my friend. Her eyes had glazed over and her mouth had formed a puckered *O*. I hadn't mentioned anything about the news guy's accusations or the newspaper articles to Zora Jane, figuring that official findings would be communicated to the family in due time. Why hadn't they contacted Kathleen first? Oh, yes. She and the children took a break from the reporters at the family cabin in Lake Tahoe.

Someone shoved another microphone in Zora Jane's face. "Can you comment on Deputy Dunn's clandestine rendezvous at a local bar with an unknown woman the night of his murder?"

A third microphone invaded her private space. "Can you confirm Dunn's death was a murder-for-hire operation? Who wanted Deputy Dunn out of the way?"

"What?" I couldn't believe my ears. "Don't be ridiculous! You're talking about a fine young man, a Christian man with an exemplary record of service in Nevada County."

They all started yammering again. Zora Jane looked as if she wanted to answer. Before she could speak, I grabbed her arm and yanked her into the house. I had to shove someone's microphone out of the way to slam the French doors shut.

"Call the sheriff's office," I said, securing the lock. "Get Colter out here. Somebody's got to tell us what's going on."

❧

To avoid the press, we barricaded ourselves inside the house for the rest of the afternoon. Blinds and drapes remained closed with only a few lights turned on which left us sitting mostly in the dark, praying and talking in hushed tones. When I peeked out a window, I spied parked news vans with cameras, microphones, and satellite equipment poised in readiness should someone venture outside.

After a few hours, Ed returned. I called Jesse and he hurried over a few minutes later. From his scowling expression, I gather he didn't relish shoving his way through the growing mob.

About dusk, Deputy Colter finally arrived.

I met him at the front door and tried to keep the sarcasm out of my tone. "Deputy Colter. How nice of you to come." I didn't say, 'finally,' although I thought it. I swatted a couple of microphones out of the way so I could slam the front door.

He apparently heard the *finally* in my voice because he looked down on me with disdain when he removed his hat. "I came as soon as I could. We have a huge operation in place to work this complicated case."

Ed hurried into the entryway, followed by Jesse and Zora Jane. "Just get to the point, Deputy, if you don't mind. What's this about the patrol car?"

Deputy Colter cleared his throat. "Deputy Dunn's patrol car has been pulled out of Rawlins Lake."

"And...what about it?" Ed asked.

Deputy Colter's smallish brown eyes scanned our faces. "It appears that Baxter was not alone."

What a gift for the obvious! I stepped closer. "Who found the car? Rawlins Lake is nowhere near where Baxter's body turned up. It's not near Half-Moon House, either. What made them look in Rawlins Lake?"

A quick frown popped out before Deputy Colter rearranged his professional mask over it. What was that? Dread? Reluctance? Unhappiness? *Why would Colter be unhappy about this development?*

Deputy Colter pursed his lips. "Someone phoned in a tip."

Jesse looked confused. "Did he say something about a fat lip?"

"No." I turned so Jesse could see my lips. "A tip."

"A tip?" Jesse frowned. "From who?"

Colter's blank expression magnified his evasiveness.

Ed stepped right in his face. "Are you gonna make us drag this out of you?"

Colter dropped his gaze to the hat he gripped with both hands and fired words rapidly. "People jog around the lake every day. A jogger noticed broken weeds and tire tracks running into the lake. He saw a large white object in the water." He lifted a glance to Ed. "The patrol car has a white top."

"So, it's a homicide investigation now?" Ed spoke louder than necessary. Steam drifted above Ed's ears. At least, I thought I saw steam.

The abrupt increase in volume blasted Deputy Colter back a step. "Nothing is conclusive at this time."

"Well, obviously Baxter chased somebody with stolen plates who then abducted him and took him to the top of that hill." The level and speed of Ed's voice continued to rise. "Someone pushed him to his death and ran his patrol car in Rawlins Lake. Good grief, man. I haven't even been to the site and I know that much." He turned to us for confirmation. "Isn't that the way you see it?"

We nodded our heads. That's exactly how it looked to me.

Deputy Colter shifted from one foot to the other. His fingers drummed his hat nervously while he lowered his gaze. "I…cannot make a definite statement about that. I came to confirm our latest discovery to you. At your request."

I stepped forward. "Okay then, how about the rumor that Baxter attended a meeting with drug dealers the night he died?"

Ed flashed a look of surprise. Jesse's mouth gaped open. But when I saw the pain in Zora Jane's face, I felt sorry I'd blurted that question out without preparing them in advance. "I—I heard that from a member of the press."

"The news people will stop at nothing to create a story. Disregard anything you hear from them."

Ed scratched the back of his head. "Are you saying he didn't attend such a meeting?"

Colter's expression said he wanted to run away and hide. "No. I… simply cannot comment. Not during an ongoing investigation."

I pushed closer until I stood directly in front of him. "Well then, how about the black van? The one Baxter stopped. Any progress locating that?"

"No." Deputy Colter's head snapped back again. "The black van has not been located."

Jesse moved to Colter's other side. "What about his belongings? His pistol, badge, and radio? Were they in the patrol car?"

"No." Colter turned to leave. Perhaps he feared we meant to ambush him.

I followed. "So that means the man in the black van probably has them."

Ed followed. "Or they might be where the original skirmish occurred."

Zora Jane hurried to catch up. "Are they looking for the black van, Deputy?"

Striding a few long steps, Colter made it to the door. Hand on the knob, he heaved a deep sigh before answering. "The way it appears to me, the driver of the black van panicked and tried to dispose of the patrol car." He replaced his hat and mumbled, "My condolences."

We watched Colter navigate through the barrage of news people, elbow crooked to shield his face.

Ed slammed the door, then scratched his head. "Didn't he say exactly what I said?"

Zora Jane looked puzzled as well. "Is he calling this a homicide?"

Jesse stared at the door, brows furrowed. "It isn't homicide if Baxter fell accidentally. But if it wasn't homicide, why would someone sink his patrol car?"

I tried to shake the confusion that fogged my brain. "Why didn't Baxter radio in a report after he stopped the van?"

Ed planted one hand on his hip, frowning. "If you ask me, there's a lot more to this story than we've been told. Brace yourself, folks. It's going to be a bumpy ride."

Colter's strange behavior fueled that suspicious feeling now growing exponentially in my mind. *Who called in the anonymous tip about the location of Baxter's body? Who occupied the black van? Why couldn't anyone find these people?*

Fed by my insatiable speculation, that pinprick of doubt soon transformed into complete disbelief. Something smelled rotten in Nevada County, and the officials sworn to uphold the law weren't moving toward a resolution. At least, they weren't reporting any progress to us.

Saturday morning when I went to drive Zora Jane into town to run errands, just to get her out of the house for a few hours, I ran into the Channel 11 news guy again. He leaned against his van in the Callahan driveway looking quite bored. On my way into the house, I stopped to chat with him. He perked up as his microphone reflexively lifted toward my mouth.

I backed away automatically. "Last week you said Baxter attended a drug deal the night he died. Remember?"

His eyes lit with anticipation. "Do you wish to make a statement regarding Deputy Dunn's drug addiction?"

"Don't be ridiculous."

I attacked the microphone, pulling it out of my face, and held it down with both hands. "I want to know where you got that stupid idea about the drugs. Did you make that up?"

He pulled himself to his full height, which was not much taller than me, as if I'd thoroughly insulted him. "Make it up? What kind of journalist do you take me for?"

"Well then, where did you get that information?"

"Surely you're aware I can't divulge my sources. Not even under threat of imprisonment. It's my right under the Constitution."

"I didn't know freedom of the press covered gossip mongers. Don't you deal primarily with fiction? Anyway, I'm certainly not threatening imprisonment. I would, but I don't have the authority." A heavy sigh escaped. "I'm only asking if Baxter was involved in a drug deal. Fact or fiction?"

"Madam!" He clutched his chest in indignation. "You cut me to the core! Fiction? Gossip mongers? Indeed! I am a journalist."

His blatant evasion annoyed me so much that I stepped right into his face. "Let's cut the banter."

My nose so close to his must have startled him into submission. "No, of course not. It's one hundred percent true. Baxter Dunn was observed consorting with known drug dealers the night of his death. He purchased illegal narcotics from them."

Once again, I stifled the desire to grab him and shake the stuffing out of him. "Who told you that?"

"Someone at the sheriff's office leaked it. Look, lady, I can't tell you who." With gentle fingers, he extracted the microphone from my fingers and stepped an arm's length away as if he knew how close I was to thrashing him soundly. "I *won't* tell you who."

"Just give me a hint then. Who would leak that information? Why would they tell *you?*"

He shrugged, dramatically. "You're not scoring points by implying I'm unworthy to receive information. Anyway, I can't tell you. My entire profession rests on this right. However, I will tell you why I'm interested." He bent to my level. "Baxter Dunn wasn't officially part of the Narcotics Task Force. He wasn't assigned to investigate drugs. He was off duty. So, what was he doing at that meeting? Why did he make a purchase? Most intriguing of all, why is all of this being officially denied by the sheriff's office?"

I fell back in surprise, questions echoing in my head. *Where were these vicious lies coming from?*

3

CHAPTER THREE

While I made dinner Saturday night, I flicked on television for the evening news. A somber-faced female news anchor reported, "…further development this weekend in the investigation into the suspicious death of Deputy Sheriff Baxter Dunn in Nevada City. The patrol car Deputy Dunn drove the night of his death was located last Friday at the bottom of Rawlins Lake."

Footage of the green and white patrol car being dragged from Rawlins Lake flashed across the screen.

"Rawlins Lake is twelve miles south of the ravine where the body of Deputy Dunn was found on March 14. Sources confirm that his death occurred around midnight last Friday, March 13. So far, investigation has uncovered possible misconduct on the part of Deputy Dunn and a group of his friends." A smiling picture of Baxter Dunn in uniform flickered onto the screen.

"Oh, come on," I said to the TV. "Just give the facts without the spin."

Swiss steak bubbled on the stove. I lifted the lid off the pan and used my wooden spoon to rearrange slabs of tenderizing beef. I intended to change the channel, but before I replaced the lid the news lady continued, "We go now to Nevada City with a live report from our correspondent Leonard Pinzer." My favorite news reporter appeared, planted in front of the Nevada County Sheriff's Office. "Leonard, how is the investigation progressing?"

Mr. Pudgy-face, I now knew his name was Leonard, replied, "Thanks, Kelly. Here at the Nevada County Sheriff's Department a massive investigation is underway. Sheriffs from Yuba County and Placer County have offered assistance. As reported, the patrol car Deputy Dunn drove the night of his death has been located. Instead of providing answers, however, the patrol car raises more questions. Why was it at the bottom of Rawlins Lake? How did it get so far from Deputy Dunn's body? What about the time line for the bizarre events of that fateful night?"

A clip of Baxter's draped body being removed from the ravine rolled as Leonard continued.

"It's beginning to look as if the death of Deputy Dunn is only the tip of a huge dirty iceberg. Two and a half hours are unaccounted for from the last communication Deputy Dunn made at nine twenty-five until his death at midnight."

The scene changed to shots of the Nevada County Sheriff's Office. "Does the sheriff's department know more than they are saying about his whereabouts prior to his death? Is the sheriff's department covering for its own? Is this a case of good ol' boys shielding the misconduct of one of their own?"

Leonard's grim face reappeared. "We'll stay in Nevada City waiting for further developments. Reporting for News 11, this is Leonard Pinzer. Back to you, Kelly."

I snapped the television off in disgust. "I can't believe it!"

Molly, our thirteen year old border collie, lifted her head from where she'd been napping nearby. Her eyes filled with sympathy and her tail thumped the kitchen floor.

Jesse rushed into the kitchen. "What?"

"I was talking to the television."

He took me by the arm and turned me toward him so he could see my face. "What did you say?"

Impatience with his inability to hear washed over me. Repeating everything had become quite tedious. "Nothing. I didn't say anything. I was just talking to the television."

"I'm sorry, Christine." Jesse's expression deflated. "I'm sorry I can't hear you. If you would quit mumbling, I could hear you just fine."

Of course then I felt like a complete heel. "It wasn't anything important. I'm sorry for being impatient with you."

He dropped my arm. His hunched shoulders tugged at my heart.

"I'm frustrated with those news people, that's all. They report Baxter and his friends' involvement in illegal acts as if it's the truth, but they never name the friends or specify what they were supposedly involved in. Someone is just out to smear Baxter's good name."

Jesse lifted the lid on the Swiss steak and sniffed. "I thought we weren't going to listen to the news."

"Right." I pulled veggies from the refrigerator to make a salad. "I'm curious about this case, though. A lot of what they've told us doesn't make sense. And only the news people seem concerned about that."

Jesse stuffed a chunk of celery in his mouth and munched. "What doesn't make sense?"

"What triggered the search for Baxter on Saturday morning? And the time line. Baxter called Kathleen about five o'clock on Friday and told her he was on his way to check something out and probably wouldn't be home in time for dinner."

Jesse watched me intently, reading my lips. "Uh-huh."

"Kathleen usually has dinner ready around six-thirty because Baxter's shift ends at six. The kids go to bed about eight-thirty. That's been their schedule since the kids were born. Zora Jane says they rarely deviate."

"Right. They're big on routine." He gestured for me to get to the point.

"So, Baxter went somewhere from five until nine twenty-five when he called dispatch to check on license plates from a black van. Where was he? I don't think he meant to be gone that long. If he had, he would've said it differently. He wouldn't say, 'I probably won't make it home in time for dinner.' He'd say, 'It's going to be late by the time I get home. Don't wait for me.' Something like that. 'Cause they like to put the kids to bed together."

"Pretty thin logic, Christine. How do you know what he might say? Do you read minds now? Not to mention everything you're talking about is hearsay. You could be wrong about his exact words. Don't think you could take any of that to court."

I ignored his negativity, knowing I had it right. "Another thing, where did he go between the time he stopped the car and the time he went off that cliff? Two and a half hours are missing. Driving from Half Moon House to that ravine doesn't take two and a half hours. Even if he drove to Rawlins Lake and back, it wouldn't take that long. I think the news guy is right. Someone needs to account for the missing time. Why aren't they on that?" I whacked the lettuce in half with my big knife, chopping the pieces like a Benihana chef.

"Hang on there, Slick. Just because the media isn't reporting it doesn't mean the officials aren't investigating it. You're jumping to conclusions again. And don't get any ideas about helping the authorities out, either. We're retired. Besides we're too old to go traipsing around investigating especially when we have no authority to do that. It's only been a week since Baxter died. The sheriff's office is perfectly capable of getting to the bottom of this without your help. You promised you'd stay out of this, remember?"

I made no such promise, but rather than argue the point and get into an argument, I slammed the refrigerator door. *Jumping to conclusions, eh? Would they ever get to the bottom of this without someone lighting a fire under them?* I had my doubts. And I surely wasn't too old to start a fire either.

Was I just waiting for a chance to jump in? If forced to take a lie detector test, I'd have to admit that I was. At any rate, right then and there, I started looking for everything I could find that might be connected to Baxter's death.

Being too technology challenged to research on the Internet, I went to the county library. Before Jesse retired, I worked as a librarian and knew my way around the Dewey Decimal System quite well. Although most information is now stored on the computer, I managed to find hard copies of old newspapers with stories pertaining to Baxter's death from Friday, March thirteenth onward. I read the local paper and Sacramento papers as well.

At home and in the Jeep, I listened to news reports on different channels when Jesse wasn't around. I also started praying for truth, asking God to show me what to do. Surely there must be something.

Over the next week and a half, I concentrated night and day on Baxter's death. Someone needed to retrace Baxter's steps. His whereabouts before and after he stopped the black van would surely be illuminating. Finding the black van and its occupants, along with Baxter's missing radio, gun, and ammo seemed crucial, but how to accomplish either one baffled me.

The rumor about the *alleged* clandestine rendezvous must figure into the equation since it kept coming up. Someone at Half Moon House might be willing to talk to me. Worth a try.

Deputy Colter definitely knew something he refused to tell. Maybe I could get him to talk, ongoing investigation notwithstanding. I called and left a message for him, saying I'd like to make an appointment.

⟡

Three weeks after Baxter died, the day for his funeral finally came. Although the atmosphere couldn't be described as joyful, a certain feeling of celebration for a life well lived permeated the space. That's usually the case when a Christian dies. Baxter's many good works would not gain him eternal life, of course. Nevertheless, we were as certain as we could be, based on his public confession of faith in Jesus' atonement and the way he lived his life. The fruit of his faith showed in his deep love for people and commitment to help as many as he could.

Baxter Dunn would be sorely missed. His death left a huge hole that no one else could ever fill. However, the certainty that he had gone to be with God eased the sadness a little. I imagined God smiling as He welcomed Baxter to heaven saying, "Well done, faithful servant. Enter the joy of eternal rest."

Our little sanctuary in Nevada City overflowed with mourners come to pay last respects. Deputy Colter was noticeably absent, causing me to wonder why.

After the pews filled, folding chairs were set along the aisles to accommodate more grieving friends. An impressive number of officers wearing crisply ironed uniforms crowded together in the middle section with hats in their laps and shoes so highly polished I could see my reflection in them.

Multicolored floral arrangements lined the platform despite the family's request that donations to Baxter's latchkey ministry be made in lieu of flowers. So many different kinds of flowers surrounded the coffin that the air smelled like a florist shop.

Jesse and I found seats behind the family. In front of us, Ed and Zora Jane flanked Kathleen. She held her youngest child in her lap. Zora Jane cradled another of the Dunn children. The remaining two huddled together at Zora Jane's side.

Ed chose a serious black suit for the service, foregoing his usual plaid golf pants. His bald head looked extra shiny. With her typical stylish flair, Zora Jane reflected the tone of the occasion outfitted in a somber black sheath with a leopard print belt. From a few rows behind, I admired the prominent black flower waving atop her black hat.

Pastor Gregg began the service with prayer and Scripture reading. In his booming radio voice, he read familiar words of comfort from Psalm 23. Then he turned to 1 Corinthians 15 to read about the fate of those who have already died in faith when Jesus returns the second time. Those verses give me chills. I imagine my mama coming in the clouds with Jesus as I listen.

Baxter's older brother, Max, read a lovely poem he wrote about their relationship. By the time he finished, people were reaching for the Kleenex boxes the women's ministry had left in the pews. Baxter's sister, Alexia, sang a beautiful old song with a contemporary arrangement about going where the roses never fade. Painting a lovely picture of the gardens of heaven, the song made me smile.

Following the song, one of Baxter's fellow officers spoke about the fine job Baxter did for the county. I recognized him as Deputy Oliver, whom I'd met at Zora Jane's house. Tall and blond, he represented American law enforcement in a wholesome, handsome package. He appeared to be somewhere around Baxter's age, in his mid to late thirties.

He gave statistics about Baxter's career. I didn't realize Baxter had made so many arrests or been decorated for so many selfless acts of bravery. Deputy Oliver got a little choked up recalling pranks they'd played. Like the April Fool's Day Baxter squeezed toothpaste onto the toilet seat of the men's locker room commode then hid to watch the reactions of his victims. Or the hours of surveillance time they passed making up names and situations to prank call the rookie lady dispatcher.

When he finished speaking, Deputy Oliver asked if anyone else wanted to recount a story of Baxter's impact on his or her life.

People trailed to the podium and recounted how Baxter helped members of the community. They also spoke of his love for children and the elderly, of his patience, gentleness, and generosity.

After we'd been there nearly two hours, Pastor Gregg returned to the podium and led us as we sang Baxter's favorite hymn, "How Great Thou Art," before he dismissed us with a final prayer.

The officers provided an impressive escort to the cemetery in their polished green and white patrol cars, lights flashing and sirens wailing.

We stood with the crowd around Baxter's grave while a group of his fellow deputies lowered his coffin into the ground. Kathleen and the children pulled red roses out of one of the arrangements to throw on the casket. Many people followed their example. Even Jesse and I contributed.

While people in the line waited for their turn to toss flowers, I noticed Deputy Oliver as he joined a circle of men in uniforms. Such an opportunity couldn't be passed by.

"I'm going to talk to someone," I said to Jesse.

Jesse turned his good ear toward me and frowned. "What?"

"I'm going over there to speak to someone," I repeated.

His frown deepened. "It sounded like you said your hair was squeaking like a siren. You didn't say that, did you?"

My shoulders sagged. Sometimes I just didn't feel like making multiple repetitions. "Never mind. I'll be right back."

Jesse reached for my arm, but I moved away as fast as I could in my Sunday shoes. My high heels stuck in the cemetery grass, scattering little grass plugs in my wake. Dedicated to my mission, I increased speed, determined to persevere.

Once I got to the group, I sucked in a substantial breath and spoke with authority. "Excuse me. I have questions about the investigation into Baxter's death. Could you take a few moments to answer them?"

The group consisted of four uniformed men, all but one around Baxter's age. I focused on Deputy Oliver first so maybe that's why he answered, but not before they eyeballed each other and stepped back to open the circle.

Deputy Oliver's eyes narrowed. "It depends, ma'am, on what you want to know. We're only peripherally involved, so we're not privy to all the facts. Also, it's an ongoing investigation, so some things we can't talk about."

I waved off his disclaimer. "First off, where did the media get the idea that Baxter went to a meeting with drug dealers before he died?"

A couple of the men cleared their throats, exchanging another glance that I read as "let's humor the old busybody." A burly dark haired man, the one who appeared older than the others, answered. I remembered him from the Callahan's house, G. Rogers. "What we might say about that is there has been a long investigation into drug trafficking in Nevada

County. Only recently has there been progress in locating the major players."

"Uh-huh," I said. "But Baxter wasn't part of the Narcotics Task Force. Wasn't he with the Crimes Against Persons and Property Unit?"

Deputy Rogers gave a condescending nod. "That's correct. However, he knew about the task force. And drug trafficking often involves loss to persons and property. Let's say it's possible he inadvertently uncovered suspicious activity while investigating something else."

"What 'something else?'"

"We're not at liberty to divulge that at this time." His smile looked a tad artificial.

I wasn't going to let them off the hook without trying harder. I turned to Deputy Oliver. "Baxter got off duty at six, right?"

"That sounds right," Deputy Oliver answered. "That's when he usually got off. But if he was in the middle of something important, he couldn't just leave to go home."

If I kept asking the same questions in different ways, maybe I'd get lucky. "What was he in the middle of?"

A couple of the officers, the two who hadn't spoken yet, shuffled and lowered their eyes.

Deputy Oliver gave a slight cough. "Mrs.....?"

"Sterling, I'm the Callahan's' neighbor."

He bent slightly as if speaking to a child. "Mrs. Sterling, Baxter developed a lead on a missing person's case he'd been following for more than a year. I was with him at the office around five when he got a call concerning the whereabouts of this person."

The repeated use of the word "person" increased my suspicion. I remembered the reference to a woman made by one of the news people. "Was this *person* a woman?"

More shuffling, more averted gazes. All except Deputy Oliver who bent lower to stare directly into my eyes. "Yes, Mrs. Sterling. He went to meet a woman. But don't you pay any attention to those rumors about an affair. Baxter Dunn was definitely *not* having an affair."

ॐ

The phone rang while I cleaned up the kitchen after dinner the next evening.

When I answered, I heard concern in Zora Jane's voice. "Christine. Deputy Rogers just called Kathleen. He's been assigned to investigate Baxter's death."

"Oh, yes. I met him yesterday at the graveside. Is he a detective then?"

"I guess so. Anyway, the preliminary autopsy results came in this afternoon. Please pray for Kathleen. She's quite upset."

Her tone brought on a flush of fear that started around my chest. "Why? What did he tell her?"

"They found a suspicious substance in Baxter's blood. The blood sample has been sent away for more detailed analysis. Toxicology reports take a long time, he said, because they go out of state or something."

"Oh, no. Did he say what the substance was?"

"Some kind of hallucinogenic drug. Deputy... rather, Detective Rogers asked if Baxter was a drug user."

My chin dropped to my chest and I squeezed my eyes shut.

A drug user! What next? How could anyone think Baxter Dunn would voluntarily ingest hallucinogens?

4

CHAPTER FOUR

Waiting in the audiologist's office for Jesse's hearing test, I tried reading one of the celebrity gossip magazines from the messy stack on the end table.

Where did they find enough gossip to fill so many periodicals? And who were these supposed celebrities? I didn't recognize a single name or face.

I paced across the small waiting room a few times. With no one else sitting I had the run of the place, but the confined space didn't allow much walking room. Feeling the need for fresh air, I pushed the door open and stepped outside. The sparkling spring air exuded joy, the kind of day that makes you think of birds singing and butterflies floating above the flowers even when you can't see flowers or hear birds.

As I wandered next door to the drug store, a newspaper rack filled with Los Angeles newspapers caught my eye. I stooped to look at the headlines.

'Alleged Deputy Misconduct Suspected in Homicide Cover-up'

"That can't be. In an L.A. paper?" I leaned closer to scan the print. Sure enough, the article concerned Baxter Dunn's death. After the headline, they didn't bother to use the word *alleged*. Presented as fact, the short blurb purported to expose a giant conspiracy by a hayseed sheriff's office in Nevada County to cover up Baxter's illegal conduct. Baxter's meeting with drug dealers and the clandestine rendezvous were both mentioned, citing "Baxter's double life." *By day, he's mild-mannered family man/deputy, Baxter Dunn. But at night, he transforms into The Party Boy of Nevada County. Right.*

The placement of the fold kept me from reading the entire article. The last paragraph before the fold said:

The Nevada County Coroner has ruled that death resulted from a fall into the ravine where Baxter Dunn was impaled on a rusty spike. The preliminary toxicology report indicates the presence of a hallucinogenic...

I straightened abruptly. "What in the world?" Shaking my head in disbelief, I turned when the door to the audiologist's office banged open and the gum popping receptionist stuck her head out to call. "Mrs. Sterling?"

I started toward the office. "Yes?"

"Linda wants to see you now."

The receptionist ushered me to one of the examining cubicles while I ruminated on the pervasive lack of respect in a generation intent on calling professionals by their first names. Jesse sat on a little bench. He turned to grant me a tiny smile of recognition when I entered.

"Mrs. Sterling." Linda Adams, the audiologist, smiled and extended her hand. "Come in."

I sat where she pointed as she produced a chart with a zigzag line drawn horizontally in blue marker along the middle. "Jesse wanted you here while we go over the results of today's testing." She tapped the blue zigzag with her pen. "This shows where Jesse tested today. Normal hearing would be at the top of this chart, so you can see he has significant hearing loss. Roughly speaking, he's only hearing a little more than half of normal."

"My goodness," I said. "No wonder he has trouble understanding what I say."

Jesse rolled his eyes. "That's only because you mumble."

I ignored that, preferring his retort to the one I'd left myself wide open for. "What caused it, Dr. Adams? He lost his hearing almost overnight."

She consulted her chart again before glancing up at Jesse. "Since this hearing loss occurred rather rapidly, I'd like to send you for a few tests to see if we can determine the cause. I hesitate to speculate at this juncture. It could be many things, heredity to injury to serious things like tumors. You indicated that both parents had hearing loss?"

"Yes. My father died at sixty-five. His hearing wasn't terrible, but getting there. Mom's hearing is getting worse, too. But she's in her eighties. My older brother can hardly hear at all these days."

Dr. Adams scanned her notes. "This may have started during your stint in Vietnam. Firing heavy artillery without earplugs would undoubtedly damage the inner ear. Or we could be dealing with genetic hearing loss which will worsen while you age, but I'd like to have the tests done anyway. Just to rule out other possibilities."

"Can you fix it?" Jesse asked.

"Let's get these tests done and then we'll be in a better position to discuss possible solutions." She wrote a requisition for several tests and dismissed us with a professional smile.

I called Zora Jane as soon as I got home to tell her about the newspaper article. "Has Kathleen heard anything about the coroner's report?"

"No, I don't think so. Not unless they just called this morning. I talked to her last night and she didn't mention it. Why?"

I recounted what I read in front of the drug store. "Where do you suppose the news people get the terrible stuff they print? Why doesn't anyone hold them accountable for printing things that aren't true?"

"Well, it did say 'alleged' in the headline," Zora Jane pointed out.

"But they slanted the whole thing toward convicting Baxter of misconduct, regardless of the fact that an official finding hasn't been made yet. It's slander against a wonderful young man. It just galls me!"

"Hmm. Ed tried to talk with Detective Rogers a couple times. He said they're investigating every lead, involving officers from other counties, too. They don't ever take the death of a fellow officer lightly. I'm sure they won't this time. But I'm afraid they're not going to share much with us until the investigation is completed. And that's what they're supposed to do. I think we ought to…"

"Don't ask me to pray for the sheriff's department right now, please Zora Jane. I'm just not feeling that charitable."

She chuckled a righteous little trill. "Okay, Christine, but you know we really should."

❧

When I returned from taking Molly for a walk the next afternoon, I discovered Sam Colter had left a voice message. "This is Deputy Sam Colter from the Nevada County Sheriff's

Office. I am returning a call from Christine Sterling. I am leaving the office today. Please feel free to call tomorrow."

"AARGH!" I said to Molly. She immediately sat at my feet, waiting for my command with adoring eyes. I knelt to run my fingers through the soft collar of white fur on her chest and then patted her black head. "I really wanted to talk to him."

Jesse dashed into the room. "What?"

"I was talking to Molly."

He pursed his lips. "I thought you called me."

"I'm sorry. Deputy Colter finally returned my phone call and I wasn't here to answer it."

"Did the phone ring while you were gone?"

A laugh escaped before I could stop it. "You poor thing. It must be so frustrating not to be able to hear."

I guess he didn't see the humor because he stalked out of the room, throwing back a glare when he exited. I sighed. I never seemed to say the right thing anymore.

❧

Wednesday morning I called Deputy Colter again. The dispatcher answered. "Nevada County Sheriff's Office, may I help you?"

"I'd like to speak with Deputy Colter please." I answered, crossing my fingers.

"One moment please."

My hand flew to my mouth to suppress a whoop. Never before had I called and been directly connected.

"Deputy Colter, how may I assist you?"

"This is Christine Sterling. I'd like to make an appointment. How about tomorrow at your office?"

The edge in his voice didn't sound friendly. "What is this in reference to?"

"About the murder of Deputy Dunn."

Now he sounded downright peeved. "As you know, an ongoing investigation into the death of Deputy Dunn is in progress. I am limited in what I can discuss concerning that investigation." I heard tapping on his end, probably his pen against his desk. "Besides, Mrs. Sterling, you are not a family member so information will not be shared with you when it becomes available."

How could I make my request sound attractive? Sweet talk? Could I pretend to be a damsel in distress? "Yes, Deputy, I know you aren't supposed to talk about the investigation." I threw in as much sweetness as I could muster without upchucking. "I greatly admire your conscientious attitude about your work. But I have no one else to turn to. You've been kind to me in the past. I just know I can depend on you now. The thing is, it's been over three weeks since Baxter died. I've tried desperately to sort things out in my mind, but I'm still so confused. It keeps me awake at night worrying. You simply *must* help me."

"Excuse me?"

"Please, Deputy Colter. I'd like to be facing you when we talk."

The tapping stopped.

"I promise not to take much of your valuable time," I said in my Marilyn Monroe voice. "And I would be most appreciative."

He cleared his throat. "I am off this weekend, but I could give you a few minutes next Monday afternoon. Around two o'clock."

"Oh thank you, Deputy Colter. I knew I could count on you. Bye, bye. See you Monday."

As soon as I hung up, I started making a list of questions for our appointment.

Early Friday morning, Jesse herded Ranger, his black Morgan stallion, into the horse trailer and drove off to a mounted shooting match in Gilroy. Cowboy mounted shooting had become Jesse's latest passion. At the matches, he joined other contestants who donned vintage western costumes and raced around orange highway cones with balloons attached. The object was to shoot all the balloons in proper order, round the barrels according to the prescribed pattern, and ride back through the finish line at full speed. After the results of each stage were added together, the person with the fastest overall time won. Being a better than average shot, Jesse had already amassed an impressive array of belt buckles and plaques. He would rather do cowboy mounted shooting than breathe.

Although I usually complained about his time away, this time I considered his absence fortuitous because it provided the perfect opportunity to conduct a wee bit of sleuthing. Since Half Moon House figured into the puzzle of Baxter's demise, I would begin my search there. With luck, I'd locate the woman he was last seen with.

At my age, I rarely ventured out unescorted after dark. Even in my wildest day—way before I married Jesse thirty-nine years ago—I never went trolling in bars. Nice girls didn't, my mother said. But mostly people frequent bars at night, so this particular hunt couldn't be done in the daytime. I wasn't sure what I'd encounter, so I took Molly along for backup.

Of course, Molly loves everyone. If someone threatened me, Molly would probably do nothing more aggressive than lick an adversary to death or perhaps even knock someone down with her wagging tail. Still, she was always great company and smart enough to go for help should the need arise.

It made me feel braver just to have her along. "You're terrific moral support, aren't you, girl?" Molly stirred and sat on the passenger seat gazing at me, tongue hanging out. Sometimes I really think she understands what I say. I scratched her head and she settled down again.

In less than an hour I arrived at Half Moon House. Built as a lodge more than sixty years ago, the historic building lay midway along scenic Highway 20 between Nevada City and Interstate 80. Addresses on Highway 20 were often measured in proximity to the famous landmark. Everyone knew where it was.

Dusk had just settled into darkness when I pulled into the parking lot. The rustic log building housed a restaurant and inn with a small tidy bar area, both of which had been recently remodeled. A female bartender wearing black slacks and a clean white long-sleeve shirt worked behind the new granite bar. No one sat on the squeaky leather seats.

I eyed the bar stool and sidled up, no small feat with short legs like mine. Why do they make these chairs so tall? After I wiggled into place, I flashed a smile. "Hello. I'm looking for a woman who met Deputy Baxter Dunn at a bar on the night of his death. I thought it might be this bar. Were you here that night?"

"Dunn?" She stopped drying a glass and tilted her head. "Was he the one got killed a few weeks ago?"

"Right."

She set the glass precisely in its place behind the bar and turned to stare into space over my head. "Yeah. I heard about that. A shame. Right before I started working here." She shook her head, meeting my gaze. "Don't know nothing about it."

"Do you know someone who might have been here that night?"

She jerked her head toward the adjacent room. "Try the front desk."

"Thanks." I eased off the stool and approached the desk she indicated, finding no one there. Peering around for a minute without sighting anyone, I hunted for a way to signal for help. No bell. I lingered a few seconds longer, standing on tiptoe to glance over the desk. "Yoo-hoo? Anybody home?"

At length, a man with a pencil stuck behind one ear shuffled over. "You want a room for tonight?"

"No, thanks." I flashed my toothy smile. "Just a little information. Were you here the night Baxter Dunn got killed?"

He frowned. "Already talked to the law."

"No, no." I grinned again. "I'm not from the sheriff's office. I'm just a friend of the family. I want to find the woman Baxter came to—"

Impatience filled his eyes. "Look, lady. I don't know anything about it. No lawman stopped here that night. I already told 'em that twice. Don't have time to go through it again." He hurried away.

I called after him. "Are there other bars on Highway 20?"

He didn't look back, raising his voice while he hurried away. "Try the Night Owl."

Only slightly daunted, I returned to the Jeep and pulled onto the cool tree-lined avenue. About a mile farther along Highway 20, my headlights illuminated a small building to the left. At the driveway, a crooked sign swinging in the wind marked the location of the Night Owl, Bar and Pool Hall.

As I veered into the tiny parking lot, I prayed. "Okay, God. Here I am. I really believe You placed this on my heart. Please help me find the woman I need to talk to."

Even as those words left my lips, a quiet voice in my head warned that I should wait for Jesse to accompany me; but since I'd already come this far, I chose to ignore the voice of caution. I switched off my headlights and stared at the bar.

Housed in a single story building, the Night Owl had rough, timber siding. No windows. Why don't bars have windows? I heard my mother's warnings playing through my brain. "Men loved darkness rather than light because their deeds were evil." Wasn't that in the Bible somewhere? This must be the kind of place my mother advised me to stay away from.

A streetlight shone on the front of the building. Based on first impressions, the owners weren't big on TLC. Shingles dangled off the roof. Tall dry weeds crowded out shrubs in planting boxes along the siding. Five jumbo sized motorcycles rested in front.

Oh, no. This is a biker bar.

Not that I knew what a biker bar entailed. I'd heard the term on television, usually associated with brawls. Again, I remembered my mother's words. "Bikers and alcohol. Not a good mix."

A neon entrance sign above the front door blinked *ntranc*, missing the E's on either end. I studied it, my inner editor wanting to take out a red pencil and correct the misspelling.

Maybe they dropped the E's on purpose. For a few seconds, I considered possible meanings for the abridged version, but nothing brilliant occurred to me.

In addition to the bikes, I counted six automobiles lined up in the parking area. That made the lot less than half full. Not very crowded for a Friday night.

Saturday night must be bar night in these parts.

I gulped down trepidation and opened the car door. "If I'm not right back, Molly, go for help."

Why did Molly's eyes look worried?

Knees shaking, I eased out of the Jeep. A few uneasy steps and I found myself at the door.

A stale smoke odor greeted me from the darkened room when I pulled on the knob. Guess they hadn't heard about California's no smoking in public places law.

Glasses jangled and a jukebox blared in the background. After my eyes adjusted to the dim smoky interior, silhouettes of people came into view. Some were sprawled along a bar to the right of the small room. Others sat on mismatched chairs at the rickety round tables scattered over the dull wood floor. A few played pool in one corner.

At first, the room buzzed with conversation, but the voices stopped abruptly when the door crashed shut behind me.

Everyone turned to stare.

For a moment, I stood stiff legged, forgetting what I had planned to say or do once I arrived. Trying to look like I belonged, I picked up my leaden feet and eased into the first empty bar stool I came to.

What do you do with your hands while you wait?

After I'd been sitting at the bar for at least a minute, the bartender, a man distinguished by missing teeth with a stained towel wrapped around his middle, drifted toward me looking quite bored. In the dim light, I could barely make out a tattoo of a ghostly schooner which dominated one forearm. An earring dangled from one side of a bushy eyebrow that met its mate in the middle of his forehead.

He planted both hands on the bar and leaned toward me. "Are you lost, little lady?"

I tried not to stare at the earring. "No. I'd like a, um, do you have unsweetened iced tea? With a slice of lemon, please."

Was that a snicker?

I peered into the darkness at the other patrons. Some met my gaze and returned to their conversations or their drinks as if they'd been caught in guilty pleasures.

"No iced tea, lady. No lemons. No mint julep neither."

"Oh. Well, how about a...7-Up?"

The bartender mimicked my request in a sissy voice,

curling one end of his mouth into a lopsided smile. I nodded firmly, so he sauntered off to retrieve my beverage.

Come on, Christine. Get a grip. Remember what you came for.

When he returned with the drink, I cleared my throat. "I'm a friend of Baxter Dunn. Do you know him?"

The bartender blinked.

"He was the deputy who got killed out near the Star Mine about a month ago."

I'd never realized how hard talking privately in a public place could be. The trick was to make my voice loud enough so the bartender could hear above the din, but confidential enough that no one else could. My technique needed work because several people stopped talking again to listen in on our conversation. I could almost feel them bend a collective ear toward us en masse.

"Already told the cops. We don't know nothing." The bartender eyed me with suspicion. "But you ain't a cop."

"A cop?" I chuckled and fluttered my hand in denial. "Good heaven's no. Of course not. I'm a friend of his, of Baxter's, a friend who's getting really frustrated with the official investigation into his death."

"Whatta you mean?" He leaned on one elbow and glowered at me, wiggling the earring on his big bushy eyebrow.

"Well, they're just not getting anywhere, are they? They haven't even found the black van Baxter supposedly stopped the night he died. They don't know what he was doing here either."

He didn't look one bit happy to help me. "What exactly do you wanna do about that?"

The man sitting to my right slid closer. "So, they're sending little old ladies out to investigate?"

I'll let that little old lady thing go for now. "No one sent me to investigate."

The bartender crooked the eyebrow on the other side of the earring, making him look more sinister than before. "Like I said, exactly what do you want?"

I guzzled my 7-Up. "What I want is… uh…information. First off, I want to talk with the woman who met with Baxter here the night of his death."

The man at my side pressed closer until I felt his hot whiskey laced breath against my cheek. "Ain't you in a little over your head, lady?"

Pool balls broke with a clatter and I jumped.

I hoped they couldn't hear my heart pounding, although it thundered against my chest so loudly I feared that people in the next county must've heard it. I pulled together all the courage I could muster. "I don't think so." I forced my eyes to meet their stares, looking from one to the other. "Is the woman here tonight?"

The bartender squinted at the man next to me. The man beside me looked me over once more and shrugged. "For sure she ain't a cop. Maybe she can do some good. That little one could use a friend about now."

The bartender nodded toward a table in the far corner. "Think you might find the package you're looking for back there. Good luck."

I dropped a twenty on the counter. Clutching my 7-Up glass in shaky hands, I approached the corner table with mounting trepidation.

CHAPTER FIVE

I had no trouble finding the package in question. She turned out to be the only female in the place besides me. When I approached the corner table, she glanced up. I stopped to gasp. For a moment the tiny hunched person looked like my former neighbor Lila Payne. But that was impossible. Lila was dead.

Camouflaged by the shadows, the woman peered at me through tangled mousy brown hair. She wasn't much bigger than a child. Dark circles underneath her eyes might indicate illness, lack of sleep, or just smudged makeup. She watched me furtively, as if trying to hide behind her hair.

How could I get her to relax? I plastered on a smile. "Hi. The bartender says you're the woman Baxter Dunn met here on the night he died. Do you mind if I sit and talk?"

She blinked several times in slow motion as if I spoke gibberish. After what felt like a full minute's pause, she waved toward the other chair at the table.

"Thanks." I sat and offered my hand, but it hung in the air unclasped so I dropped it into my lap. "My name's Christine Sterling. I'm Baxter Dunn's friend. Actually, he was the son in-law of very close friends. I'm dissatisfied with the official investigation the sheriff's department is conducting because they haven't discovered anything useful yet so I decided to ask a few questions of my own."

She didn't acknowledge the greeting, only closed her eyes and sighed, sending a strong puff of alcohol laced breath that flooded the air between us.

Oh, great, she's drunk. "You are the woman Baxter Dunn met here the night he died, aren't you?"

She tilted her head to one side as if the weight made it impossible to hold it straight. It appeared that she started to say something, but it turned out she'd opened her mouth to beckon her drink. Fumbling with a half empty glass, she finally managed to find her mouth and wash down a couple of gulps. When she set the glass on the table, liquid sloshed out.

She'd obviously had enough. I struggled with a desire to slide the glass out of reach. "Do you remember Baxter Dunn?"

I think she nodded. But it could have been that heavy head thing again.

"You do?"

Like an elevator descending, she lowered her forehead until it banged on the table. A noise accompanied the bang, perhaps a groan.

"Did you say something?" I bent closer. "No? Well, do you think you could tell me your name then?"

She rolled her head over where I could see part of her face. The lips moved, but sound didn't come out. Not anything I heard anyway. I leaned in and pushed a clump of hair off her forehead. "Say it again, dear. Your name."

After a few seconds, the word came out hoarsely, just above a gravelly whisper. "Mary."

I clapped my hands. "There we go. Good start. What's the rest of your name, Mary?"

Would it help to play charades with her? Second word. Sounds like...

"Wilson."

"Great. Thank you." I laid my hand on her arm and patted firmly, hoping to keep her awake long enough to answer a couple more questions. Impatience nibbled at my gut. Maybe I should slap her instead. "Now, Mary Wilson, did you meet here with Baxter Dunn about four weeks ago, the night he got killed?"

She perked up, as if a shot of caffeine just kicked in. "Basker... the cop?"

I ignored the slurred misrepresentation of Baxter's name. "Right. The deputy sheriff. You met him here, remember?"

She peered over one shoulder at the men seated around the bar. They carried on, laughing loudly and glancing our way. My fumbling attempt to interview this drunken woman had obviously given them cause for hilarity.

Her head wobbled like a newborns when she turned toward me. "Can't tell you that. It's a secret. Shh!" She tried to put one finger to her mouth when she shushed. Lacking coordination, the finger missed her mouth by at least an inch.

This wasn't going well. A long sigh leaked from my lips. "Could you give me your address, Mary? Maybe I could come see you in the daytime after you're feeling better. Would that be okay?"

I pulled out paper and pen from my purse. With further coaxing, I managed to drag out what I thought must be an address. I told her I'd stop by one afternoon.

Mary's head lolled on the table, eyes fixed and glassy. I wanted to gather her up like a sleeping child and tuck her into my safe warm guest room to sleep it off. Although she was a small person, chances were good that I couldn't lift her. The main problem was that I'd be hefting dead weight.

I flicked a glance at the other bar patrons. No one looked friendly enough to help. I would have to leave her, so I collected what little composure I still retained and beat a hasty retreat.

❧

My wild foray into the black leather world of biker bars left me a bit unnerved. So much so that I didn't venture out again all weekend, except to go to church on Sunday. Sitting in the pew, I debated the necessity of repenting my trip to the bar and decided to ignore the nagging voice of my inner mother.

I greeted Jesse with long hugs and deep appreciation when he returned on Sunday evening. Thankfully, he didn't verbalize questions about my weekend activities. I caught a look now and then that told me he'd like to ask, but perhaps he was afraid to hear the answers.

The time for Monday afternoon's meeting with Deputy Colter came at last. Jesse needed medical tests at the hospital, so I dropped him off and continued to the sheriff's office alone. Unsuccessful at keeping anxiety at bay, I arrived a full ten minutes early and sat in the waiting area, fiddling with my hands. At last, the door opened and Deputy Colter stuck his head out, glaring at me.

"Mrs. Sterling?"

I stood.

"This way, please."

I followed him through a busy area that confirmed my idea of what dispatch central must look like and came to a long hallway with doors on either side. Deputy Colter opened one. I entered to find a conference table with eight comfortable chairs around it. I seated myself while Deputy Colter closed the door. He stood near the table, arms crossed over his chest, obviously encouraging a short meeting.

Before he spoke, he took out a large white handkerchief and polished the star badge pinned above his pocket as if to establish his authority. He still wasn't smiling. "Okay. Here we are. What can I do for you today?"

I pulled my list of questions from my purse and shook out the folded yellow legal paper dramatically, hoping to lighten the mood. "I just have a *few* questions."

His dark expression didn't budge.

Humor wouldn't get me anywhere, apparently. I drew in a whopping breath and exhaled before reverting to my helpless woman routine again. "Thank you so much for taking time to meet with me, Deputy. I've been trying to understand this senseless murder, but I just get more and more confused. You know so much about these things. Can you help me sort it all out, please?" I batted my eyelids slightly.

He squinted over his prodigious nose, as if trying to assess my degree of levity. "C-O-D has not been officially ascertained yet, so Dunn's death has not designated a homicide. And, as I told you before, I cannot reveal any specific details of the investigation."

"Oh, yes. Well, certainly. But you have already mentioned some things to us and those are the things I want help deciphering."

"Like what precisely?"

"You said Baxter chased the man in the black van to the area of the Star Mine where the man exited his van and ran. Baxter followed him to the top of that hill above the mine dump. They struggled and Baxter fell into the ravine."

"I said that is how it appeared to me. That is not the official version, as you know. P-C has not yet been established."

"P-C?"

"Probable cause."

"Oh. Well, when I first spoke to you, you said you noticed

irregularities. What irregularities?"

He stepped closer and leaned against the table, speaking in his condescending tone. "I cannot comment on that."

"Okay. You said they found Baxter's patrol car in Rawlins Lake. Why would someone abandon the car in a lake if Baxter's fall was an accident?"

"I cannot comment on that either." He tapped the table with his pen. "Now, if you will excuse—"

"But can't you agree, hypothetically, that it would be unlikely for someone to go to the trouble of hiding the car in the case of an accidental death?"

He tapped a few more times. "It might not be likely." Tap, tap, tap. "Hypothetically."

"Is there something about the car being found that bothers you, Deputy?"

"Bothers me?" The pen hovered above the table as if stuck in the air. "Why do you ask?"

"I don't know. Something about the way you talk; it sounds like you have mixed feelings about the discovery of the patrol car. What I want to know is, why?"

He cleared his throat, and frowned. In the slight pause, the tapping resumed, but faster. "Mrs. Sterling, let me assure you, I have no personal agenda. Why would I?"

"That's what I wonder." I bent closer. "Why would you?"

"Well, I… do not…have a personal agenda."

"Hmm." I consulted my written questions. "Are the investigators concentrating on the time line of the night Baxter died? That seems to be a critical piece of this puzzle."

He regained his stuffy posture, brushing off a speck of lint from his tie as if relieved to be off the hook. "The investigators are well aware of the facts of this case."

"Have the missing gun, radio, ammo, and badge turned up yet?"

"No comment."

"It's been over a month. Are they working this case every day?"

He stopped tapping again. His small brown eyes bored directly into mine. "Mrs. Sterling, the department is conducting a full and proper investigation. Thoroughness is paramount."

I ignored the condescending attitude. "Do *you* consider this a homicide, Deputy Colter?"

"No comment. Please excuse me, Mrs. Sterling. I have work to do." He turned toward the door.

I still had questions on my legal pad, so I stayed in my chair. "The news media says this story was leaked to them by someone in the sheriff's office. Any idea who that would be, Deputy?"

His head snapped around to stare at me. Arms akimbo, he stood above me, glaring. Before he replied, he caught himself and closed his mouth. That same odd expression crossed his face, an expression I couldn't decipher. He cleared his throat. "I caution you again, Mrs. Sterling, this is none of your affair. Do not meddle in official business." He stooped near to spit hot words directly into my face. "I cannot emphasize this strongly enough. Stay out of it! Is that clear?"

❧

Frustrated over the lack of progress my interview with Deputy Colter engendered, I decided to check out Mary Wilson's residence. Maybe I'd find answers there. Besides, I still had some time to kill before I needed to pick up Jesse.

The address she gave took me northwest of Grass Valley to a peculiar area known as Rough and Ready which holds the dubious distinction of being the first (perhaps the only) town ever to secede from the United States of America and then vote themselves back in. In 1850, unhappiness over the imposition of a tax on mining claims caused the citizens to form the "Great Republic of Rough and Ready," complete with a constitution, president, and cabinet. The fledgling republic held together for three whole months before deciding to rejoin the United States.

I'd already experienced the residents of Rough and Ready as an independent, sometimes less than law abiding group, non-conformists to mainstream society like the bikers at the Night Owl. Perhaps the bikers descended from the secessionists of 1850.

After winding around hilly roads for some twenty minutes, I eventually came to the street Mary specified and turned into her driveway.

Mary Wilson's ramshackle house occupied a flat graded space between the lower front of the property and a small hill behind. Add-ons jutted out at odd places. Weathered and rickety, the small building needed painting and general maintenance. A sizable rip zigzagged through the rusty screen door and the light fixture beside the door appeared naked without its shade. Litter clung to trees and weeds around the property as if someone turned a garbage can upside down, scattering the contents into the wind. A corroded car occupied the shade of a large oak tree, looking quite appropriate in such a setting. I wondered if the car still worked. Houses in this area seemed to collect scrapped vehicles the way more affluent neighborhoods acquired new trees or fountains.

I parked on a dirt area that resembled a parking space and climbed out. A slight wind blew through the leaves, but nothing about the house indicated life inside. I pounded on the door anyway.

After a long pause, shuffling preceded the opening of the door. Through the screen, Mary blinked at me. She appeared much the same as she had in the Night Owl, perhaps a little more alert. From the looks of her hair, I must have awakened her from a nap.

"Hi, Mary." I hung my 'good neighbor' grin like a welcome sign on my lips. "Do you remember me? I met you at the Night Owl last Friday night. I'm Christine Sterling."

A fluffy gray cat meowed loudly, rubbing against her leg. She reached down to pick it up and cradled it like a big round baby. "Sorry. Don't remember what day this is. Was I in the Owl last Friday?"

Well, at least she wasn't drunk. That was a good start. "Sure you were. That's where we met."

She tilted her head to stare at me while massaging the cat. "You were in the Owl?"

"I'm a friend of Baxter Dunn's. Do you remember him? He's the officer who was killed about a month ago out near the Star Mine."

"Yeah. What about him?"

The screen door separated us. "Do you mind if I come in, Mary? I'd like to talk to you about your meeting with Deputy Dunn the night he died."

She paused, processing the request perhaps. "I guess that wouldn't hurt. You don't look too dangerous." With one hand, she pushed the door. "Come on in."

I squeezed through the opening she provided and followed her into a tiny, messy living room. Stale cigarette smoke hung in the air like fog. Didn't she ever let air in?

Mary paused in the center of the room, looking confused. "Sorry. I haven't gotten around to tidying up today." I didn't know where to sit. Stuffing popped out of the overstuffed chair in places, coils of several springs exposed, but the couch looked just as uncomfortable. She pointed to the chair. "Just push that stuff out of the way."

With one hand, I slid assorted debris out of the way and sat. From the state of disarray in the room, I guessed no one had tidied up for decades.

Mary deposited the gray cat on the cluttered floor and arranged herself on the sofa opposite me. The cat protested with a loud meow and an insulted expression. Mary paid no attention. Plopping on top of a pile of clothing, she tucked her bare feet underneath as if they were cold. "What do ya wanna know?"

"How did you meet Baxter Dunn in the first place?"

"He came with a couple other cops when I got arrested." She splayed her long fingers to study her green pained fingernails. Then she picked a dented pack of cigarettes off the end table. Pulling a cigarette out, she lit it, took a big drag, and absentmindedly blew a cloud of smoke toward me. She looked like a child experimenting with nicotine.

I waved smoke away from my face, blinking as my eyes started to water. "Arrested? For what?" I coughed. "When was that?"

She waved smoke too. "Sorry. Uh… maybe a year ago. I don't know. Could be longer. I lived with a guy who sold drugs. A real weirdo. Into some strange junk. I went along for the ride, but got sucked into the arrest anyhow."

So Baxter *had* been on a drug bust. But why?

"That happened about a year ago, you say? Did you see Deputy Dunn after that? Talk to him or anything?"

She flicked ash into an ashtray already brimming over with butts and ashes. "He started coming around the Owl a few months ago. Wanted to talk about the old man."

"You mean your boyfriend? The one into strange stuff?"

"Yeah. I talked to Deputy Dunn a few months ago, I think. Didn't have much to tell him. But then the guys would tell me he'd been coming around asking for me when I wasn't there."

"You only talked to him twice at the bar? A few months ago and then again on the night of his death?"

She frowned. "Why are you repeating what I say?"

"What did he want?"

She stubbed out the cigarette and observed me as if I wasn't speaking English. "I told you. He just wanted to talk about the old man. That's it. End of story. I broke off with that dude when I got arrested so I had nothing else to say. Like now."

The interview in which I'd placed such hope had raced nowhere on an express train. I couldn't think of anything else to ask Mary. Dejected, I drove back into town to pick up Jesse while snippets of my conversation with Deputy Colter muddled my brain.

"I have no personal agenda." That's what he said. Personal agenda, personal agenda. Why did Colter word it like that? *Perhaps Deputy Colter has a personal agenda after all.* But if he did, I couldn't imagine what it might be.

6

CHAPTER SIX

The teakettle screamed. Zora Jane scooped spoonfuls of Earl Gray tea into her favorite teapot. A sharp yelp from the kettle and she poured, what she termed, passionately boiling water over the tea leaves.

I knew the routine. A perfect cup of tea required waiting exactly five minutes. But not the freshly baked Snickerdoodles. The scent of cinnamon overpowered the room, tempting me to my second cookie. Which, I hate to admit I ate, while carrying the piled plate of cookies to the great room.

I'd stopped over to see how Zora Jane was holding up. Stunningly attired in tapered black jeans with a long zebra striped velour top tied up on one side and matching zebra striped thongs on her feet, clearly Zora Jane was holding up just fine.

A precise five minutes later, I held a cup of tea. Blowing air gently between my lips, I flattened the steam curls. Not wishing to burn my tongue, I returned the cup to the coffee table.

Zora Jane laughed. "Drinking tea requires—" She raised her head.

My eyes followed her gaze.

A late model Cadillac limo slowed down on Mustang Hill Road. As if someone was pausing to confirm an address, the sleek black vehicle lingered a moment before turning into the long driveway. We watched while the Cadillac drove slowly up the hill until we lost sight of it turning into the circular driveway in front of the Callahan's house.

"What now?" I asked. "Were you expecting someone?"

"No. But let's go see who it is."

We hurried to the entryway, arriving at the front door when a lady emerged from the back door of the Cadillac.

I called her a *lady* because no other word would have fit. From the delicate but deliberate way she set her foot on the ground to the very top of her well-groomed head, this stranger oozed genteel breeding from every pore.

Once she descended from the car, she stood still as if accustomed to posing for paparazzi. The cut and fabric of her gray suit shouted dollar signs. After a moment, she fluffed the ruffled collar of her burgundy silk blouse and brushed a wrinkle from her A-line skirt. The thick platinum band that curved around her throat shimmered in the sunlight when she floated toward us.

Besides the uniformed driver who emerged from the car to open the back door, two other occupants exited the vehicle. A studious woman partially hidden behind large black glasses followed a young man carrying a complicated video camera.

"Oh, my goodness!" I said when the lady came close enough for me to recognize her. "Do you know who that is?"

Zora Jane cocked her head, stare blank.

"*That* is Constance Boyd."

Zora Jane pursed her lips and shook her head.

"*The* Constance Boyd. On TV. You know, 'The Constance Boyd Show.' "

"Oh," she said.

Zora Jane didn't waste time watching television. Still, she must see the news now and then. *Could it be possible she didn't recognize someone at this level of celebrity status?* No matter. I didn't have time to educate her. The one-and-only, nationally acclaimed, Emmy winning Constance Boyd sashayed down the front walkway of the Callahan's' house. She looked more beautiful in person than she did on television, if that was possible. I suddenly understood the meaning of dumbfounded.

Constance Boyd climbed the porch steps in soft black leather pumps that must have been a premium Italian brand. A huge diamond ring caught the sun causing a dazzling explosion of light when her delicate hand reached toward us. "Hello. I am Constance Boyd." The way she said it, she obviously expected us to know already, offering her name as a mere formality. Intelligent brown eyes surveyed us. "We've come to offer our respects to Kathleen Dunn. Would you please inform her that we are here?"

Zora Jane took the offered hand without hesitation. "Kathleen was here this morning, but she's not now. Perhaps I could help you. I'm her mother, Zora Jane Callahan."

With a voice as well modulated as a finely tuned violin, Constance said, "What a pleasure to meet you. May I offer my sincere condolences for the loss of your son-in-law?"

Zora Jane dipped her head in a single nod.

Constance's words spread like melted butter. "This must be a difficult time for you and your family, but Baxter Dunn's story seems important to share with the world. Perhaps you would allow me to do that."

Zora Jane did not answer right away, so I interjected. "Important in what way, Miss Boyd?"

She turned as if noticing me for the first time. "And you are?"

"I'm the Callahan's' neighbor, Christine Sterling. I live just over there." I pointed in the direction of my hill.

Instead of glancing where I pointed, she acknowledged my words with a cursory nod. "Ah, yes." Then she turned back to Zora Jane. "Will Mrs. Dunn be returning today?"

Zora Jane paused before answering. "I don't know."

Constance Boyd shifted her feet. Surely she was not accustomed to being kept standing on the porch. "It is most important that I speak with her." She glanced at her entourage. "I'm doing a little piece about the work of rural sheriff departments in America. How often their officers unselfishly place themselves in harm's way for the public good, yet how underpaid and underappreciated they are. I plan to include your Deputy Baxter in my program." She flashed her Ultra-Brite smile. "May we come in and talk with you about this? Then perhaps I could speak with Kathleen later."

Zora Jane gestured toward the house. "Please come in."

Constance motioned to her underlings. Apparently, they understood her hand signal because they waited outside without a word while she paraded into the house like a high fashion model on a Paris runway.

She tossed out a compliment about the cozy atmosphere of the house while she seated herself in the middle of the sofa, smoothing the front of her gray suit. Sounded insincere to me. Her smile looked plastic too. "Mrs. Callahan, as I said, I am aware you have suffered a great loss. Please forgive me if anything I mention seems insensitive to your grief. That is not my intention. However, I need to establish the facts to put together my show. I'm sure you understand."

Zora Jane nodded.

"Splendid. Do you mind if I tape our conversation?"

Zora Jane appeared more comfortable than I felt. "No. I don't mind. Would you like a cup of coffee first? Or tea perhaps?" Her smile, as always, was genuine. "I've just baked a batch of cookies."

"No, thank you. Not just now." With her perfectly manicured fingers, she extracted a small silver tape recorder from her Italian leather handbag.

Zora Jane seated herself in one of the green recliners, so I sat in the other.

Constance turned the tape recorder's face toward Zora Jane and pressed a small button to activate it. The machine seemed awfully tiny to be a quality tape recorder. I couldn't hear the slightest sound to indicate a recording in progress.

Modern technology, how amazing!

"First, I need background information if you don't mind." Constance Boyd smiled at Zora Jane again. Her smile showed off perfectly shaped lips in just the right shade of wine lipstick to complement the burgundy silk blouse. "Please give me your son-in-law's full name, place of birth, and age."

Zora Jane closed her eyes and emitted a slight sigh. "Baxter Charles Dunn, deputy of the Nevada County Sheriff's Department. He was born in Truckee, California. His parents were Ted and Ida Dunn of Truckee. The Dunns had three children, a girl and two boys. The other children live in Southern California. Baxter was the second child, born on Valentine's Day. His birthday suited him perfectly because he was such a sweetheart, February 14. We just celebrated his thirty-seventh birthday."

An almost imperceptible catch in her voice underscored the freshness of her grief. Zora Jane glanced at me, eyes brimming with tears about to fall. I patted her arm. She grabbed a tissue, blew her nose, and continued. "Thirty-seven years may not be long, Miss Boyd, but Baxter made the most of his life. Many people were blessed through his care. We thank God for allowing us to have him for so long. In addition, he left four lovely children. They will continue to remind us of the fine man Baxter was."

Constance tilted her head, hands folded primly in her lap. "I understand he was very civic minded. What sorts of activities was he involved with?"

"He coached his daughter's softball team and helped with high school football. He was passionate about children, helping children. He started an after-school program for latchkey kids in town. They have quite a large group now, nearly a hundred, over at the Presbyterian Church every afternoon after school. So often these days, both parents have to work. Many children are raised in single parent families and the parent often works outside the home. Kids get in trouble when left unattended. That concerned Baxter greatly, after seeing so many turn to crime when they didn't have adequate adult supervision."

Constance nodded. "That's quite admirable."

Zora Jane repeated a few stories Baxter's friends shared at the funeral. During Zora Jane's pauses, I added details. We told about his fine record of service with the sheriff's office.

"Let's see. He taught a Sunday school class at our church and worked with the young people there." Zora Jane looked at me.

"He took that group of teens to Mexico last summer to build a church. Don't forget that."

Tears welled in Zora Jane's eyes again.

I leaned toward her. "An example of Christian manhood, wasn't he?"

"He certainly was." Zora Jane dabbed her eyes with a tissue. "Best of all, he loved the Lord with all his heart." She looked directly at Constance. "Do you know Jesus, Miss Boyd?"

I did a double take and caught myself before the gasp escaped my lips. Such boldness! How would Constance Boyd respond?

Constance shifted slightly in her seat. "I was raised in church." Her perfect smile stiffened.

I stared back at Zora Jane. Would she let it go?

Zora Jane placed one hand on Constance Boyd's arm. "Church is good, certainly. God desires our worship. Church is essential for growth, teaching, and fellowship. But I'm talking about the eternal state of your soul. Do you have a relationship with Jesus?"

My eyes ping-ponged back to Constance who exhaled through lips parted into a little *O* before answering. Her expression communicated how unaccustomed she felt to defending the eternal state of her soul. "I was baptized as a child."

Zora Jane acknowledged that answer with one nod. "Baptism is good, too. Jesus commanded it, to proclaim our salvation publicly and identify us with God's people. But baptism won't save you either."

Constance crossed her legs and brushed something off her skirt. "I am a good person, Mrs. Callahan. I'm sure you've heard of the many ways I use my fortune to benefit society. I started several world-renowned charities. Just one of my foundations alone, The Boyd Network, has contributed almost a hundred million dollars to combat poverty in this country. We've raised the standard of living for countless children, by providing needed medical care. Some of these children would have died without our assistance. Many would never have been able to attend school but for the work of the foundation. I know God is pleased with my work."

I couldn't wait to hear how Zora Jane would counter *that* statement.

"How wonderful that God has used your foundation to bless so many children. But Romans 3:12 says, 'There is no one who does good, not even one.' We can't do *good* apart from

God, because we're all sinners. Let me tell you straight from God's mouth, 'For all have sinned and fall short of the glory of God.' You'll find that in Romans 3:23."

The Bible verses lay in the air a moment while what appeared to be conflicting emotions crisscrossed Constance's beautiful countenance. Then she gathered composure and snapped off the miniscule tape recorder with an overly dramatic flourish, wrenching back control of the conversation. "Yes, well, we've gotten off track here, I'm afraid." She stood and marched toward the door with evenly measured steps. "Rebecca?"

In an instant, the studious assistant appeared, pen and clipboard ready.

Constance turned back to Zora Jane. "I'd like my photographer to snap a few shots of the exterior of your house and property. Then I must meet with Baxter's widow. Baxter's parents, also. Please arrange that."

She ordered it as if she'd already established that Zora Jane would cooperate. Apparently, no one ever questioned her right to call the shots. Rebecca busily copied instructions.

"I must have a few pictures of the church he attended."

Rebecca scribbled again.

Constance Boyd smiled, her perfect white teeth sparkling. "It's been simply enchanting. Thank you for your generous assistance. Once again, I'm sorry for your loss." She extended her hand in a dainty fashion. The camera whirred and popped while the photographer snapped photos of the handshake.

Zora Jane sandwiched Miss Boyd's hand between both of hers so she could look directly into those beautiful brown eyes. " So glad I could help. Jesus loves you, my dear."

Without another word, Constance Boyd flounced to the Cadillac. Rebecca conferred with the cameraman. He hefted his heavy equipment onto one shoulder and wandered around the property taking pictures in front and back. He posed Zora Jane on the deck and took a few more.

When he finished, Rebecca handed Zora Jane a sheet of paper. "Here's a list of people Miss Boyd will interview." She pointed to the bottom of the page. "Call me at this number with the particulars."

Zora Jane stared at the paper. "Oh."

"We expect to hear from you tonight." All efficiency and no finesse, she turned and followed the cameraman into the car.

My ire flashed watching them drive away. "Of all things! They ordered you to make arrangements. Can you believe it?"

Zora Jane frowned. "I wonder what kind of story she plans to do about Baxter."

"She said she wants to do a story about the work rural officers do and how under appreciated they are. That sounds okay, doesn't it?"

Zora Jane shook her head. "Well, I think we need to pray about whether we should participate or not. Something feels off to me. Maybe I should run it by Ed to see what he thinks."

I couldn't imagine what would be wrong with lifting Baxter's exemplary life to national scrutiny. After all, there are so few heroes these days. Baxter certainly qualified for hero status. What could bother Zora Jane about Constance Boyd's plans?

Catherine Leggitt

7

CHAPTER SEVEN

Thursday when I arrived in town to run errands, I spied Leonard Pinzer leaning against the corner of the post office. The ever-present cameraman lounged on his stomach in the grass nearby, pulling dandelions from the lawn. I squeezed the Jeep into a parking space and hopped out.

They seemed lost and pathetic, so I stopped to say hello. "I thought you'd be long gone by now."

Leonard jumped to attention when I approached. "Hey. You're the Callahan's' neighbor, right?"

"What are you doing here? Still hoping for a scoop on the Baxter Dunn case?"

"Constance Boyd's in town," he said with an air of importance.

"I met her yesterday at the Callahan's. Who would've guessed that someone of her national status would be interested in doing a story about our Baxter?"

He wrinkled his forehead and tilted his head. "You're glad she's doing an exposé on Baxter?"

My stomach lurched. "What do you mean *exposé*?"

"The story they're doing about the steamier side of rural

sheriff's departments. You know, the drugs, the affairs, the bribes, the illegal stuff, how they protect their own no matter what the cost to the community. They're digging deep. And with her notoriety, people are talking. Some folks will do anything for that one minute of fame."

"What?" I couldn't believe someone so exquisite had duped us. "Are you sure that's what she's doing? Maybe you got it wrong."

A grin spread over his face. "Man, you should see yourself. You just went white."

"Who's she talking to? Where has she been?"

"Had a long chat at the sheriff's office today. Talked with a few officers, I think, a couple of Baxter's friends. From what I heard, Detective Rogers, who's heading up the investigation, won't talk to her, but good old pompous Colter sure gave her an earful." He chuckled.

I didn't see anything funny about that. "Where is she now? Is she still at the sheriff's office?"

"Nope." He pointed across the street. "She's been at that restaurant for a couple of hours. Guess she and her little groupies got pretty hungry after all that dirty digging."

The restaurant across the street arguably served the best food in town, expensive and creative. "You're just waiting around so you can follow her to her next stop?"

He puffed up his chest like a fat bantam rooster. "That's the idea."

"You're going on the air with this tonight?"

"I'm a reporter. That's what I do, report."

"But it's all lies. Don't you care about that? All that stuff—the rumors and innuendo—none of it's true. Doesn't it bother you?"

He cocked his head and studied me. "How do you know it's lies? Maybe it's true. Maybe you're the one who doesn't know the real Baxter Dunn."

My blood pressure zoomed toward the red alert zone. I started to defend Baxter again, but I feared I might say or do something I'd regret later. Strangling the pudgy news guy wouldn't exonerate Baxter. I clenched my jaw and skedaddled.

When I got to the car, I glanced back. Leonard had resumed his lean against the corner of the building, with a giant smirk now covering his chubby little face.

I drove around the block a couple of times, trying to decide what to do next. Each time I got back to the post office, the news guy was still on the corner. I thought of staking out the restaurant so I could follow Constance Boyd myself.

But what would that accomplish? Her people probably kept her well insulated from the local riffraff. How could I stop her from talking to people anyway?

Perhaps I could catch Deputy Oliver at the sheriff's office instead. From what he said at the funeral, he sounded like Baxter's friend and what I desperately needed at the moment was an ally within the department.

The receptionist informed me that Deputy Oliver was in. For a few minutes, I paced in the waiting room before he stuck his head out the door. "Mrs. Sterling?"

Basking in the potential favor of his handsome smile, I followed with rising hope. He led me through the noisy dispatch area toward the hallway with many doors and, at last, into a small cubicle at the far end.

With a hospitable gesture, he indicated that I should sit, so I did.

"What can I do for you today, Mrs. Sterling?"

I cleared my throat. "It's about Baxter Dunn's death. Rumors are flying about him and the way he died. I'm very disturbed about the misinformation out there because Baxter was the son-in-law of my friends, the Callahan's. I hoped you would tell me what's going on."

"Oh. Well." He looked at his hands for a moment and then back at me. "Your friends have been advised of the official findings to date. Why don't you ask them?"

"I'm not explaining this right. The news people are reporting about his involvement in drug dealing, affairs, and illegal activities. Constance Boyd's in town digging into stuff, looking for dirt. I know for sure Baxter would never take part in such things. You do too, if you were his friend. Why is the press allowed to report all that stuff if it isn't true?"

He screwed his lips tight. "Freedom of the press, Mrs. Sterling. Whether we like it or not."

"It's slanderous!"

He raised both hands in a gesture that communicated the impossibility of the situation.

"You *were* Baxter's friend, weren't you?"

"I like to think so."

"Then you know he was a fine, upstanding person."

He stared at his hands again.

"Help me understand where all this stuff is coming from. Someone from the sheriff's office is leaking false information to the press. Who would want to slander Baxter's reputation?"

"There is an ongoing investigation, Mrs. Sterling."

"I know, I know."

He paused, glancing away. Then he turned back with a frown. "Where did you get the idea that someone in the sheriff's office is leaking information?"

"The Channel 11 news guy told me."

"Hmm. What did he say exactly?"

"He knew the story about the drug deal and the meeting with the unknown woman. Apparently, he accompanied some other officers on a drug bust last year. I talked to the woman he arrested. Why would Baxter have been on a drug bust anyway? You said he wasn't on the Narcotics Task Force."

His eyes sparked. "You talked to the woman, Mrs. Sterling?"

I felt a lecture looming. Why was this upsetting to him? "Isn't there something you can do? Anything?"

Deputy Oliver sucked in a long gulp of air and let it out slowly. When he spoke again, his voice had softened. "Look, Mrs. Sterling, a certain situation has been developing for some time and because of that I have an idea who might be talking to the press. Baxter knew about it too. It's a highly sensitive matter involving internal affairs. I will look into it but I won't be able to share any of it. That's going to have to be okay with you."

"If you could just let me know the slightest little bit now and then, I promise I will hold it in strictest confidence." I wrote my name and number on a little scrap of paper from my purse.

He met my eyes when he grasped my hand. From the strength of his handshake, I knew he'd help as much as he could. But would that be enough?

❧

Zora Jane called later that evening. "Christine, please pray."

"What's happened?"

"Constance Boyd. Kathleen saw her on the news spreading awful rumors about Baxter. Kathleen's very upset."

"I was afraid of this." I shook my head. "I talked with the news guy from Channel 11 today." I repeated our conversation.

"Oh no! I knew that woman couldn't be trusted."

"Did you get all those interviews with the family arranged like they asked?"

"I said I would."

"So, of course you did. Has she already talked to Kathleen?"

"First thing this morning."

"She's been a busy little bee, hasn't she?"

"I feel such a call to pray, Christine."

I wanted to say, "So what's new? You pray about everything. Do you notice it's not helping?" But of course, I didn't.

Are you listening, God? Do you see the way Your child is being defamed? Why don't You do something?

❧

On Friday, Dr. Adams explained to Jesse that all his medical tests came back negative. An underlying diagnosis to explain his growing deafness had not been identified.

I frowned. "Shooting your guns probably doesn't help though."

Jesse glared at me.

Dr. Adams didn't look amused. "I advise staying away from any kind of loud noises."

"I always use earplugs." Jesse's indignation was only mildly veiled. "I had special ones made to fit my ears exactly."

No one seemed to notice when I rolled my eyes.

She consulted her file. "So, the next thing we need to talk about is hearing aids. How do you feel about wearing those?"

"What?" Jesse asked.

We all laughed.

Jesse frowned. "How big will they be?"

Ah, vanity! Thy name is Man.

The audiologist explained about the various kinds of hearing devices available, made recommendations, took measurements, and completed our order. I tried to catch

Jesse's positive attitude. He so wanted to be able to hear again. I wanted that too, but the high probability that hearing aids might not work for him muted my enthusiasm.

❧

Strange dreams often plague my sleep and I usually remember them when I wake up. That night I had a particularly odd one.

The setting was a crowded grocery store. An old-fashioned meat department like the ones I remember from my childhood dominated one end. A long line of impatient shoppers waited in front of the glass display case to make their selections from the rows of perfectly marbled meat arranged within. A large, walk-in freezer extended along the wall.

When my turn arrived, the butcher instructed me to select a frozen slab of beef from the freezer. After lugging my selection to the counter, I arranged it on a large sheet of butcher paper covering one tray of an enormous brass scale.

Deputy Colter stood on the other side of the counter. Over his uniform, a long butcher's apron tied around his middle. His normally large nose had swelled to cartoon proportions. Attached to the apron, Colter's oversized badge sparkled like an electric light. He took out a hunk of meat much larger than mine and plopped it on the opposite side of the scale.

"Exactly the same," he said with a sneer.

I studied the meat he'd deposited. Its slimy surface glistened in the light. No longer red, the color had darkened to a dark brown. To inspect it more thoroughly, I bent toward it. Dark red blood puddled around it. The pungent odor of rotting flesh made me gag. Considerably heavier than my selection, the scale dipped lower and lower on his side.

"No," I said. "They're not the same. Look. Yours is heavier."

"I say they're the same." He glowered at me. "What I say is what counts. I know the truth."

Curious onlookers gathered. Bodies jostled against me with people peering over my shoulder to view the scale. Most of them held bulbous black microphones. Their murmuring swelled to a roar when they all spoke at once.

"What's she trying to do, cheat?" "Can't she see?" "Get new glasses, lady." "It's as plain as the nose on your face." "There are irregularities. Can't she see that?"

I faced the crowd. "No. Look! They're not the same! His side is heavier. Doesn't anybody see that? Just because he says it's true doesn't mean it is. Look at the scale!"

The multitude clambered closer until they squeezed in so snugly I feared I might suffocate.

⁂

I bolted upright in bed, gasping for air. My heart thumped forcefully to the beat of *personal agenda, personal agenda, personal agenda.*

Jesse stirred. "What time is it?"

"I... just had a weird dream." I drank in a long breath, trying to quiet the thumping.

"You're okay." He rubbed my back and yawned.

"No, Jesse. I saw Deputy Colter in my dream. He was weighing meat."

Jesse yawned. "You have weird dreams, Christine. Go back to sleep."

Of course, I couldn't. Instead, I lay there for an hour replaying the dream.

"It looks like an accident." That's what he said. But that's not how it appeared to everyone else. The media version blended innuendo and lies, focusing on supposed illegal activity on

Baxter's part. The official version from the sheriff's department hadn't been finalized yet. Deputy Colter hung onto a version all his own, that it had been an accident. That didn't fly since they found the patrol car. Why did Deputy Colter insist on sticking to the accident story? What was he trying to cover up?

None of it made sense. Truth isn't subjective to different perspectives. How could anyone believe there could be more than one Truth?

❧

Constance Boyd's appointment to interview Baxter's parents was set for Monday morning. They agreed to meet at the Callahan's house for the interview since they had planned to visit with Ed and Zora Jane anyway. Zora Jane invited Jesse and me as well.

At exactly ten o'clock, the shiny black Cadillac drove into the Callahan's driveway. The chauffeur opened the back door and out stepped Miss Boyd dressed in an expensive looking green pantsuit. Zora Jane greeted her wearing a pair of orange paisley pants with an orange velour top. The shoes were orange, of course. She reminded me of an orange Popsicle.

Thankfully Miss Boyd's broadcast would be in living color.

"How nice to see you again, Miss Boyd." Zora Jane gestured toward the house with a flourish. "Won't you come in?"

"How gracious of you to make your home available for this interview." Constance Boyd flashed her perfect teeth. The studious assistant and cameraman bustled into the house without smiling.

Ida and Ted Dunn, Baxter's parents, sat stiffly on the sofa. Ed and Jesse lounged in the two green recliners. Other chairs formed a semi-circle facing the sofa. Constance Boyd settled into the prominent overstuffed chenille chair, with the assistant and cameraman on either side of her, sitting on dining chairs.

To protect her? From us?

Perhaps.

Zora Jane made introductions. I plopped onto one of the dining chairs and Zora Jane sat beside me.

Constance Boyd smiled at the Dunns. "I appreciate your coming all this way for our interview today."

"Have you been here all weekend, Miss Boyd?" Ted asked.

"I have," she said in a conversational tone. "It's a lovely area. We've enjoyed our stay very much."

I couldn't resist. "Have you gotten what you came for?"

She turned her brown eyes to study me a moment. "Everyone has been most cooperative."

Ed got right to the heart of the matter. "We're concerned about your motives. What you told my wife seems to be different from the type of interviews you're conducting in town."

I agreed with a passionate nod.

Constance Boyd raised her perfectly shaped eyebrows. "My motives?" She fluttered a hand as if such a gesture could dismiss all doubts. "Please don't worry. In a small town, rumors are certain to abound. We merely checked a few things we'd heard to see if a shred of truth could be found."

I leaned toward her. "And did you find a shred of truth?"

Her perfect smile froze. "I fear we've gotten off on a wrong note. I came today to hear a bit more background on Baxter's early life. Please don't dwell on idle gossip. I assure you, after all these years in the business, I know what to use and what not to use in a story." She bared her white teeth. Her expression put me in mind of a cobra hypnotizing his prey just before the kill.

Zora Jane cleared her throat. "Let's begin with prayer then." Without waiting for permission, she closed her eyes. "Lord, thank you for Miss Boyd and her interest in our Baxter. Please direct her ways. Help her discern truth from rumor and lies."

In the silence that followed, I squirmed in my seat. Jesse adjusted his chair. Ed coughed a little *ahem*.

I peeked at Miss Boyd. She frowned at first, creating furrows in her unlined brow. She started to speak, then thought better of it and gave a simple nod to her cameraman.

The cameraman set up his video equipment, adjusting it to the Dunns' position on the sofa. Mrs. Dunn still sat too low, so he gave her a pillow to sit on.

Constance blinked at us. "I must ask the rest of you to step outside while I conduct this interview." The assistant directed us with gestures.

Looking over my shoulder, I saw Constance perch in perfect posture on a chair opposite the Dunns, smoothing the front of her dress and checking her makeup in preparation for the interview. While we craned our necks to watch, Rebecca closed the French doors.

Ed looked concerned. "We should've stayed in there to run interference."

Jesse gave his back a light pat. "Oh, they'll be okay. Ted and Ida have level heads."

"We should've stopped this interview all together," I said. "She's going to misquote everyone when she puts the story together. We won't even recognize what we actually said by the time she gets finished with it."

They all frowned at me.

"I think we should—" Zora Jane started.

Right then I couldn't bear the notion of praying for Constance Boyd. "Don't say it!"

Jesse playfully shielded his face with his hands.

Ed shook his bald head and chuckled softly.

"Well, I'm going to." Zora Jane knelt beside one of the chaise lounges on the deck and closed her eyes.

With both men's attention while we waited, I used the time to share information I'd gathered, leaving out any reference to Mary Wilson and the biker bar. I didn't want a scolding.

After a few minutes, Zora Jane finished praying and joined us. We had a lot of catching up to do. Most importantly, I wanted them to understand how insanely convoluted this case had become. What in the world could be happening in our quiet little community?

8

CHAPTER EIGHT

The next week, while Dr. Adams fitted Jesse with his new hearing aid, I alternated between sitting and pacing in the small waiting room. Jesse had decided to purchase only one aid to begin with, reasoning that his adjustment time would be cut in half that way. He expected to struggle and his apprehension had rubbed off on me.

Would he ever be able to hear again? Were we spending all this money for something that wouldn't help him?

When I returned to my seat, I picked up a Hollywood magazine, which seemed to be the most literary of the available selections, and paged through without comprehending a single word on a single page.

Jesse lived in a world of distorted and muffled sound as if his ears were permanently plugged. At times, he heard clanging that no one else heard. It must be awful. What if I couldn't hear music? I thought of my grandchildren's beautiful laughter. Cats purring. What if I never heard birds singing again? Or water bubbling down the waterfall into our pond?

Dr. Adams opened the waiting room door. "Christine? Come on back, please."

Jesse sat in a tidy office lined with bookshelves full of medical books. He turned and smiled when I entered. "Go ahead. Ask me something."

I mouthed, "Can you hear me?"

"Very funny," he said. "Really now. Give it a try." He acted like a six year old on his first trip to Disneyland.

"Can you hear me now?" I repeated out loud.

"That's not much of a test," he said. "I can always hear you when you look right at me. Go stand over there with your back to me and try it."

I complied. "Can you hear me now?"

He laughed in triumph. "Sounds like a cell phone commercial."

I faced him. "Oh, Jesse! Can you really hear?"

"There's a whistle when you talk, but I can make out the words okay."

Dr. Adams retreated to her desk where she jotted a few notes in Jesse's file. "The device will take some getting used to. We may still have some adjusting to do. If you have any problems, don't hesitate to come back. It usually takes a little tweaking before we get everything in proper alignment so you get maximum benefit."

"What?" Jesse asked.

Dr. Adams frowned in concern until she saw the amusement in Jesse's face.

Jesse grinned. "Hey, thanks a million. This is quite encouraging."

❧

When we settled into the car again, Jesse turned to me. "Now that I can hear, I can help with this investigation you're spearheading."

"Really?"

He nodded. "You missed a lot of pertinent information when you interviewed this Mary Wilson."

My pride took a hit while I buckled my seat belt. Conscience too. I really should tell Jesse about how I found Mary. Maybe some other time. "Like what?"

"Like how about the name of the wacko boyfriend, the one Baxter asked about. And how about a description of the wacko boyfriend."

Oh, nuts! Didn't even think of that.

Jesse started the engine. "Where was Mary when Baxter couldn't find her for two years? And how about the black van with the stolen license plates? Did you ask about that? Maybe she knows who it belongs to."

"You're so smart!" Never hurts to stroke the male ego. "Gotta admit, I never thought of any of those questions."

Jesse beamed as if he'd been awarded first prize at the spelling bee. He sang while we drove northwest toward Rough and Ready.

> *I wanna know for sure that you'll be my girl.*
> *Come on baby let the good times roll.*
> *Get along home, Cindy, Cindy, Get along home Cindy Lou.*
> *Tell me that you care. Tell me that you'll always be there.*
> *I spent a lifetime looking for the right one …*

Not knowing one complete song never stopped Jesse from singing. He knew plenty of snippets to compose a medley. When he started to serenade, I never tried to join in because he might move on to a completely different song at any moment when he ran out of words and I never knew what tune he would use next.

Hearing him sing, I relaxed, sighing in contentment. Ever since his hearing started to fail, he'd been grumpier than usual and hadn't been singing much. How pleasant to have him back to normal, well, at least normal for Jesse.

After winding around curvy roads for more than fifteen minutes, we arrived at Mary's. The house appeared the same as before, unadorned and commonplace.

Jesse parked on the dirt driveway beside the house. "Let's ask for God's help first."

I bestowed a wide grin on him. Nothing makes me quite as happy as when he takes his rightful spiritual leadership role.

Jesse put his hand on my knee and prayed. "Lord, thank you for better hearing. Please give us the right questions to ask Mary today. Help her be cooperative and unafraid."

I finished the prayer. "And help us get to the truth about what really happened to Baxter that night."

"I could hear you with my eyes closed." Jesse smiled his delight. His radiant smile always dazzled me. As usual, I got lost staring at it, but he soon turned away to inspect the house. "Sure is quiet out here."

"Yeah." Climbing out of the Jeep, I took in the neglected scene. The wind blew a lonely howl in the tops of the trees. Knowing a little about Mary's life, the sound seemed a perfect background. "Quiet and sad."

Jesse pointed to the rusty vehicle. "Do you think that's her car?"

"Don't know. Does it look drivable?"

Exploring the possibility, Jesse peeked in the driver side window and shrugged. "There's a lot of dust on the seat. Doesn't look like anyone's driven it for a while."

He knocked on the door. We waited at least a minute and then I knocked again.

Jesse frowned. "Maybe she's not here."

"Give her time. She's probably sleeping off a hangover."

Just then, I heard muffled footsteps. The door slowly opened. On the other side of the screen, Mary blinked at the streaming sunlight.

"Hi." I gave a wide grin. "Remember me? I came out last week to talk with you about Deputy Dunn."

She kept batting her eyes without saying a word.

How far gone was she today?

"This is my husband, Jesse Sterling." I nodded toward him.

Mary blinked a few seconds longer, probably dazzled by his smile. Then she heaved a sigh so long and deep that her shoulders raised and lowered. "I told you what I know about the cop."

"I know," I said as encouragingly as possible. "I appreciate that very much. But we need to ask a couple of other things. Won't take long."

"Whatever." She shrugged one shoulder lazily and pushed the screen door, stepping back to let us through. We followed while she padded toward the same living area where I sat on my last visit.

"Shove that stuff off and grab a seat if you want." She curled up in the big chair and picked at a tuft of stuffing that stuck out through a jagged rip in the upholstery.

I moved aside a mound of clothing and settled next to it on the sofa. Jesse pushed a few items onto the already littered floor so he could sit beside me.

My gaze traveled in a semi-circle around the room. "Do you live alone?"

"Me and a couple cats."

All of a sudden I wondered a lot of things about Mary that I hadn't considered before. "Have you lived out here a long time?"

She shook her head. "Not long."

Jesse asked, "Is that your car out front?"

Mary glanced in the general direction of the vehicle, although she couldn't see it through the wall. "It's registered to the old man. He let me use it."

Jesse raised his eyebrows. "Does it run?"

"Not very often." Mary tugged her drooping sweatshirt over her bare shoulder. "I don't know how to fix it and mechanics cost money."

I nodded. "How do you make ends meet? Do you have a job?"

As Mary probed the chair, a clump of stuffing popped out of the arm. She looked surprised and stuffed it back inside with one finger. "I get some help from the state and then I waitress down at the Owl. Part-time."

Jesse arched one eyebrow. Did he judge her? I knew how he felt about young healthy people receiving welfare.

When she shrugged, the oversized sweatshirt fell off her shoulder again.

"Did you say 'waitress'? Do they serve food there?"

Out of the corner of my eye, I saw Jesse shoot me a questioning glance.

Her listless eyes turned toward me. "Not food. I just serve drinks sometimes when they get really slammed. They pay me under the table."

Oh, sure. Waitresses serve drinks as well as food. "Oh." But she didn't look old enough to serve drinks in a bar.

Jesse cleared his throat. "Let's see if we got this right. You haven't been here long, but you were living here with a boyfriend the first time you met Deputy Dunn. Right?"

A single nod conveyed her answer.

"Deputy Dunn came to arrest you and your boyfriend."

"Well, me really, cause the old man wasn't here when the

cops came. Who did you say you work for?" Brows knit in a frown, she looked at me, then Jesse.

Maybe she would clam up if she thought too much about who we were. "We're not working for anyone." When I get nervous, I babble. "We're friends of Deputy Dunn's family. A bunch of rumors and lies are circulating about him. Maybe you've heard them. The story is all over the news. We're disgusted with the current investigation. What's being reported gets further from the truth every day. We just want to give the sheriff's department a reason to start down a different road."

"How do you know what's being said isn't true?"

The fat gray cat wandered into the room again and jumped into her lap. It purred so loudly I could hear the sound from where I sat. While Mary absentmindedly scratched its ears, she cocked her head as if she couldn't imagine a cop who wasn't dirty.

"Baxter couldn't possibly be involved with drugs. We saw him with his family. We saw him at church. He wasn't the kind of person who'd get into the drug scene." How could I convince her? "Baxter was a Christian. Do you know what that is?"

Mary wiggled her head slightly, side to side. "Never had much use for religion."

"It's not religion, it's a relationship. Religion is what people make up, trying to reach God. Being a Christian is about connecting to God through Jesus Christ." I paused, amazed at the words pouring out of my mouth. Zora Jane must be rubbing off on me.

"He was a fine, upstanding man with high standards and morals," I continued. "Christians live by God's standards. Baxter worked hard to be like Jesus. He cared about the community, about health and safety. He wasn't the kind of man they're talking about on the news."

Jesse nodded. "Also, Baxter wasn't on the Drug Task Force. So, why do you think he came with the other officers when you got arrested?"

Eyes lowered, she stroked the cat. "Now that you mention it, he didn't seem like part of the team. Two other cops did the arresting. Dunn just stood there, asking questions about the old man." She stopped stroking and regarded me as if she'd just realized something. "Actually, that's all he *ever* talked about, the old man."

I nodded. "What's your boyfriend's name?"

She straightened in the chair. "*Ex*-boyfriend. Frank de la Peña." She whispered his name as if it were a secret she'd promised not to tell. Fear flashed into her eyes. "Most people call him Kingfisher."

"Why?" Jesse asked.

"Kingfishers are birds. Big heads, colorful. They're murder on fish because they have these huge, strong bills, see? That's Frankie. He's little, but smart. Big head, colorful personality, but you don't want to cross him. He's strong and..." Mary shivered involuntarily and shrank back into her chair.

I bent forward. "You're afraid of him?"

Her dark gaze darted toward the window. "Afraid? You bet! You should be too. That's one bad dude."

Jesse leaned toward her. "Why?"

Mary tilted her head and her voice lowered to a whisper. "That dude's into really weird stuff. He's not afraid of nobody."

Jesse frowned. "Weird stuff? Is that what you said?"

Mary nodded slowly, eyes darting back to the window.

I followed her gaze, but didn't see anything. "What kind of weird stuff?"

We had to strain to hear her whispered answer. "Says he gets visions from God. People listen to him 'cause he uses God's words. Big words, words I don't understand. He says God told him to get people ready."

That didn't sound good. "Get people ready for what?"

"He says… he says…" Her body squirmed as if she was trying to shrink deeper into the chair. "Holocaust. A big war's coming like we never seen before. If you're not with him when the war comes, you'll die."

Jesse and I blinked questions at each other. Was she delusional?

Jesse frowned. "Do you know where Frank lives now?"

"Back in the woods, past North San Juan off Benedict Road. Him and the other one, they named the place *Satori*. I think that means enlightenment. It's a big place, an abandoned sawmill. He took me out there a couple times. They talk like it's gonna be famous someday."

Scary!

Jesse's expression conveyed genuine interest. "They live there, you say? Who's the other one?"

She straightened again, eyes glimmering with emotion. "Weird guy… calls himself Bodhi. It's some kinda Indian word, I think. Not his real name. That's all I ever heard them call him. I haven't seen him much, but what I saw, they're just alike. They got a big gang up there. I don't know how many. Hundreds. Maybe more. Doing military drills, you know, getting ready for war. Frankie's mean. Crazy mean. They both are. I don't know who's the leader, Frankie or that kinky-haired freak. Just know you don't want to cross 'em." While she spoke, she became more agitated, rising unsteadily to her feet at the end of her warning. "You won't say I talked to you, will you? I shouldn't have told you any of this. You can't say anything about me. Don't even mention my name."

We stood with her.

"Don't worry, Mary." Jesse reached to comfort her. "We wouldn't want to make trouble for you."

Shaking his hand off her arm, she motioned for the door. "You better go. I don't want no trouble."

"How about that car? Would you like me to fix it?"

I jerked a look at Jesse. Was this generous offer a stalling technique or did he really want to help? Clearly, someone needed to come to this child's aid. So much of her life was substandard.

But she wouldn't accept his help. "Just go."

The screen door slammed behind us. Hearing the sound, Jesse threw his arm around me and pulled me into the dust. "Was that a gunshot?" He lifted his head to peer into the trees.

I would have laughed, but my face was in the dirt. Spitting out as much dust and pebbles as I could, I rolled him off me. "That wasn't gunshot. The door slammed."

He helped me to my feet looking rather sheepish. "Sorry. It was loud. Guess I overreacted"

"It's okay." Brushing off my clothes, I gave him an encouraging smile. "But you know what? We forgot to ask about the black van." I yanked the door open again. "Hey! Just a minute, Mary. Do you know anyone who drives a black van?"

"Just Frankie."

She slammed the door again.

This time Jesse only flinched. "This hearing aid magnifies sound like you wouldn't believe."

But I had already keyed in on Mary's important revelation. "Holy guacamole, Batman! Did you hear that?" I punched Jesse playfully in the arm. "Good ol' Frankie drives a black van. When we find Frankie, we find the black van. And when we find the black van, we'll find out what Baxter was doing when he stopped it that night. All we gotta do is find Frankie."

"Yeah." Jesse's expression was worried. "All we gotta do is find Frankie."

On the drive back through town, we stopped at the sheriff's office. I hoped to find Deputy Oliver in again, but no such luck. Deputy Colter happened to be on duty, so we asked to speak with him.

Before long, the door popped open and Colter strutted toward us, looking quite annoyed by this disturbance in his busy schedule.

"The Sterlings." He pronounced our name as if it had a bad taste. His shoulders drooped. "What can I do for you today?"

"We hoped to speak with Deputy Oliver about the progress of the Baxter Dunn investigation."

"Deputy Oliver is not in charge of that investigation. That would be Detective Rogers." He turned abruptly.

I feared he would leave before we learned anything. "We know where you can find the black van."

He jerked back toward me. His eyes sparked and his breath puffed in shallow bursts as if his head might explode at any moment. "Have you been snooping around after I specifically told you not to?"

Afraid he might strike me, I moved out of his reach. Jesse stepped in front of me at the same time. I guess he also worried that I might have provoked a punch.

Chin out, Jesse confronted the wild beady eyes. "We asked a few questions, that's all."

I peeked out from around Jesse's middle. "The media is telling lies."

Deputy Colter's complexion reddened. "I specifically warned you not to interfere in this investigation." His eyes squinted until only tiny slits appeared where the orbs used to be. "You are in over your meddling heads." His hands tightened into fists. "This is your final warning! Dangerous things are happening in this county. Stay out of it! If you do not, I will slap you in jail for obstruction." He spit the words out, emphasizing each one. "Do you understand?" Then he turned on his heels and marched out of sight.

I gulped air in hopes it would calm my racing heart. "Was he threatening us?"

"Sounded like it." Jesse put his arm around me and led me out of the waiting room. "Either he's afraid for our safety, which I doubt since he isn't the compassionate type, or he has some reason for wanting to scare us away."

Were those the only possibilities? What reason could Colter have for wanting to scare us away?

An even more curious question shrieked like a siren in my brain. Why didn't Colter ask where to find the black van?

Deep in my own ruminations, I almost missed Jesse's lecture. "So I don't want you traipsing off to this *Satori* place. Got it?"

"What?"

Jesse spun me to face him and gripped my shoulders in his hands. He bent to my eye-level. "I'm being very clear about this, Miss Snoopy Nose. You are not to try to find that place on your own."

"But Jesse!"

He shook his head. "I knew you had that in your mind. It's too dangerous. No way."

"Who's going to go then? Who else cares?"

No matter what I said, his mind was made up.

CHAPTER NINE

As soon as we reached home, I called Deputy Oliver to tell him about the black van. Maybe he'd be more interested than Colter in finding the occupants.

"Mrs. Sterling," Deputy Oliver said as soon as we were connected. "Thank you for calling. I hoped to talk with you today."

"Oh?"

"I heard you stopped by to see me this afternoon and I've been thinking over what we spoke of the other day. You said someone in the press received information from the sheriff's office. Is that correct?"

"That's right. He wouldn't tell me who though."

"Do you remember exactly what he said?"

"I don't think I can report like Archie Goodwin reported to Nero Wolfe."

"How's that?"

"Verbatim. I can't do that. I wish I could. Maybe I could've a few years ago, but my memory isn't what it used to be." I was rambling again, although I couldn't say what made me nervous about this particular conversation. "I believe he said someone at the sheriff's office leaked information to him. He said this person told him that Baxter consorted with known drug dealers the night he died, purchased illegal drugs, and that all of it had been officially denied by the department."

"That's it?"

I struggled to pull up another memory, but none came. "I don't remember anything else. Sorry."

"What's the newsman's name?"

"Leonard Pinzer. He's been hanging out waiting for Constance Boyd to drop some interesting crumb. I think he works for Channel 11."

"Yes, I've met him."

"Leonard is hard to miss. He's quite… tenacious!"

Deputy Oliver chuckled. "That's a nice way of putting it."

"Do you have any idea who's leaking information?"

"I might, but I need proof before I accuse him. I hoped you'd remember something more incriminating."

Nothing came to mind. "Can't you tell me the identity of the leak?"

"Sorry. I can tell you to get ready for a big TV broadcast. Constance Boyd is winding down her, I guess you'd say her investigation."

"So she's leaving soon?"

"That's what we heard. She scheduled another press conference for tomorrow afternoon. Wanted more pictures too, I think. Then she's going back to New York. Her people have been here almost three weeks already. She flies in for a day or two between broadcasts." He sighed. "She's stuck to this case tighter than Spandex running shorts on a fat man. Frankly, I'm relieved she's almost finished. The way she throws her national celebrity status around you'd think she was queen of the world. Most of us have refused to talk to her." He paused and cleared his throat. "Actually, that's more than I should say, Mrs. Sterling."

"My lips are sealed. We'll pray for your success."

I couldn't believe I offered to pray. I was beginning to sound just like Zora Jane.

As the phone disconnected, I realized I never mentioned the black van. I started to, but it just felt wrong. Well, I would have to scout that out myself. If I did find the actual vehicle, then I'd really have something to report.

Right then I couldn't wait to share the news about Constance Boyd's departure. Without hanging up, I punched in the Callahan's' phone number. When Zora Jane answered, I launched in. "Constance Boyd plans to broadcast her story soon. She has one final meeting at the sheriff's office tomorrow afternoon and then she's leaving town."

Zora Jane sighed. "Oh, dear. That will be some story. Since what really happened hasn't been determined, she will have to embellish what she's found to fill in the gaps. We might be in for an hour of distortion and unsubstantiated rumors."

"You can bet her version will be full of lies."

"We need to pray."

This time I fully agreed with her. Evil pooled in Nevada County like an oil spill, dark and noxious. Gossip churned the collective emotions. Oppression blanketed our community. God's Word proclaimed victory over Satan's minions. Being God's representatives as Christians, we needed to unite in prayer and plead for God's intervention.

That's why we planned a prayer meeting at the Callahan's' house for the next morning.

Jesse and I arrived for prayer just before nine o'clock. Intent on the importance of our mission, for once I didn't notice Zora Jane's outfit.

She began without hesitation. "Before we pray, we need to search our hearts for anger or bitterness against the media for how they've handled Baxter's death. We must be clean when we come before the Lord with these petitions. If God reveals that we're holding bitterness, we must ask for forgiveness. Let's take a few moments now to examine our hearts."

In the silence that followed, the anger and resentment I held in my heart against the media blitz and the people who fed off it loomed large in my mind.

Forgive me, God, for being judgmental and angry. Cleanse my heart. Give me Your love for these people even if I can't love what they're doing.

"Now," Zora Jane continued, "we'll pray for them. I'll mention the ones we know by name. When you hear them named, pray only blessings on them. We must not ask God to harm them in any way, including loss of their jobs. They make their livings being journalists. Their families depend on that."

Ed nodded. "That's true. Reporting the news is a legitimate occupation. When it's done with compassion and dedication to Truth, it serves an important function to keep the public informed."

Zora Jane's smile looked saintly. "So we'll ask God to prosper them, give them success in their careers and their personal lives, and to save their souls. We'll ask Him to grant them wisdom and understanding of the people they're interviewing and give them a passion for Truth. Not merely intellectual curiosity, but a genuine yearning to present the Truth." She stopped for a moment and regarded us before speaking again. "We are also going to make a specific request. We will ask God to postpone the airing of this show until the investigation is complete. Whatever the eventual outcome, we want the news people to have time to compile all relevant material in a non-biased manner."

Kneeling, we began to pray. Periodically, Zora Jane named one of the news people by name or suggested something to pray about. We prayed for Constance Boyd and her people and for Leonard Pinzer and the local news group. Mostly, we prayed silently for the next hour, beseeching God on behalf of the media. When we rose, I sensed the spirit of God and felt the power of communal prayer. Hope shone in Ed and Zora Jane's eyes.

Zora Jane grasped Jesse's hand. "Thank you so much for praying with us today."

"What's next?" Jesse asked.

"I think we should try to talk with Miss Boyd," Ed said. "Ask her point blank to postpone her show."

I raised my eyebrows. "You think she'll talk to us? Just like that?"

"Have faith in God," Ed said. "All we have to do is find her."

Finding Constance Boyd turned out to be relatively easy. We drove to downtown Nevada City, spotted Leonard Pinzer and his faithful cameraman sidekick lounging outside the Brownstone Inn, and there she was, having a late breakfast surrounded by her entourage.

After about half an hour, she emerged in the middle of four people whose rigid expressions and shifting gazes implied that their sole purpose in life was to shield Miss Boyd from oncoming danger. Her uniformed chauffeur walked in front like a burly bodyguard. Rebecca, the spectacled assistant, and an older woman we'd never seen before flanked either side while the cameraman dawdled in the rear, his impressive equipment dangling over one shoulder like a hunter's trophy.

Ed approached the group, striding boldly. The chauffeur stepped toward him, arms out to block his path.

Ed extended his hand and smiled. "Miss Boyd? May we have a moment of your time?"

Constance Boyd stopped to peer warily at Ed, shielding her eyes from the bright sunlight. Apparently, she recognized him because she stepped away from the bodyguard to meet him. "Mr. Callahan. How lovely to see you." She took Ed's hand. "What can I do for you?"

The entourage huddled behind, shielding her rear flank.

Zora Jane, Jesse, and I caught up with them. Constance glanced at each of us in turn, offering what I considered to be her public smile.

Zora Jane caught her gaze. "We've been praying for you, Miss Boyd. We heard you're almost finished with your investigation. Will you be returning to New York soon?"

The smile froze on Constance Boyd's face. "I have another meeting or two, then I'll be leaving."

"We have a request," Ed said. "Please postpone airing this piece on Baxter until after his this case has been marked closed."

Constance blinked. "Postpone it?" A choked laugh escaped. "You must be joking. I've just spent three weeks gathering information. Time is money, you know."

Leonard Pinzer and his cameraman joined us without another word. Leonard jerked his fat black microphone toward Constance and the cameraman hoisted his video camera to his shoulder. The green light flickered on.

"We appreciate how hard you've worked on this project," Jesse said. "That's why we're sure you'll see the wisdom of waiting. Right now, you've only collected part of the story. If you wait until the official investigation and trial are over, you'll have the whole truth."

Zora Jane and I nodded in unison.

The assistant peered over the top of her glasses with raised eyebrows.

"I will do an update when the trial is completed," Constance said. Her coterie collectively glanced at us for a response.

I stepped toward her. "All you have right now is gossip and innuendo. You need more than that. You need to know *why* and *how* when you report this to the nation. Otherwise, your story might be slanted in the wrong direction."

An ugly frown transformed Constance's sleek countenance. Apparently, I'd hit a nerve. She flung her words at me like darts. "Are you insinuating I produce stories without proper research? How dare you? We've been researching for three weeks. Also, I do not slant my stories. I do not deal in sensational journalism unless strictly based on fact. Perhaps you did not realize that incredible facts spike ratings." Her eyes transmitted daggers that sliced the air between us. "Perhaps *you* don't wish to believe the facts of this case."

I stood my ground.

Zora Jane stepped between us, always the peacemaker. "Please, Miss Boyd, as the family and friends of Baxter Dunn, we implore you. Do not air the story at this time. We will accept whatever the truth is, but you must promise to report what really happened. If you go on air now, you will perpetuate a great disservice to a remarkable young man and to all who knew him. I am certain you do not want to broadcast lies."

Without the slightest warning, the face of TV's national news star flared red with fury. Constance Boyd whirled abruptly and shoved her way through the crowd behind her. She flounced away, flinging words over her shoulder like a volley of pebbles. "Small town. Small minds. I've been in broadcasting for twenty-five years! How would you know what's best for *my* show?"

Her entourage hustled after her. Leonard Pinzer and his lanky cameraman vacillated, apparently unsure which story to follow. They soon opted for celebrity over small minds and raced after Constance Boyd as she pranced down the sidewalk. We stood still, disappointment settling over us like a smothering blanket.

God, didn't you hear our prayers?

Standing with us after the others departed, the stranger who'd been walking on the far side of Constance studied us thoughtfully. Her gaze lingered on each of us before she spoke. "You've made a good point. Right now, we don't have the whole story. We have a lot, and much of it is quite sensational, but perhaps it would be a better story if we waited until after the trial. Assuming there will be one eventually."

We all spoke at once.

I said, "You're so right. Truth always makes a better story."

Zora Jane said something like, "Oh, praise God!"

I think Jesse said, "You'd be laying yourself open to slander lawsuits by the family if you aired this clap-trap she's collected."

Ed asked, "Can you talk her into waiting?"

Chuckling lightly, the woman held up one hand to stop the barrage of words. "Hang on now. You'll have to speak one at a time."

"Who are you, anyway?" Ed asked.

The woman extended her hand. "I should introduce myself. Priscilla Stuart, producer of The Constance Boyd Show, at your service." She dipped her head in a curt nod.

Ed grabbed her hand and pumped hard. "We're sure pleased to meet you. Do you think you can convince her to hold off on this story?"

She winced extracting her hand from Ed's overenthusiastic grip. "Maybe. It could take a year or more for a trial. Being a diva, she won't like to wait. But I think she'll listen to reason once she cools down. Even if she doesn't, I have enough clout with corporate. I think I can manage a delay."

We thanked her, all speaking at the same time again, grateful beyond measure that God had indeed heard and answered our prayer. He didn't answer the way I thought he would, but His way was much better.

Now if God would only lead us to what really happened the night Baxter Dunn died.

10

CHAPTER TEN

Heedless of Jesse's warning that I must stay out of the case, the first chance I got I herded Molly into the car to search for *Satori* and the black van. Thoughts of North San Juan filled my mind while I drove along Highway 49 to the cutoff. Where did North San Juan come from? If there was a *North* San Juan, shouldn't there be a town of *San Juan* somewhere nearby? Yet I'd never heard of one. Could there be ruins of an ancient civilization hidden in the forest? I would file these questions with my long list of other unanswerable issues such as why God created weeds.

North San Juan wasn't on the way to anywhere. Getting there required a deliberate turning off the main highway. Perhaps that explained the general dilapidated state of the buildings. Clearly, the entire town had been built in another era. Bricks were broken, strips of paint curled, siding had chipped off. Front windows sported cracks. Missing glass let in the weather.

Although I assumed I could find *Satori* without help, I stopped at a small market to confirm directions and eased my stiff legs out of the Jeep. My ankles cracked and my knees refused to bend. How long had I been driving?

Three dusty motorcycles languished in the bright mid-morning sun in front of the Dew Drop Inn. I would not be dropping in there for directions; I'd had quite enough of biker bars for the time being, thank you very much.

The Hotel of the Rising Sun flanked the Dew Drop Inn. Farther down the road from Dee's Whole Earth Market and Deli, an antiquated gas station and auto parts shop made up the rest of the town.

A faded sign in the hotel window proclaimed, "Give peace a chance." *Let me guess, hippies settled North San Juan.*

"I'm going into Dee's, Molly," I said to my faithful companion. "If I don't come out in a couple minutes, send in the drug-sniffing dogs, okay?"

By way of answer, Molly yawned and flipped her tail a couple of times. She'd been sleeping in the sun next to me during the forty-five minute drive from our house. Evidently, she didn't have energy for a full wag. I gave her a pat on the head and locked her in.

Across the street I couldn't help noticing the first splash of color in this otherwise drab town. Flaming red hair topped a woman wearing shorts and an abbreviated top. Well past the age when shorts constituted attractive attire, her outfit illustrated the term *muffin top*. A colorful tie-dyed top, not quite reaching her middle, exposed rolls of flesh forced up and out by the waistband of the tight shorts.

When I moved toward the grocery store, the woman shielded her eyes, appearing to watch me. By the time I reached the door, more color had materialized. A man of even larger proportions joined the redhead. Rolls of belly protruded over his biker leathers. He wore a red kerchief tied on his head. While I entered the store, the two leaned against the wall of the bar, staring...*at me?*

I stifled a desire to wave.

Must not get many strangers in these parts.

Pulling open the grocery door, a gross mixture of odors assaulted my nostrils. Rotten meat, sour milk, and rancid oil permeated the air. The distinctive, pungent smell of Pine Sol indicated that someone had made a perfunctory effort to clean up. The floor could definitely use more attention. Dirt hid in cracks and corners where countless boots had mashed it in. Always a big red flag in a grocery store.

I wonder how often the health inspector visits North San Juan.

Groceries lined rows of shelves in a disorganized fashion, brands and items I wasn't used to seeing: miso, tempeh, incense. Except for the clerk, I had the store all to myself. Perhaps the residents of North San Juan weren't out and about this early.

Behind a cluttered counter, a lanky teenage boy wearing a black shirt emblazoned with an *Easy Rider* logo peered at me over the top of the biker magazine he'd been studying. He looked too young to have seen the original movie. Maybe they'd remade it.

"You need help?"

I stepped toward him. "Actually, I do."

He scowled, shrugged his skinny shoulders and focused on his magazine. "What?"

"I'm looking for a place called *Satori*. It's an abandoned sawmill off Benedict Road. Somewhere north of here. Do you know it?"

He slammed down the magazine and bent over the counter to look me over head to toe. "You don't look like someone who oughta go there."

From the back room, a woman called. "Are you talking to someone, Ralphie? Is someone out there?"

Without taking his suspicious little eyes off me, Ralphie answered. "Some old lady wants directions to *Satori*. Don't think they want just anyone going out there."

What's with the old lady comments? *How'd you like this old lady to throttle you, young man?*

A hard faced woman barely old enough to be his mother appeared from the back room just when I decided someone should teach this young man a little lesson in courtesy.

"What do you want to go out there for?" she asked, wiping her hands on her stained apron before addressing the stringy state of her hair.

"I—uh—I…" *Wish I'd thought of a clever cover story. Help me, God. What should I say?* A clever cover story didn't drop into my head, so I spoke the truth instead. "I'm a friend of Baxter Dunn's. He died out near the Star Mine last month. The sheriff's department hasn't solved his murder because they're looking in all the wrong places. I just want to know what really happened."

She tilted her head, eyeing me with disdain. "You're not a cop."

"No, of course not." I laughed lightly. "I'm not making official inquiries either."

She shuffled behind the counter in worn Birkenstocks while pinching clumps of hair back into the brown scrunchy from whence they'd strayed. When she finished, she picked up a pair of granny glasses and adjusted them on her nose. "Why do you think you'll find answers at *Satori*?"

"There's a black van there."

"And…"

"Deputy Dunn radioed about stopping a black van the night he died. I think maybe it's the one Frankie de la Peña drives."

She cocked her head to one side, eyes sparking with mistrust.

One more try. "What sort of place is *Satori* anyway?"

Pinching her expression into a frown, she planted her hands on her hips. "They masquerade as a religious organization, but it's not any kind of religion I ever heard of. You ask me, it's just some kind of ego trip. Grownup boys who'd rather fight than work."

"Oh…well, I want to go out there."

"Nosy people sometimes get their selves in trouble."

Ralphie snorted.

"Please." Right then I wasn't above begging. "Help me. I won't make trouble. I just need to find the truth."

She considered that briefly and then waved both hands in the air, as if absolving herself of responsibility. "Go for it, then. But don't say you weren't warned. That's a bad bunch out there. Try not to hassle 'em. Stay out of sight if you can."

"Thank you." I gave an enthusiastic nod. "I certainly will."

She gave me directions, specifying that I should look for a "Y" in the road and a sign announcing the "Gleason Mill."

The directions the woman at the grocery store offered proved essential; I'd never have found the place without them. Locating Benedict Road wasn't much trouble, although it was farther from the North San Juan turnoff than it appeared on the map. Once I exited onto Benedict Road, however, the woods pressed in on each side while the road curved every ten feet or so, making long-range visibility nearly impossible.

Benedict Road narrowed after about a mile. At first, side roads angled off where houses peeked through the trees. These gradually became farther and farther apart until no more appeared. Perhaps a half mile after that, the pavement ran out and a bumpy dirt road took its place.

How do they get in and out of here during the winter rains? There must be another way in. Lumber trucks would never be able to navigate this lane.

Deep potholes scored the road. The Jeep bucked and jolted when I tried to drive over them. It took concentration to maneuver around them. I decreased speed significantly, but still bounced and rattled as if I drove a wooden cart pulled by a horse. Molly let out a whine of discomfort.

"I know, girl." I patted her head. "I don't like it either. Hopefully, these bumps won't last much longer."

The dirt path twisted and turned through dense woods. I hadn't passed any indication of civilization for at least a mile when I came upon a wider space of road where the dirt path made a "Y." A weathered sign with an arrow pointed to "Gleason Mill" ahead.

"Thank you, God, for the helpful woman in North San Juan."

Braking to veer to the right as she had directed, I caught sight of another beat-up sign nailed to a tall pine tree. In large red stenciled letters it read:

PRIVATE PROPERTY
STAY OUT!
TRESPASSERS WILL BE SHOT
NO QUESTIONS ASKED

When I slammed on the brakes, Molly fell off the seat and thumped to the floor.

"Sorry, girl!" Pretty strong language! What now, God? Should I go ahead or turn around?

Driving a little farther, I braked and turned off the ignition. After the dust settled, I stepped out and slowly scanned the dense forest that surrounded me, looking and listening for movement.

Silence. Not even a leaf stirred.

Fixing my eyes on the Jeep, I looked for some assurance I was still on planet earth. Molly sat motionless in the driver's seat staring. Only her panting tongue moved. Was her brow furrowed?

She blinked, forcing my mind back to the task at hand. My exploration could take a while, so what was I going to do with Molly? Why didn't I think of this before? I couldn't leave her in the car and go off without her.

The Jeep presented another problem. I rearranged the car facing toward Benedict Road under a leafy arbor just in case I needed to leave in a hurry. Partial camouflage seemed preferable to none at all.

Normally, I didn't put Molly on a leash because she always obeyed when I called. But since I was sneaking in and didn't want to risk being heard, I hunted through the back of the Jeep until I found the purple leash I kept for emergencies. Clipping it on Molly's collar, we set off for the sawmill.

Through the trees, the noonday sun hovered nearly straight overhead. Despite the mild spring air, before long I worked up a sweat. Being sweaty made me grumpy. My face got red and my clothes stuck to my skin. And why didn't I wear proper hiking shoes? Molly didn't look as if she enjoyed the walk either. Maybe the leash bothered her.

Presently, we came upon a fenced area with an iron gate that was locked. Of course. I'd have to climb over it. Climbing fences always challenged me, having such short legs. But this time I managed with only minimal discomfort from the jump down.

"Ouch! That stings!" I clapped a hand over my mouth when I remembered my need for stealth. I'd let go of the leash and when Molly saw me on the other side of the gate, she scooted underneath.

Ahead I saw the rundown sawmill buildings. Several had collapsed walls. I peeked in the windows of one of the larger buildings, but only could only see lots of rusted machinery. The saw must have been housed inside. The next building hosted piles of wooden crates.

Ammunition? Mary had said they were getting ready for war. Guns, maybe.

Old logging machinery and tools were stored in the two small shacks. Why put some of the machinery indoors and leave the rest outside?

Tiptoeing to the next set of windows, I came upon a low structure that resembled barracks. Rows of bunk beds lined one wall. A wood stove at either end promised heat on cold winter nights. Sparse rustic furnishings lent a monastic atmosphere to the space. I counted beds, thirty-six with top and bottom with each having the same heavy woolen blanket and pillow.

Not the Ritz, but serviceable if you don't mind Spartan surroundings.

By then, we'd reached the far end of the compound without encountering a single soul. That worried me, but Molly padded contentedly at my side, not even straining on her leash, as if she enjoyed our stroll.

Where did everyone go?

Most likely playing war games in the woods.

By now, the skulking had become stressful. Squatting fatigued my leg muscles. Jesse liked to remind me that I wasn't as young as I used to be. My shoulders ached from holding my body so tense. My eyes strained to scout in all directions before moving a muscle. Not to mention the mental fatigue from worrying that at any moment someone might discover us lurking behind the buildings.

Molly whined a couple of times when I stopped too long. I considered returning to the car the way I'd come. Although I'd seen evidence that people currently occupied this compound, I'd yet to come upon any vehicles. That's what I really came to see, the vehicles.

Where is that black van?

When I got to the crossbar section of the "U" on the far end of the compound, I craned my neck to peek between the two farthest buildings.

A small black surveillance camera caught my eye when it moved a few inches with a faint whirring sound. The camera hung under the eaves of the next building to my left, pointed away from us. Did that indicate the relative importance of that particular building?

A large pile of fur on the veranda rearranged its position with a grunt and a groan. *Oh, no! A dog! A German shepherd guard dog.*

I struggled to keep from screaming.

Now what? Dogs have keen hearing. Why hadn't he heard us already?

A mere fifty feet separated Molly and me from the dog. I tucked Molly safely behind me where she'd be harder to see. Shade at the back of the building gave us partial covering. I hoped the two dogs wouldn't see or smell each other.

How had I missed that dog when I started my trek along these buildings? Christine, Christine! How do you do it?

No one knew our whereabouts. *This is what you get for going against your husband's wishes.* That was wrong. A headache stabbed my brain. *Why hadn't I told someone where I planned to go?* We might never get out of here.

Retreating to a safer position at the rear of the building, I pressed my back against the wall. Molly plopped at my feet, watching my face. Tilting my head upward, I prayed to God for wisdom. *Oh, Lord, help me. I know I should've asked You before I came out here today. But I didn't. Again. Why do I think I can do these things on my own? Please forgive me. I know asking for Your help now is like asking You to keep the cow from escaping after the barn door has been left open all night. I'm a sinful creature, Lord. A wretched, sinful creature.*

I poked my head out around the buildings once more. The scene hadn't changed. Beyond the next building another long building stood. Most likely another barracks. The final building on that side appeared to be two stories tall with a large double barn door. Two beat-up pickup trucks rested in its shade, the only vehicles I'd seen so far. There must be others. That larger building might be tall enough to park cars inside. If I wanted to find the black van, I'd probably have to look in there.

Now or never. I sucked in a long breath, put my head down, and raced along the back side of the building where I knew the dog and camera guarded the front. Then I continued to the long building without pausing to look around, dragging Molly behind me.

On the other side, loud voices shredded the afternoon silence like sharp bowie knives. I froze mid-step.

CHAPTER ELEVEN

Hearing the voices, I yanked Molly toward me and held her securely. In total trust, she sat watching me, panting as if she needed a drink. I should have thought to bring water.

In slow motion, I peeked out along the side of the building.

A man with masses of tightly curled hair hurried through the doorway of the building housing the surveillance camera. His flowing robe reminded me of a Hawaiian muumuu, but not as colorful. The German shepherd yawned, stretched, and stood as if waiting for instructions.

Mr. Curly Hair twitched erratically. What chemical had he ingested? He read aloud from a paper he held in one hand, but from my vantage point the words sounded like a rapid-fire machine gun, fast and clipped, although I couldn't tell what he said.

When the man arrived at the edge of the veranda, he stopped abruptly, jerking his head back toward the doorway. A shorter man dashed out, dark hair partially hidden under a ball cap. Attired more conventionally, his averageness made a peculiar contrast against Curly Hair's weirdness.

The two conferred over the paper a moment before a third man burst from the door. A long dirty lab coat draped his tall frame with combat fatigues showing underneath. He wore an army hat atop his shaved head. They rushed out en masse. I guessed the building they exited must be an office of sorts. I watched while they crossed the quadrangle to enter one of the storage sheds with the German shepherd trotting behind.

Thank you, Lord!

As soon as the shed door shut, I bolted across the open space, pulling Molly after me. We darted between the cover of the parked trucks, pausing to scope out the quadrangle. With no one in sight, we raced for the double doors.

Old lady, indeed! How's that for speed?

I tugged on one of the doors. It opened and we scooted inside. When we reached the safety of the inner darkness, I slid the door shut.

The darkness made visibility difficult at first. I waited a moment panting, pressed against the sliding door in case someone spotted our mad dash. When no one appeared and my eyes adjusted, I turned to examine the contents of the building.

Just as I surmised, rows of vehicles. Pickups, vans, and military jeeps made up the lot. Some were painted in camouflage pattern, some black or other dark colors. None were white or light colored. A few seemed old and beat up, several newer. I walked between the row closest to the door looking for the black van without success and wishing I'd brought a flashlight.

Turning the corner, I started down the second row with Molly trotting behind me.

Here we go. This must be the van section. Blue van, green van, camouflage van... black van. I stopped. A quick scan along the remainder of the row confirmed there was only one black van.

Given its sordid history, I expected to be greeted by some kind of evil machine, but the van seemed innocuous enough. Quiet and cold. I stepped to the back to look for the license plate, but didn't find one.

How could I prove Baxter stopped this particular black van?

When I peeked in the driver's side window, part of a license plate stuck out from under the seat. Sliding inside, I pulled it out so I could read the entire number. Why was it on the floor? Would this be the stolen plate or the one that belonged to this van? How would I know unless I had the sheriff's department run the number? Have to take it with me, I guess. *That's not right. God just protected me from the German shepherd and kept me from being seen.* The least I could do was to act honorably.

Did I have paper and a pen to record the license number? No, of course not. I'd have to rely on my often flawed memory. *U8LCW5, U8LCW5, U8LCW5.* How would I remember that? *LCW—little curly worm—you ate little curly worm—5— don't know how to remember the 5. Well, I have five fingers.*

Repeating my mnemonic like a mantra, I pulled Molly toward the door.

The deputies would have to impound this vehicle now. I'd see to that.

When I peered out a slit between the sliding doors, no one was in sight so I beat a hasty retreat from the compound under forest cover.

However, when I rounded the corner to the place I'd left the Jeep, two burly men in camouflage uniforms leaned against the front fender. I blinked at the sight of them, trying to catch my breath.

The tallest one straightened. "What're you doing here, ma'am?"

"I…I…" *Think fast, Christine.*

"What he means is, where have y'all been?" The shorter man's southern accent sounded as thick as his sunburned neck.

Still panting from my dash through the forest, I pointed to the north, away from the compound. "Just had to take my dog on a small walk. She's been in the car for a while and… "

The first man guffawed. "Why don't I believe that? Do you believe her, Pete?"

"Nope."

"So." They stepped closer to where Molly and I stood. "You got about thirty seconds to spill the truth. What're you really up to?"

The truth? How could I tell them that? Might as well stick to my fib. "We got out to take a walk. Honest."

In my heart, I sent up fervent prayers for help, but God didn't answer. *Why would He help a liar anyhow?*

The men took a couple more steps toward me until we stood toe to toe. My heart thumped so loudly I thought the noise would summon the entire army. Molly whined and cowered behind my legs.

"See, we been waiting for you a long time. Either you got lost out there or you were doing some snooping where you ought not go. And you never mentioned getting lost." The biggest soldier lowered his voice to address his friend. "Which truth do you believe?"

I made one last attempt at bravery. "Look, if you don't mind, I need to get on home now." I gestured for them to step out of my way.

The two towered solidly in place.

A dribble of perspiration trickled down my backbone.

"My, uh, husband is expecting me. He knows I've come out this way. I'm sure he's looking for me." Why not pile a couple more lies on top of the one I'd already told?

"Whatta ya say, Pete?" the tall one snarled. "Don't think we want a nosy woman trespassin' on our property. Think she oughta be taught a lesson, don't you? Something she ain't likely to forget." Roughly, he snatched Molly's purple leash out of my firm grip.

Through the swirl of struggling and confusion, the tether to my beloved dog slipped through my fingers. I heard myself scream.

✒

When I shoved the gearshift into park outside our front porch and raced through the front door, my sobbing had reached epic proportions. "Oh, Jesse! Someone's taken Molly and it's all my fault!"

Jesse looked up from the kitchen island where he'd been hunkered over the newspaper I'd forgotten to bring in that morning. "What happened to you?"

"Jesse! They took her. We've got to get her back." I tugged his shirtsleeve, hiccupping from forty-five minutes of hysterical wailing.

"Hey. Wait a minute. Slow down. What's going on?"

The version I blubbered out was only slightly slanted so I wouldn't give him extra reasons to berate me for deliberately disobeying his orders. When I finished, he shook his head. "This could only happen to you, Chris. See? I told you."

"I know." I grabbed a paper towel and blew my nose. "But they took Molly! Did you hear that? We have to rescue her before they hurt her. Please come with me."

Jesse retreated a step. "Come with you? You think you're going back to that place?" Shaking his head, he said, "No, no, no. We will not be going back. And you certainly will not. Those people are dangerous. Do you understand?"

To say he wasn't pleased would be a gross understatement. He let me have it for a couple more minutes. I nodded and tried to look sorry, impatient for him to finish his tirade.

We had to get Molly back. How could I convince him? "Okay, okay," I said when his verbal flogging finally ended. "You're right, of course. But we were never in the slightest danger until the absolute end. There were places to hide. And I found the license plate number. Look." I grabbed a yellow legal pad and wrote out *U8LCW5*. "See?"

"The license number? Sorry, I'm not following. What does this have to do with Molly? Have you taken to collecting license plate numbers now?"

"This is *the* license number." I sighed dramatically. "From the black van that is right there waiting for the deputies to impound it. Don't you get that?"

"I get that you've put yourself in serious danger again without considering the consequences, possibly compromised evidence in the process, and lost our dog. Promise me you won't do this anymore. I mean it, Christine."

I threw my arms around his neck. "You know me, Jesse. I'll try not to do it again. I'll really try. From now on, I'll include you in all my wild schemes." Despite my attempt at lightening the mood, I felt time ticking in my chest. Every minute we delayed finding Molly, the greater the chance became that we would never get her back. "Please, Jesse. Help me rescue Molly."

Jesse pried my desperate arms from his neck. "Maybe we should take this story to the news media."

"Ha! Those idiots will just mix it up."

The cogs of Jesse's analytical process rolled. "We have to be careful about sharing this information."

I followed his logic. "Right. Deputy Colter didn't show any interest in the black van."

"Deputy Oliver always seems to be Baxter's friend, but

he doesn't have direct access to the case. And I don't think he has enough clout in the department to process this evidence properly."

"Maybe not."

"Then there's Detective Rogers. He's supposed to be heading the investigation. The fact that he refused Constance Boyd's interview definitely swings the scales in his favor. But look what was in the paper today." He tapped the front page.

The bold lettered headline proclaimed, "Official Findings Confirm Dunn's Illegal Activity Contributed to Death." I read the headline out loud. Tears bubbled into my eyes, taking my mind off Molly for the moment. "Who's telling these crazy lies?"

According to the article, toxicology results confirmed the substance found in Baxter's blood as the powerful drug PCP, originally developed for use as an anesthetic, but discontinued in medical applications due to the varied and unpredictable nature of its side effects. The state of the drug in his system indicated it had been ingested within an hour of his death.

Based on this report, Baxter's death had been ruled an accident resulting either from his negligence or from actions he perpetrated. In the official version, Baxter went to The Owl to purchase the drug while off duty. Under the influence of the illegal substance, he instigated a brawl with several persons he met that night. Eyewitnesses supposedly corroborated this part of the story; however, these unknown people were simply called "unidentified eyewitnesses." These supposed witnesses left the bar with Baxter in pursuit. Later, he radioed dispatch about chasing a black van with stolen plates.

A high-speed car chase ended near the site of the Star Mine where a foot race ensued, concluding on the ledge above the mine dump. Around midnight, after a brief, but violent scuffle, Baxter fell to his death in the ravine, impaled on a rusty spike below. The person or persons Baxter had been fighting drove his patrol car into Rawlins Lake, hoping to divert attention away from the actual site of Baxter's death. His body probably wouldn't have been found for a long time, hidden in that remote ravine, except for the anonymous tip.

"This is packed with speculation," I said with an emphatic slap to the counter. "Where's the evidence? Who are these eyewitnesses? Why would anyone hide his patrol car in the lake? This garbage reads like Colter's version. What's going on at the sheriff's office?"

Jesse's brow scrunched into furrows. "I agree it doesn't make sense. If Baxter purchased illegal drugs from those people, why would he radio the license plate in? He wasn't on duty. How would he explain the car chase? Also, whoever was with him on that ledge disposed of the patrol car for fear of getting caught. What's that based on?"

"This is total rubbish. Come with me to get that license plate and we'll keep going up the ladder at the sheriff's office until we find someone who will know what to do with it."

Somehow, I managed to convince Jesse to accompany me to *Satori*. Perhaps he wanted to get Molly back as badly as I did. Before he could change his mind, I ran to change my shoes. We collected Jesse's telephoto lens and camera and set off in the Jeep.

Just after three o'clock, we parked near the place I'd hidden the car earlier.

Standing on the road to the compound, I pictured Molly's pleading brown eyes as the men dragged her away. My eyes brimmed with tears. *I've come back to get you, Mol. Hang on. Don't be afraid.*

If only it wasn't already too late.

Afternoon shadows lengthened while we hiked. We retraced the route I'd taken in the morning, climbed the gate, and passed the rusty trucks and machinery. When we sighted the compound, we slipped into the woods away from the road. This time, we hiked through the trees at the right side of the road.

Instead of being deserted like before, the compound buzzed with activity. Men in army fatigues leaned against buildings or sat in groups on the ground. Most had rifles slung from straps on their shoulders and belts loaded with ammunition. They laughed and gestured wildly. Cigarette smoke swirled above their heads.

Jesse and I crouched behind a fallen tree to observe.

While Jesse snapped a few pictures, I counted fifty men in the compound. Shortly, another wave of at least that many marched between two of the buildings. Within minutes, a third group arrived. Apparently, the original unit had been waiting for the others because when they came into sight all smoking materials were extinguished and the soldiers on the ground stood. The disorganized crowd of soldiers packed the compound, but in short order they formed straight lines and waited quietly at attention.

Mr. Curly Head and the other two I'd seen earlier bustled out of the office. A short, dark-skinned man with a large head approached the group from the opposite direction. He wore a long robe similar to the one on the curly headed man. Remembering Mary's description, I figured the short man must be Frank de la Peña. He unlocked the door to the building beside the office and the four filed in ceremoniously. The lines of soldiers marched after them. In no time, the compound was deserted again.

"Okay, let's go," I whispered, starting to rise.

"Christine!" Jesse pulled me back down. "We can't go in there. That's an army. Didn't you see them? They have guns. We've got to get out of here!"

"But—"

After a quick glance toward the compound, Jesse yanked me away from our surveillance post and we took off on a run.

As soon as we got out of sight of the compound, I braked abruptly, forcing Jesse to pull up too. "Hold on a second. We came to find Molly. We need to do that. They'll be busy for a while with their meeting. We could be in and out in a flash—"

"No." Grim-faced, he wheeled away and plodded purposefully ahead.

I ran after him. "Come on, Jesse. It'll be okay."

"No!"

"Why not?" I grabbed his arm and jerked him around to face me.

"I'm afraid, that's why. They have guns, Christine. This was a really stupid idea. I don't know what I was thinking when I let you talk me into it. We're in way over our heads. We are old people. There's nothing we can do here. We'll take the license plate number to the sheriff's office and let them deal with it. We're not going to sacrifice our health and freedom, maybe even our lives, for this investigation. We have no authority here. We don't know what we're doing and we're no match for an army with guns. Besides, our dog is probably already dead. Drop it, Christine. Do you hear me?"

He whirled and lumbered toward the car.

12

CHAPTER TWELVE

Jesse shoved me into the car a little rougher than necessary and slammed the passenger door. Then he jumped into the driver side and yanked his door shut. With both hands on the steering wheel, he lowered his head. I thought it best to leave him alone for a moment and continued sobbing as silently as possible so I wouldn't disturb him.

When he straightened at last, his voice shook like his hands. "This was a very bad idea. If someone watched us go in and they find out who we are…"His voice trailed off, causing me to imagine a horrible, lingering, tortuous death. Not to mention what they might do to Molly. Had they already used her for target practice? We must get her out of here fast.

"Okay. Think." His hands gripped the steering wheel until his knuckles whitened. "First off, we can't stay here."

"But we can't leave Molly!" I tugged on his arm.

Too late. Jesse had already started the Jeep and swerved onto the dirt road.

"Jesse! You're not going to leave her here. What if they… kill her?"

His expression stayed grim. "We have no choice, Christine. We don't know where they've taken her. We are two unarmed people who actually were trespassing on private property. Don't forget that. We had no right to spy on them. No right at all." His voice trailed into a mumble. "Why did I let you talk me into this?"

Jaw set, he jammed his foot on the gas pedal and we lit out of there like a rocket in spite of the potholes.

❧

By the time we reached the outskirts of Nevada City, my teeth had finally stopped chattering from our rapid flight over the bumpy dirt road. My heart beat more normally, too. The initial panic had waned, replaced by a huge pit of intense sorrow. Memories of my anguish when Molly went missing along with Lila Payne last year filled my mind. A wave of nausea crested in my stomach. How could our dog be gone again?

I couldn't tell how Jesse fared. His face looked wooden, eyes staring straight ahead.

Talking to him wasn't working, so I babbled to myself. "I think we should go see Deputy Oliver. We need help."

No reaction.

"Jesse." I reached a hand to his arm.

He jumped. "What!" His head jerked to glance at me. The car careened into the wrong lane. "What?"

As I righted myself, I pointed to the road. "I'm saying that I think we should go see Deputy Oliver. He was Baxter's friend. At least he sounded that way."

"No. We've got to find Mary Wilson. She's been out here. She'll know how to approach these people. Mary can get in."

His idea sounded crazier than mine. I frowned my disapproval.

But Jesse didn't seem to notice. "Look, Christine. We can't go to the sheriff's office. We don't know who we can trust there. Colter warned us to stay out of this investigation and had no interest in the black van. You don't know this Oliver fellow well enough to know if he's trustworthy. According to the newspaper, the guy heading the investigation released the information concluding that Baxter's death was accidental. Obviously, there's something wrong with his thinking. There's no one left but Mary. Maybe Mary can get a message to Frankie pleading with him to give Molly back if we let this thing go. No more snooping. We're in way over our heads and we have no muscle to back us up."

Dark possibilities swirled through my head. When Jesse steered toward Rough and Ready, I gripped the door handle with all my might.

Mary Wilson answered our determined rapping quicker this time. Perhaps she'd been looking out the window when we drove in. More likely, she'd been preparing to go out. Her hair appeared better arranged in a messy up-do, piled on top with stray ends sticking out like feathers. She'd applied a deep red lipstick that made her mouth look bolder. Not exactly a style that enhanced her appearance, the brash mouth made her look like a little girl playing grownup.

Her look of anticipation deflated significantly when she spied our faces on the other side of the screen door. "Oh, it's you."

"Were you expecting someone?" How could we make that up to her? "Sorry. We won't take much of your time if you're on your way out."

"I am." She reached for the door.

Jesse pulled the screen door toward him, holding the rapidly closing door open. "Wait, please. We need to talk to you. It's very important. Could we come in?"

Mary hesitated. Seeing the serious set of Jesse's jaw may have caused her to step out of his way. He can be formidable as well as dazzling. I followed Jesse, accidentally releasing the screen door so quickly that it flapped shut with a loud clap. This time Mary didn't lead the way to the seating area, but stood defensively against the wall, arms folded across her chest as if she hoped we'd be quick about whatever we came to say.

Jesse glanced at me and then at Mary. "We need your help. We went to the sawmill. The one you told us about. They took our dog."

"What?" The what wobbled out in a small laugh of disbelief. "How?"

I released pent up air. "I was spying on them, looking for the black van. I didn't think they knew I was there. Please. You've got to help us get our dog back."

Her eyes widened. "Are you crazy? They won't give you the dog. No matter what you do."

A gasp escaped my lips.

"Why would you mess with those people? I told you they were bad." She raised both hands as if to fend off a predator. "I can't help you."

Jesse stepped toward her. "But you know them. You know the layout of the place, where they might keep our dog. Please, Mary. We may not have much time."

Fear invaded her emotionally barren face. "No! I… can't."

My eyes filled with tears. "She's a wonderful dog, our Molly is. We've had her for thirteen years. She's more like a family member than a pet. Molly's a border collie, the best dog we ever had. Smart. You wouldn't believe what she can do. I swear she knows what I'm talking about most of the time. I wish I'd brought a picture to show you. You'd really love her. She's worth saving, I promise."

When my tears started to flow, her eyes softened. "You don't understand these people. They're cruel."

"Okay then. Just give us advice," Jesse said evenly. "Maybe we should call them. Do they have cell phones out there?"

Mary focused on the space between Jesse and me. "I don't know. Honestly. I just don't know." Then she shook her head harder. "If they have phones, I don't know any numbers. Cell phones don't always work out there. There's dead spots because of the mountains. I think they use radios."

Jesse pressed her. "Should we walk in with a white flag and announce ourselves and why we've come? Promise never to bother them again?"

"I don't think they'd let you in."

"How about if we write a letter? You could deliver it for us."

She shook her head, staring at the floor.

I shrugged. "We should go right to the police then."

She looked up abruptly. "Police? Definitely no. Frankie has too many guns."

Jesse frowned at me.

Mary crossed her arms over her chest like a shield and rocked slightly on her heels. "It's…a huge place. Some of the buildings have dugout rooms underneath. There's at least one that links up with an old mine shaft. I think that's where they have their secret ceremonies."

A shiver passed over me. Secret ceremonies? What kind of group was this?

Jesse keyed in on a different word. "Mine shaft? Where's the mine shaft located? Maybe we could go in where it comes out to the surface."

"I think it links to the Star Mine; the shaft entrance is blocked. If I remember right, it's close to the main entrance. But I don't think you should try going in that way. They keep guards there most of the time."

I thought of the narrow, pot-holed road. "There must be another way out to the sawmill. You couldn't get trucks loaded with logs over that curvy road, especially during a storm."

Her face brightened. "Sure. There's another way. It takes a lot longer, that's why they don't use it much. That's how you should go in. But you probably couldn't find it all by yourselves." She dropped her arms and gazed from Jesse to me. "Maybe I should go with you."

Had she forgotten her misgivings about these cruel, insane men? Once she decided to help us, her spirits perked up noticeably. When she pulled her black purse off a hook near the door, she actually smiled. I followed her to the Jeep, too grateful for her assistance to ask why she was helping us.

In the twilight we passed through North San Juan, turning past the gas station to head north. From my seat in the front passenger side, I leaned around so I could see Mary in the back seat. She huddled against the side of the car looking out the window. Tight black spandex pants were partly covered by a long bulky burgundy sweater underneath a wide, mesh, bolero jacket. Was she trying to hide her figure?

She turned her head and saw me studying her.

I flashed my kindest smile. "You don't seem like the sort of girl who'd get involved with folks like Frankie. How'd you meet?"

"Frankie? He seemed fun, at first—wild and completely unpredictable. Had an unusual kind streak that appeared when you didn't expect it. We met at a street fair a couple years ago. He was…nice to me." She resettled herself, tucking her feet underneath herself. Heavy eye makeup gave her eyes a dark exotic appearance. "I was new in town then, came out to stay with friends. Things were…bad at home. So…I left."

Mary lowered her head and peered at me through thick eyelashes, perhaps waiting to see if I would censor her.

Her vulnerability made me want to gather her in my arms instead. "Do you mind me asking how old you are?"

"Twenty-one."

I knew she lied, but I didn't call her on it. "So, you met Frankie and had lots of fun."

She glanced up. "Yeah, lots of fun. Then he started using more and more. When he gets high, he gets ugly. After a while, 'God' started talking to him."

My Miss Goody-Two-Shoes tone slipped out. I couldn't help it. "Does he really think he hears God when he does drugs?"

With a shrug, she shook her head. The bulky sweater fell off one shoulder. "I guess." She tugged the sweater in place and pushed her little black purse out of the way to make room for her feet. "He started wearing this funny robe all the time and got crazier and crazier. I don't know where the soldiers came from. Maybe he got them off the Internet. Frankie spent a lot of time on the computer. All of a sudden, men started coming. They'd have big meetings. Him and that curly-haired freak would get all heated up preaching to them. Really weird. After a while, I quit going to the meetings because it scared me, all the killing and torture talk. It was gross."

Jesse kept his eyes on the road. "What kind of drugs do they use?"

With arms crossed, she dug her fingernails into her arms. "You name it, they used it. The curly-haired guy is some kind of scientist, I think. He runs the lab where they make drugs. That's why they have guards. To protect the drugs." She stopped talking and whispered. "I shouldn't be talking about this."

Jesse glanced at me and raised one eyebrow. "Do you still want to go in there?"

I nodded sluggishly, aware of a chill that started inside.

Mary tapped Jesse's shoulder. "Slow down. There's a turn coming up. To the right."

Jesse maneuvered right onto another winding road that we never would have seen in the dark without her help. No one spoke, all eyes on the road. So far, even though unmarked, this roundabout route seemed better maintained and wider than the way we'd taken earlier.

Mary stared out the window. "The superstitious parts scared me too."

I looked back at her. "What do you mean, superstitious?"

She shrugged. "Friday the thirteenth's always real important. So are black cats. Halloween's like a major holiday, meetings always start at midnight. You know, stuff like that."

I couldn't imagine what stuff like that might be.

Jesse shot me a quick look. "What day was Baxter killed? Wasn't it...?"

"Friday the thirteenth. He died about midnight."

He glanced at me again. "That's got to be significant. Don't you think?"

I stared at Mary.

"Could be." Mary nodded, dark eyes widening. "Maybe it means Frankie knows how Baxter Dunn died."

13

CHAPTER THIRTEEN

The headlights soon illuminated a large weathered sign announcing the Gleason Mill, and Mary confirmed we were nearing the sawmill grounds. Thick clouds covered the nearly full moon that should have provided light for our path. The darkness felt so dense I wondered how in the world we'd ever manage to navigate through the thick woods.

Mary pointed. "Park there. In those trees."

Jesse complied and then turned to study her. "I hope you have a plan in your pretty little head."

"I've been thinking about that." She paused, nibbling savagely on her fingernail. "I've been here a lot of times, but you realize they never let me roam around on my own, don't you?"

We nodded, not taking our eyes off of her.

"One good thing is that Frankie's a dog lover. If he knows they took your dog, chances are good that he will take care of her." Mary extracted a cigarette pack and lighter from her black purse. "There's a well-guarded tunnel under the lab where they store their valuable stuff. They might put your dog there." She shook out a cigarette and tucked the pack back, her young forehead puckered with furrows. "Frankie has a lot of dogs. He would keep yours with the others, in the big dog cages." She glanced at us. "But he moves those around sometimes. Twice that I know of. Last time I saw them they were in the tunnel behind that big car garage. You'll know when you get close, 'cause you'll hear dogs barking."

Jesse's expression conveyed his reluctance. "Okay, I guess that gives us someplace to start."

"Do you think we can get in there without being seen?" I asked.

She flipped her lighter over in her palm. "Maybe Jesse could if he wore fatigues. They might not question someone who looked like one of the soldiers."

"Where would I get fatigues?" he chuckled.

I didn't like this plan.

"One of the bunk rooms usually has boxes of them. That's on the other—"

"I saw that bunk room," I interrupted. "I could get in there. But wouldn't the soldiers be there now?"

"Could still be at dinner. They eat together in the sawmill building. There's a big dining room in the back. The kitchen's there, too."

"Okay." I unbuckled my seat belt. "Point me toward the bunk room and I'll be back in a flash."

"No," they said in unison. Jesse grabbed my arm.

"Why not?"

Mary spoke first. "I'll go. I'm younger and faster."

I frowned. *Was she insinuating I'm old and slow?*

"No offense," she said quickly. "It's just that I can get in and out without any trouble since I know where I'm going." In a flash, Mary had opened the door and slipped off into the night.

Jesse rolled down the window and whispered, "Hey!"

She didn't come back. Would she smoke her cigarette out in the forest? With all the trees and dried needles? I should follow her and make sure she didn't.

But Jesse raised the window and turned to me, putting an abrupt end to my thoughts. "I was going to give her my penlight. It would give her a little light. But she didn't stop, so, I guess our job is to pray for her now."

We asked God to protect Mary and roll back the clouds so she could find her way.

Somewhere near the end of the longest hour I've ever spent, Mary opened the back door and jumped into the car. With a "Tah dah!" of triumph she held up the fatigues, hat, and boots she'd pilfered. Breathing quite rapidly from her race through the woods, she smiled. "Piece of cake. I didn't bump into a single soul along the way."

"Then why did it take you so long?" I gathered the garments from her.

She took a deep breath. "It's farther to the compound than I remembered. I almost got lost before I found the buildings. Maybe I should've told you to park closer, but at least out here they're not patrolling the road."

I patted her arm. "Thank God you have a good sense of direction."

"Well, that's the funny part." She chuckled. "I usually don't. I get lost a lot. When I followed the dirt road, I walked too deep into the woods. All of a sudden, I got totally turned around. It really scared me. I thought of whistling to you. Maybe you'd come and find me. I know how to whistle real loud like a boy. My brother taught me. Anyway, then I felt someone guide me. Someone I couldn't see."

Jesse and I gazed at each other.

I smiled. "We were praying."

Mary shrugged. "Maybe there is a God, because at first I thought I got lost. But just when I started to get scared, the clouds moved away and the moon lit up my path. Just like someone pointed the way."

Jesse took the fatigues behind a tree to change by the light of the moon. To my surprise, the clothes fit, although he complained about the boots being a bit loose. When he secured the hat and stepped back for our inspection, the transformation was stunning. He could indeed pass for one of the soldiers.

After I'd adamantly refused to be left behind alone in the car, we set off together for the compound. Mary lit our path with the tiny dot of Jesse's penlight.

God's answer to our prayer and Mary's favorable response made me think of the eternal state of her soul. "Mary," I said, falling in step beside her. "We prayed for God to light your path and He did. Did you know God answers prayers?"

"I guess I don't know much about God."

I put my arm around her thin shoulders. "Let me tell you about Him."

She nodded, eyes bright.

As we trudged through the forest, I started from the beginning. "God created a perfect world. Evil didn't exist. Everything was good because God is good. God created Adam and Eve to live in His perfect world and take care of it. They could do anything they wanted except one thing."

Mary whispered, "God told them not to eat the apples."

"You've heard this story. That's right. God forbid them to eat the fruit from a special tree in the middle of the Garden of Eden. Do you know who came to talk to Eve in the garden?"

"The Devil. Right?"

I squeezed her shoulder. "Yes. One day Satan called to Eve. He told her God had lied. She could eat the fruit and not die. This is the sad part, Mary. Eve believed what Satan said and took a bite. She persuaded Adam to eat too. When they chose to eat, they disobeyed God. That's what sin is, doing what God says not to do. Sin and evil entered the world. Ever since, people have been born sinners. All of us. God's rule is that sin must be punished by death. Everyone deserves death because of sin."

In the small glow from the penlight, Mary kept her eyes on my face. "I've never heard it explained like that before."

Jesse continued. "The story doesn't end there. God doesn't want us to die. He loves us. He loves you too, Mary. God made a way for people to live with Him forever and ever instead of getting the punishment of death that we deserve. Do you know who God sent to die in our place? I bet you do."

Mary stopped. "Jesus?" She only whispered His name but neither one of us needed hearing aids to hear it. The Holy Spirit was at work.

"That's right, Mary. Jesus did everything that needed to be done so our sins are forgiven."

Tears trickled down Mary's face. "I'm full of... bad things... things I shouldn't have done. Sometimes I think I can't do anything right, even when I try. I always feel guilty, like I'm a bad person. If I ask God to forgive me, will He do that? No matter what I've done?" She searched my face as if she knew that her life depended on my answer.

Barely touching her chin with my fingers, I told her the truth. "Yes. You can ask God for forgiveness no matter what you've done and He will forgive you instantly."

"I want God to forgive me," she said just above a whisper.

Jesse huddled with me around this dear child while we took turns leading her in prayer.

We hugged each other when we concluded. I wiped a few tears away.

Mary grinned. "I feel… lighter. Happier."

"Like a lifetime of sin has been lifted off your shoulders?" Jesse laughed. "Come on. Let's find Molly."

After several minutes, the four of us neared the complex with boldness. Of course, One of us was invisible. But very present, all the same.

Soon, a rooftop peeked through the trees. Floodlights on tall poles illuminated the quadrangle. From the edge of the forest, we studied the buildings. Using hand signals, Mary guided us to the side that housed the vehicles.

Jesse kissed me long, more passionately than usual. That scared me.

"You come right back," I whispered.

He smiled and saluted.

God, protect him please!

ᕒᘴ

Mary and I cowered in the middle of a thick stand of birches. A few times, we heard voices and marching feet, but we didn't budge. Soldiers patrolled at regular intervals. The noises sounded like military maneuvers.

What if they'd caught him? Could we save him? Would our cell phones work to call for help?

"Shouldn't he be out by now?" I whispered in Mary's ear. "How long has it been?"

Shadows hid her face so I couldn't see her expression. "Not that long."

I shivered and wished I'd brought a coat. My fingers felt frozen.

A door slammed.

Between the buildings, a group of soldiers gathered in a huddle. Straining to listen, my body stiffened with fear. But we were too far away to hear what the men said.

"Which building did they come out of?" I whispered as close to Mary's ear as I could get.

She shook her head, not being able to see any better than I could.

Another door slammed and the soldiers collectively turned toward the long building. A new man joined them. They conversed for a minute or two, before exchanging salutes. The newcomer strode purposefully out of sight in the opposite direction.

Something about that stride looked familiar. Could that be Jesse?

Leaves rustled nearby.

We froze again, barely breathing.

Presently, Jesse tiptoed past, stopping directly in front of us to peer around.

"Pst! Jesse!" Tears of gratitude formed in my eyes.

He turned. "There you are! Good hiding place."

We disentangled ourselves from the trees and followed him away from the buildings. When we had gone a little distance, he stopped to grin in the moonlight. Apparently, his charade had exhilarated him.

"Well?" I whispered. "Did you get into the parking garage? Did you find Molly?"

He shook his head.

Mary joined us, crowding close.

"The door was locked. I got all the way into the underground lab though. Man! You should see the setup. It's quite extensive! But Molly wasn't there."

"How'd you do that?" I asked. "Get in, I mean. With all the soldiers around."

"Piece of cake!" He grinned again. "I pretended I'd come for an unannounced inspection. I threw around a few names real fast. Names I read from a file I found when I first went in. I accused them of sleeping on the job because I could walk right in without anyone stopping me. No one questions an impromptu inspection when they think their career's on the line. I guess enough new people come and go that they don't question orders from someone they never saw before."

"Shh!" Mary said.

She tiptoed toward the compound.

"I didn't hear any..." I started to say but then I heard voices and a deep dog bark.

The German shepherd!

"This way!" a muffled voice yelled.

Jesse grabbed my arm, tearing through the woods so fast I could hardly stay on my feet. I felt like a rag doll being yanked through a tornado.

"Jesse!" I tried to stop him but the wind caught the word in my throat. "Mary! We can't leave Mary!"

He didn't hear me, blazing through the undergrowth and vaulting over logs. Branches tugged at my hair and clothes, trying to slow us down. Still he raced on.

Were we running in the right direction? I didn't recognize any landmarks. *Why didn't I leave a breadcrumb trail to follow?*

When Jesse finally stopped, I couldn't hear the dog barking any longer. Sweat dribbled down my face. I panted so hard I didn't think I could ever breathe normally again.

"Jesse!" Hands on my thighs, I turned to peer at him and said between gulps of air, "We can't leave Mary. We have to go back and get her."

He dropped his head. "Oh, no! Mary." His legs buckled and he fell to his knees.

Guess he just remembered we arrived as a threesome.

"I'm sorry." He shook his head. "I panicked. Everything was going so well and then I heard the dog. Sorry."

We allowed ourselves a short respite to return to normal breathing before venturing back the way we'd come. Back toward the compound, the dog… and the soldiers.

14

CHAPTER FOURTEEN

Jesse and I crouched in the cab of a rusty crane on the east side of the compound. We peered tentatively out the window. A clear view of the buildings spread out below. Floodlights lit the quadrangle as bright as a sunny day in the desert.

"We need a diversion," Jesse whispered.

"Like what?"

"A good fire would do nicely."

I shivered in the chilly night air. I'd never gotten over my fear from the night our kitchen caught fire just after my seventh birthday. "No! Definitely not a fire. Not in these woods."

He frowned at me. "Got a better idea?"

"We should have come prepared for diversionary tactics."

"Ha! Wait, the flares!" He climbed down the backside of the machine, holding his hand for me to come. I slid into his arms.

"What flares?" I whispered once I reached him.

"We've got highway flares in the Jeep. You know, in that roadside emergency kit."

Trudging through the trees in silence, we followed the road once we passed the compound, bringing us back to the car. Sure enough, in the rear of the Jeep, three unused highway flares nestled in the emergency kit.

"So… what do you propose to do with these?" I asked with no small measure of trepidation.

Jesse put his hand on my shoulder. "We better ask God's help." He bowed his head. "Lord, we're going back for Mary and hopefully Molly too. We need protection for ourselves, for Mary, and for Molly. Please give us wisdom, courage, and supernatural speed. In Jesus' name."

I mentally echoed his words, wondering about the speed part.

"Okay." Jesse picked up one of the flares. "Here's my idea. I'll circle around to the south end of the compound in the trees and make loud noises when I light the flares. Then I'll hightail it out of there."

"Meanwhile, I'll be here at the north end watching," I said, catching his enthusiasm. "When they see the flares, they'll send someone to investigate. Maybe they'll send a lot of people. As soon as they clear out, I'll run in and find Mary."

"No, no! You will not run in to find Mary. You are not fast enough and besides you have no idea where Mary is."

"Then how will you—"

"You will be waiting here in the car where you're safe. I'll circle back around the compound. Then I can dash in and search from the north side."

"You think you're fast enough for that? Racing all the way to the south end and back?" I shook my head. "I'm sorry, Jesse. You're two years older than I am, remember? And your knees are bad. You're not that fast, either."

I watched Jesse pace, just a few feet one way and then back the other like a caged tiger. "You're right. You're right. Of course. Where would I look for Mary and Molly anyway? Okay, let me think about this a little longer."

I slumped onto a stump, resting my tired head on my knees.

We'd have to come up with a better plan if we hoped to find Mary and Molly. Shivering in the cold, I wiped away a couple of stray tears. Why didn't I remember to bring a jacket?

Presently, Jesse stopped pacing and plunked down beside me. "Okay. Men who practice war games in the forest all day have to sleep sometime... most of them anyway. We'll wait until one or two in the morning. They should be asleep by then. I'll circle down to the south end, make noise and light flares like I said. It'll take some time for them to respond. During that time, I'll come back to the north end where you'll be watching. You'll report how many have gone into the woods or whatever else happens."

"Okay," I said. "That's better."

"If it looks like I can go in to look around, I will. Otherwise—" He embraced me and kissed my forehead. "We'll have to get help."

Jesse and I climbed into the backseat of the Jeep to rest a few hours before venturing toward the north end of the compound. Snuggling close together for warmth, Jesse fell asleep within seconds, his even breathing giving way to light, even snores, just like at home. I felt reasonably comfortable and protected with Jesse's arm around me, but the tension of the situation kept me awake. I closed my eyes anyway, hoping to give them a break.

The sounds of the night forest whispered and wailed in the stillness around our Jeep. Wind in the trees, scurrying creatures, pine cones falling, branches snapping. After a couple of hours, I could no longer keep my eyes shut.

As I contemplated the stirring shadows, I refused to consider the possibility of being discovered by roving guards. Instead my imagination created all sorts of monsters converging on our unprotected vehicle. To keep from scaring myself into a coronary, I whispered hymns. To my delight, I discovered quite a few stored in my brain from childhood. It's amazing how much courage those powerful old words impart.

According to the luminous dial on Jesse's wristwatch, he woke just before one-thirty. "Oh!" He bumped his arms on the roof when he attempted to stretch in the small space. "I forgot where I was."

I moved out of his way. "It's amazing that you actually slept." Lack of success in that department always left me feeling deprived. I climbed out and extended my arms over my head.

Jesse followed me out. "You didn't get any sleep?"

"Not a wink."

He flexed once he'd grounded himself. "Kind of a small space for sleeping, wasn't it?"

I nodded. "Good thing that didn't bother you."

"Sorry, Christine."

He flashed a tired version of his incredible smile and I forgot about being jealous of his ability to sleep when I couldn't.

Mustering cheerfulness, I offered a salute. "What now, Captain? Your army awaits instructions."

He pointed in the general direction of the compound. "Onward to the battle, troops."

We'd just spotted the first glow of the stadium lights when a piercing whistle split the night silence. We froze.

I turned toward the sound. "What was that?"

Jesse's faulty hearing made the direction of sound impossible to decipher. He circled, listening. "I don't know."

The piercing whistle shrieked again, closer this time. A boy's whistle. Just like my cousin David tried to teach me in the fifth grade.

I suddenly remembered our conversation in the car. "Mary!" I pulled Jesse's sleeve. "Remember when she said her brother taught her to whistle like a boy. That's got to be Mary." I pulled Jesse toward the sound. "This way, hurry."

We barreled through the woods. Soon, we heard one final whistle blast, closely followed by crashing noises. A tiny figure raced toward us.

Mary.

Rarely have I felt such relief in a reunion.

We chattered simultaneously and locked arms in a threesome bear hug.

"Where have you been?"

"What happened?"

"Are you all right?"

Mary's little laugh trilled into the air." I'm fine. Except I thought you went off and left me."

I squeezed her arm. "We would never leave you. But where did you go?"

"Didn't you hear my whistle?" She glanced behind her. "We'd better get out of here. And fast. I think it's about…"

The end of her sentence drowned in an explosion so powerful that I felt the jolt from my feet to my scalp. Mary dragged me from my surprised stupor toward the Jeep. The blast apparently rendered Jesse motionless because Mary dropped my arm after she'd gotten me moving and ran back to where Jesse stood as if his feet had melted into the ground. Grabbing his arm, she tugged him along until they caught up to me.

"We've got to get going!" she yelled. "Now!"

Something about her urgency penetrated our stupefied minds enough that we turned from the explosion and sprinted toward the car. From the safety of the front seat, I watched a red pillar of fire rising high into the night sky.

Those old buildings were as dry as tinder. They'd all burn to the ground before the firemen arrived. Would Molly get out? What about the soldiers? Surely we should stay and assist.

❧

Jesse broke his own speed record racing away. Still numb with shock, I held on with both hands. We hurtled through the darkness for several miles. In fact, no one spoke until we reached North San Juan.

Then I spoke first. "We need to tell someone about the fire." Back at the mill during the long sleepless night, I had checked my cell phone. It displayed "No service." "Do cell phones work here?"

Jesse tugged his flip phone out of his pocket. "I've got service." He handed the phone to me. "Don't give your name, though."

Taking his phone, I called 911 and reported an explosion at the old Gleason Mill. "I think the buildings are burning. People are sleeping inside."

"Don't stay on too long," Jesse whispered. "They might try to trace the call."

Right away, I closed his phone, disconnecting the call. "That feels wrong. I should have identified myself."

"Maybe later." Jesse glanced into the rearview mirror at the tiny form huddled on the back seat. He pulled off the road just past North San Juan and extinguished the lights. "We need to hear what happened first." He turned toward Mary. "Tell us."

She sat stiffly, arms locked across her chest. "You, you ran when the dog came into the woods. I didn't know what to do, so I asked God to help me. I took off in the opposite direction, thinking they couldn't follow all of us at the same time. I guess they actually gave up without following any of us. Then I hightailed back around and hid in that stand of trees where Christine and I were before. From there, I had a fair view of the compound. The guys and the dog came back after a little while. They must have figured they had nothing to worry about 'cause they all shuffled off before long."

Sirens shattered the night's stillness. Mary stopped talking while we observed a fire engine whizzing past us. The truck turned toward the mill, lights blazing.

Jesse turned back to Mary. "Go ahead."

"I only saw the regular patrol guard come and go. When the voices pretty much died down, I thought it must be lights out for the guys and decided to find your dog."

Dread over what she might tell us filled my stomach. "Oh, Mary, you didn't."

"Did you find her?" Jesse looked worried too.

She shook her head. "I checked one of the mine shafts first. They must have put her in the big dog cages in the other one. Either that or…"

I filled in the blank with the terrible possibility I'd been trying to keep from considering. "Or she's gone."

Mary hung her head and nodded.

Jesse kept staring at her. "But you searched for her."

"I looked everywhere I could think of. I'm small, so I can squeeze into places where no one would think a person could hide." She laughed a nervous, mirthless laugh. "When I got to the lab, I almost got caught. I knocked over some chemicals that started dripping together. I knew they weren't supposed to do that so I ran out fast. Didn't think it would make such a big explosion though. I whistled for you, but you didn't come. I kept whistling and heading toward where I thought we parked the car." She paused to look from Jesse to me and repeated, "I thought you left without me."

"I told you. We would never leave without you." I reached back to squeeze her little hand. "We were trying to figure how to get you out. But you're quite a resourceful young woman, aren't you? And very brave."

Jesse eased the car onto the road. For several miles as we jostled along the winding highway in silence. I heard the tremble of emotion in his voice when he spoke again. "Did anyone see you, Mary?"

"I don't think so."

He glanced in the rearview mirror. "How about the surveillance camera? Did you run in front of the camera?"

My heart skipped a beat when she paused.

"I—I did go through the compound once," she said. "Not through the center. Just the very edge. I forgot there was a camera there. I don't know if it saw me."

For the first time, I realized that I'd also scurried through the compound on my way in and out of the garage building. Did the surveillance camera catch *me* on tape? The bottom dropped out of my stomach.

Even if they saw me, what harm could that do? They didn't know me.

But Mary! *Please, God! Please don't let those people identify Mary.*

15

CHAPTER FIFTEEN

The story of the explosion at the sawmill had been buried on the back page of the local section of the newspaper. A mere blurb recorded a nocturnal disturbance in a wilderness area near North San Juan. Apparently chemicals stored in a warehouse at the former site of the Gleason Mill spontaneously combusted. The blast resulted in several injuries, but no casualties.

I tapped the article. "Could that be true?"

Jesse had just loaded a scoop of cereal with peanut butter into his mouth. He crunched while he concentrated on a different section of the paper. When he finished reading, he chewed a little longer before looking up. "Did you say something?"

"That explosion at the mill. It was huge. We saw it. There must've been a fire in those dry old buildings where the soldiers slept. The paper says there were no casualties. Do you believe it?"

Jesse gave a half-hearted shrug and went back to chewing.

"Also, how can they determine the cause so quickly? It just happened the night before last. I thought they had to investigate these things." I reviewed the short article. "Anyway, I don't believe it."

Jesse groaned and slammed the paper down, milk from his cereal bowl sloshing onto the table. "Christine, please. No more sleuthing. I'm way too old for this kind of excitement."

"But—"

"I mean it, Christine. Nobody asked us to find Baxter's killer, did they? You took this investigation on yourself. You're not a professional investigator and now they've stolen our dog. The deputies told us to lay off and we ran into crazy people with guns. A lot of guns, mind you, a whole army of guns. *And* explosive chemicals. This is not a game. It's dangerous. Do you finally get the message? Whether there were casualties or not, eventually someone's going to get badly hurt."

While his scathing tirade slammed me, I slouched lower in my chair. When he finished, he popped the newspaper open between us. All along I thought he was on my side. Maybe this wasn't the time to discuss our next move. Perhaps he'd feel like taking up the search again if I gave him a day to rest. Racing through the woods in the middle of the night might be asking a bit much of two relatively sedentary retired people.

Question was, could I wait for him to be ready? I frowned at the paper barrier that separated us. Time wasn't on our side. Even if we never discovered how Baxter died, there was a bottom line here: we must find our dog. And soon.

If Jesse wouldn't help, what should I do? While I cleaned the kitchen, I considered my options. Maybe I could write an anonymous letter to the newspaper. Or the sheriff's office. I could get on my knees and beg Detective Rogers to help me find Molly. In truth, there weren't many options and I quickly rejected all but one. Jesse would not approve, but I had to return to *Satori* for my dog, and to do that I needed Mary's help.

❧

No one answered my quick raps at Mary's house. The unfastened screen door flopped in the breeze, but the front door beyond it didn't budge when I turned the knob. My eyes swept over the yard. Wind rustled the treetops, but nothing else moved.

I yanked the screen door farther open so I could pound on the door. "Mary!" No answer. Not a sound from inside. The screen door banged shut when I released it to peek in the windows.

Through the narrow open slit between the curtains in the front window I saw the seating area, which appeared just as messy as the last time I sat there. But nothing stirred there.

I followed the side of the house to the kitchen window. Standing on tiptoes, I could just barely see in. I tapped on the glass. "Mary! Are you in there?"

Mary's large gray cat hurried toward the window, wild eyed and bushy tailed. He jumped onto the kitchen counter, mouthing a big meow. The cat's empty food dish sat on the kitchen floor. Maybe he wanted me to feed him.

Stacks of unwashed dishes lined the counters while a pile of dirty pots teetered on the stove. An upended Cheerios box scattered cereal loops across the table onto the floor. Probably the cat foraging for food.

But no Mary.

I unlatched the gate to the backyard and picked my way through scratchy weeds. Tall fox tails poked stickers through my pants legs, so I stopped to pull them out before continuing up two concrete steps to the back door. When I grabbed the knob, it turned. A shiver of foreboding crept down my spine. I pushed the door open a few inches.

A puff of hot air surged over me like a summer wind. The house was stifling. Had someone left the heater on?

"Mary! It's me, Christine Sterling." I paused in the doorway leading to a mudroom. My voice wobbled a little. "Mary? Are you home?"

The cat rushed against my leg, with a loud screech, as if he'd been starved. In his haste, he knocked over a plastic trashcan. The lid clattered to the floor. I glanced toward the kitchen. Such a loud noise in this muted atmosphere would surely bring Mary running. Where was she?

"Mary?" I said, weakly. Please answer me.

I took a tentative step into the kitchen. From this perspective, the disarray looked more like the path of a struggle. The scattered cereal wasn't the only mishap. A chair at the kitchen table had been overturned. Underneath the chair, Mary's little black fringe purse peeked out. Knives cluttered the floor. The cat's water dish had been overturned and floated in a puddle.

Debris covered the living room floor. I tiptoed through it. A violent struggle had left its mark. Pictures dangled off center on the walls, knick-knacks lay in pieces scattered here and there. An overturned lamp littered the floor, its shade bent out of shape. Someone had put up a fight. I stared down a hallway that must lead to bedrooms, not wanting to see what hid behind those doors.

"Mary?" I whispered.

My feet froze in place. I should call 9-1-1. Scouting the room for a phone, I didn't see one. The phone might be hidden under the piles of clothing and newspapers. I didn't move to look for it.

I should get my cell phone out of my purse… that I'd left in the Jeep. Why did I leave my purse?

I suppressed a gag reflex. Blinking away unbidden tears, I forced myself to baby step toward the hall as an unfamiliar sensation of disjointedness overwhelmed me. Some rational voice deep within me screamed, "Stop! Run away! Now!" I considered the benefits of running to the car, speeding home as fast as the car would go, burying my head in a pillow, pulling the comforter over my head, and never coming out again.

The other part of me, the nosy meddling part, must have been in charge of my feet because, like it or not, they inched down the hall as if propelled by a mind of their own. In slow motion, I crept toward the bedrooms. My head swam in a thick fog, vision slightly blurred.

My feet stopped at the threshold of a closed door.

Didn't I already learn this lesson about entering a stranger's house uninvited after I broke into the Payne's house last year?

Dear God, what am I doing here?

A strong metallic odor assaulted my nostrils. I covered my nose and mouth with one hand and tapped lightly on the door.

"Mary?" I barely whispered.

No answer.

My head dropped forward, thunking wearily against the door. I wanted to stay away, but the force of my head hitting the door inadvertently pushed the door open.

The door moved, squealing like a trapped mouse.

I didn't want to look inside, but my eyes peeked anyway.

Mary's little body lay on the bed, unseeing eyes fixed on the ceiling. She wore the same black Spandex pants and oversize burgundy sweater she'd been wearing when we dropped her off after our sawmill raid. Ruby red lipstick smeared one cheek. Heavy black eyeliner had trickled from the corner of one opened eye and dried. She rested in a large pool of blood that must have dripped from the deep red gash on the side of her head. Who would have guessed that so much blood could come from such a tiny person?

Staring at the lifeless body paralyzed me. At first I quit breathing. Then survival reflexes kicked in, causing me to gulp a full breath of noxious air. The horrible smell unleashed a coughing spasm. A surge of nausea threatened to expel my breakfast.

It must be a dream. Mary couldn't be dead. I didn't know what to do. My legs wouldn't budge, my arms felt leaden. The disgusting smell overwhelmed me, the kind of smell I knew I'd never forget. No matter how hard I tried. My heart raced with wild abandon. I needed to do something, if I could only move.

On the bed beside Mary's body lay a bloody object. I couldn't identify it from where I stood. I bent to see it better. It was some kind of tool, a hammer. Not a garden-variety claw hammer like I used to hang pictures, something specialized. I didn't want to touch it. My feet wouldn't move from the doorway and I didn't want them to. Whatever the tool might be, I knew, even without touching it, it must've caused the gaping gash on Mary's head.

Drops of salty sweat dribbled from my forehead, although the coldness that gripped my soul felt chilly enough that I wondered if I'd also died. I blinked hard several times. The tears stung my eyes. Flies buzzed in the silence, an army of flies on the move.

Buzz. Buzz.

Louder and louder.

I waved wooden arms in front of my face to shoo them away.

The flies lit on the bed and walked into the blood.

I bolted from the house, heart undulating in terror. Such loud and fierce pounding. At any moment, my heart might break loose and explode from my chest.

When I'd almost reached home, I called 9-1-1 from my cell phone. How I made it that far in my semi-conscious condition must be conclusive evidence of God's grace. By then, my vision had cleared and my hands had stopped shaking enough to punch in three numbers. With those tiny buttons, cell phones were not made for old people with tear-filled eyes.

Waiting for the dispatcher to answer, I watched my hands tremble. When I finally heard her voice, it sounded far away, as if it came through a hollow tube. I struggled to understand. Through a torrent of sobs I gave my name along with Mary's name and address.

The dispatcher's flat voice reassured me. "Calm down, Mrs. Sterling. Try to focus. Did you see anyone else in the house while you were there?"

My nose dripped like a faucet in a rundown motel. Hunting for a tissue, I searched through my purse in vain, swerving wildly while I foraged. "I didn't see anyone. Just a cat."

"Do you have any idea who did this to Miss Wilson?"

I paused, suddenly certain I knew the responsible party. But how could I tell without also revealing how I'd come to that conclusion? The scene in Mary's bedroom flashed before my eyes. The sticky red blood… Emotion overwhelmed me.

"Mrs. Sterling?" The emotionless voice continued. "Are you still there?"

With one hand I swiped my nose, gathering the moisture. *Now where do I wipe my hand?* "I'm here."

"Do you know who harmed Miss Wilson?"

"I… I'm not sure," I said. "Sorry. I really don't know for sure." Not a total lie. I couldn't be certain.

At last I made it to my front gate and thrust a finger at the gate opener on my console. "I'm home now. Got to go."

"Just a moment, Mrs. Sterling."

More bad news? I paused. "Yes?"

"An officer will come out to take your statement, probably this afternoon. Will you be available?"

16

CHAPTER SIXTEEN

Under any other circumstances I would have curled into the fetal position in my closet and closed the door on the rest of my life. The numbness that took over my emotions dulled all sense of horror. It must have been a gift from God because it propelled me from shock into action.

I didn't cry much while telling Jesse about Mary's death, although I did insist on having the conversation with his strong arms wrapped protectively around me. Without speaking, he held me on the green sectional in the living room, his handsome face alternating between expressions of compassion, sadness, and, I'm sure, a strong desire to thump me soundly on the head for my willfulness.

His silence continued after I finished.

It made me uncomfortable. I sniffed. "I guess you're angry with me."

He smoothed the hair from my forehead with one finger. "No. Not very."

"You should be. I need to listen to your wisdom."

Jesse pressed his lips together. The fact that he didn't say "I told you so" made me love him more than ever.

"So… what do you think?" I pushed out of his embrace so I could look into his eyes. "What should I do?"

"You did all you could."

"It's my fault, isn't it?"

"What's your fault?"

"That Mary is—"

His eyes told me he thought so too, but he tried to soften the news a little. "She… wanted to help us."

"We talked her into it." I dropped my head. Tears flowed again. "*I* talked her into it. She'd be perfectly fine right now if I'd just left her alone." I finished my sentence on a wail.

Jesse gathered me into his arms again. "We don't know how *perfectly fine* she would be."

It wasn't supposed to turn out this way. Burrowing into his shoulder, I sobbed. I had only wanted to find Molly. Never did I think someone might get hurt, let alone die. How did I botch things so badly?

✍

A couple of hours later, I lay curled on the bed under my comforter, trying without success to nap. Someone buzzed at the gate. I wandered downstairs to see who rang. Jesse looked out the window about the same time.

"It's a sheriff's car." He paused as if struggling with whether to let the detective in or not.

The buzzer blared again.

With a deep sigh, Jesse pressed the button to open the gate.

While he answered the door, I cleaned off signs of grief and gathered fresh tissues in case tears erupted again. A well of tears sloshed around inside me, on the verge of overflowing. They'd probably have to be let out sometime.

When I returned to the entryway, Jesse stood at the door with one of the deputies I remembered from Baxter's funeral. Seeing me enter, the deputy started toward me. "Mrs. Sterling?"

I nodded.

"I'd like to ask you a few questions about Mary Wilson."

"Already?" I shot Jesse a nonverbal plea. *Rescue me.* But he only stared at the tile floor, so I turned back to face the deputy. "You're… here so quickly. I only found her a few hours ago."

Jesse gestured for us to sit in the living room, but the expression on his face wasn't friendly.

The officer handed Jesse his card as if unsure whether I'd be able to process the information printed on it. "I'm Detective Joe Anderson from the Nevada County Sheriff's Office." He settled into the white leather cowboy chair across from us. "Why did you visit Mary Wilson today, Mrs. Sterling?"

I didn't know what to say. "I… we—"

Jesse draped an arm around my shoulder. "My wife has just endured a most shocking experience. Perhaps we could come to the office in a day or two to talk about this."

Detective Anderson turned to Jesse. "A woman has been murdered. The first few days after a murder occurs are critical times to gather evidence. Your wife may know something vitally important to this investigation. The sooner I hear her story, the sooner we can apprehend the person or persons responsible." He pulled a pen from his pocket to signal that I should begin.

Thoughts and images raced through my brain like cars at the Indy 500. "I don't know where to start."

He didn't give a hint of a smile to encourage me. "Start with when you met Miss Wilson."

After several starts and stops, I told the story of our brief acquaintance from how I first met Mary at the Night Owl all the way through our nocturnal adventure and the explosion at *Satori*. At the end, I explained how I saw her the last time.

By then, I couldn't stop the tears. Maybe they would never stop again. Even with Jesse sitting right there, I didn't skip anything in the telling except the part about finding the black van and Mary's conversion experience. Although I may have spun the story to make me sound less snoopy and more like I'd been doing my duty as a concerned citizen. I'm not sure why I didn't share about finding the van. Maybe because I hadn't yet ascertained where Detective Anderson stood on the good cop/bad cop continuum.

Jesse listened with bowed head and hands clasped together. Detective Anderson remained expressionless throughout my discourse, jotting notes now and then. When I finished, I felt wrung out like a dishrag. I leaned back to rest my aching head on Jesse's shoulder.

The detective cleared his throat. "Did you touch anything in the bedroom, Mrs. Sterling?"

Panic crept into the pit of my stomach. "I don't remember. Being at the house is kind of a blur. The shock of finding her… like that."

He leaned toward me. "Are you sure you don't remember?"

I searched my memory bank. The painful scene flashed into mind. "I… touched the doorknobs on the front door and the back door." Mentally I tried to reconstruct my movements through the house. "I may have knocked on the bedroom door. But—" I shook my head slowly. "No. I don't remember touching anything else."

Jesse straightened. "Why?"

Detective Anderson snapped his pen closed, shoved his notebook into his pocket, and prepared to leave. "I do need to take a fingerprint impression, if you have no objections."

I shrugged. Why would I object to that?

Out of his pocket, the detective pulled an ink pad and a paper and made copies of all my fingerprints. "That's all I need at this time, Mrs. Sterling. We may want to ask additional questions later."

Jesse followed him to the door. I heard a quiet exchange of words, but I couldn't understand them.

After the door closed, I joined Jesse in the hall. "What was that about?"

"I don't know." Jesse's eyes, full of questions, searched mine. "Sounds like they found fingerprints on the murder weapon and they want to compare them… with yours."

"What?"

Blackness engulfed my vision. A deafening roar drowned his answer. I felt myself falling. I reached for Jesse just before I slumped to the floor.

❧

Monday morning Detective Rogers requested my presence at the sheriff's office.

Within a short time, a patrol car pulled into our driveway and a young deputy got out to escort me. My heart pounded a rhythm in my ears while I descended the steps toward him. Jesse locked the front door behind us and folded his long legs into the back seat of the patrol car next to me. My mouth felt as dry as the Sahara Desert in the summer. Fear paralyzed me so completely I couldn't even babble small talk.

We rode several miles in silence before Jesse flashed his dazzling smile. I'm sure he did his best to make it as big and beautiful as usual because he knows I love his smile; however, it looked a little plastic that day. "It's going to be all right." He patted my hand. "They just want to ask you a few questions."

Questions? I had a few of my own. "I've never been summoned by the law before." I blinked away the tears that formed in my eyes.

Jesse reached toward me and wiped a tear off my cheek. "Then think of this as a new adventure."

"I feel like I did something wrong, but I don't know what." At least they didn't handcuff me. For that I would be eternally thankful.

At the sheriff's office in Nevada City, a woman in a crisp uniform ushered me into a room that could have come straight off a movie set. Grimy gray walls with one metal light fixture dangling ominously over a rectangular table in the center. A faint odor of stale sweat lingered. I imagined a criminal hunched in the metal chair while angry cops pummeled him with questions. The air weighed heavily with echoes of their voices.

I twiddled my fingers on the metal table while waiting for Detective Rogers entered. He had an imposing stature, but no one would call him fat, more like brawny and broad. Probably about my age or a little younger. He smiled a professional smile, not overly solicitous, more of a greeting. A younger officer, Deputy Wright, trailed after him into the room and grinned a toothsome smile when introduced. After that, he leaned against the door frame and melted into the background.

Detective Rogers lowered himself into the chair across from me. "I appreciate you coming today, Mrs. Sterling. You don't mind if I tape our conversation, do you?" Not waiting for my answer, he produced a voice activated tape recorder and set it up on the table.

"What's this about?"

Instead of answering my question, he succinctly stated pertinent information identifying this session into the recorder and leaned back until the front legs of his chair had lifted off the ground. "Please tell me how you know Mary Wilson."

I explained all over again. My hands shook while I told about finding her, but this time I didn't cry.

"Did you touch anything in the house?"

"No, I don't think so. If I did, I don't remember."

"Okay." The chair legs tapped the floor when he shifted forward. He leaned his elbows on the table to move closer. "Tell me, why are you so interested in the murder of Baxter Dunn?"

"Why?" I repeated his question because I didn't know where to begin. "I… don't believe the things the media is reporting about him." I sat up straight, perched at the front of my chair like an unrepentant child at the principal's office. "If you knew him at all, you'd know he would never get involved with illegal activities." I bent toward him, speaking louder as I got rolling. "Baxter Dunn was a wonderful person, an outstanding citizen, and a fine officer of the law. He loved this community and he loved his family. He did his best to live an exemplary life. How could you believe—?"

Detective Rogers held one palm in the halt position. "Simmer down, Mrs. Sterling." He chuckled. "I'm on your side. Baxter Dunn was a great guy and a fine officer."

My tirade had just started to pick up at the speed of a freight train. His statement derailed me. "What?"

"I agree with you." He scratched his head. "You know, I've spent hours working on this investigation. It's a doozy, this one. Keeps me up at night. Nasty rumors everywhere, more than on any investigation I can remember. Hard to sort out the truth. Don't know where all the lies are coming from. I invited you down here because the further I dig into this case, the more your name keeps popping up, first with Dunn and now with Mary Wilson's murder. I want to know about your involvement."

"My involvement?

He nodded. "Yes, ma'am. I assume you think Mary Wilson is somehow connected to Baxter Dunn. With no formal training in investigation, you seem to have come to that conclusion. I need to know more about it. Let's start with why you went looking for Mary Wilson in the first place."

"I didn't know her name, but the news people said Baxter was seen with a woman at a bar out on Highway 20."

"So you took it upon yourself to find this woman?"

"I waited several weeks, but you people weren't making any progress solving Baxter's murder. I got frustrated and I thought if I found her, I'd ask what Baxter questioned her about and find out what he was doing the night he died."

"Why didn't you turn her in? You knew we were looking for her."

"You didn't look very hard, did you? Because I found her on my first try."

Rogers shook his head, half smiling. "At what point did you intend to share your discoveries with us?"

In my nervous state, I'd been gasping shallow gulps of air. It made me feel a little lightheaded. I forced myself to drink in one long breath and expel it in slow motion. "I… didn't know if I could trust you."

"You didn't know if you could trust me," he repeated and shook his head again. Then he leaned back, crossing his arms. "So you found Mary Wilson. What did she tell you?"

"She said Baxter came to arrest her a year or so ago. She and her old boyfriend, Frank De la Peña. Frank wasn't home, but Mary got arrested."

Detective Rogers nodded. "The Kingfisher. Was that why you went out to *Satori*?"

I returned the nod. "Mary said Frank lives at the Gleason Mill outside North San Juan. She said he drives a black van."

Detective Rogers straightened in his chair. "A black van?"

"Right. So I went to *Satori* to find the van."

He raised his eyebrows. "Did you find it?"

I grinned.

"How'd you get in there?"

"I just walked in with my dog. They didn't see me. I found quite a few vehicles in one of the larger buildings. The black van was one of them. A license plate was stuck under the passenger seat. Let's see now. You-ate-little-curly-worm something…U8LCW…" I looked at my fingers. "Five. Yes, that's it. U8LCW5" *How's that for a little old lady's memory?* "But the awful part is that…" I started to tear up and the words wobbled out. "They stole our dog."

"Let me get this straight. You took Mary to *Satori*…to get your dog back?"

I nodded. "I have to find her. She's part of our family."

He opened his mouth to reply, but apparently changed his mind and closed it again. Instead, he slumped back in his chair and stroked his chin.

I fidgeted with my hands.

After a long interval, he glanced back at me. "I head the investigation into the death of Deputy Dunn. Why didn't you come to me when you found the black van?"

"We tried. Jesse called your office, but you weren't available. Zora Jane, that's Baxter's mother in-law, she said you wouldn't talk to us because we weren't directly involved. You haven't told them much and they're family. Plus, when we tried to talk to Deputy Colter—"

He straightened so abruptly that the chair legs clattered on the floor. "When did you talk to Colter?"

"Several times. The last instance was here. Let's see, what day would that be?"

"What did you tell him?"

"We tried to tell him about the van, but he wasn't interested."

"What do you mean he wasn't interested?"

"We mentioned to him that we might know where to

find it. He told us to mind our own business. We didn't get a chance to tell him anything else."

Detective Rogers plunked back down in his chair, chin lowered to his chest. I wondered if he'd fallen asleep, but then his eyes popped open. He stretched a hand out for the tape recorder and pushed the off button. "Mrs. Sterling." He cleared his throat. "The media has reported a great deal of false information concerning our investigation into Baxter's death."

"Yes, it has." I started to launch into my tirade again, but stopped when I saw the expression on his face. "You mean, you didn't give them that information?"

He shook his head.

"So the official findings when they reported the cause of his death in the newspaper? Was that true? Any of it?"

"We haven't released official findings on the C-O-D yet."

Budding hope immediately replaced my shock. "Baxter ingesting a hallucinogenic drug and falling to his death in a drug induced state is not the official report?"

"He did have drugs in his system. But we're still investigating how the drug got into his body and how it contributed to his death."

"He wouldn't use drugs voluntarily."

"We know he didn't have a history of using."

Relief flooded my soul. "Oh, my goodness! I'm so glad to hear you say that." Tears of joy spilled over my lower eyelids. I swiped one cheek with my hand and sniffled. "How can the media get away with reporting lies?"

"Very early on, the investigating team made the decision not to comment on what the media reported. We haven't confirmed or denied any of it officially. We don't know where they're getting this misinformation or why they've chosen to defame Deputy Dunn. But these rumors may prove useful later. In strictest confidence, I tell you that it is possible there is internal misconduct. If so, we must tread carefully. We need to be certain we apprehend everyone involved. You must not interfere. Do you understand that you must not speak to anyone about what I've said? If you do, I'll be forced to deny this conversation."

I nodded, unsure I fully understood the ramifications of what he had shared. "Can you tell me what you know so far?"

Before speaking, he clasped his hands across his slightly protruding belly. "I'm sorry. I can't say any more. My best advice is to let us work. We're trained to investigate. I'll be on the lookout for your dog. I know how important she is to you. We'll discover the truth, no matter how long it takes us. I promise you."

I could have kissed him. "What a relief! I've been so worried. I thought you wanted to talk to me because you found my fingerprints on the murder weapon."

Apparently, he hadn't spoken with Deputy Anderson. "Why would your fingerprints be on the murder weapon? I thought you said you didn't touch anything in the house."

"They wouldn't. Shouldn't be. Deputy Anderson came to interview me right after I found Mary. He took my fingerprints because he said they needed to compare them with the ones on the murder weapon."

Detective Rogers pulled his chair closer to the table, snapped the tape recorder back on, and placed a pair of magnifiers on his nose. He shuffled through papers in the file folder he'd left on the table. After several minutes, he stopped to read a few items. "Uh-huh. They found a fingerprint on the murder weapon but I don't see that they compared it to yours."

Papers rustled again.

"Ah." He studied a page in silence before his eyes met mine. "The fingerprint match was inconclusive because they only found a partial print. What they're saying is that this print has characteristics in common with yours…" His eyes returned to the page. "But not enough for a positive match."

I nodded. "Well, there you go. Not a match."

He set the folder down and adjusted his magnifiers. "How would your print get on the murder weapon anyway, Mrs. Sterling, if you didn't touch anything in Mary's room?"

I rolled my eyes. "Well, it wouldn't." The whole thing was ridiculous! "I did *not* touch anything in that room."

But someone thought I did. Who?

17

CHAPTER SEVENTEEN

My picture glared from the front page when I unrolled the next morning's newspaper, not a particularly good picture, either. The picture looked as if someone had surprised a fat woman with her hand in the cookie jar. *Note to self: throw away those jeans.* Above the photo, a bold headline proclaimed: "Grass Valley Woman Suspected in Wilson Death."

I gasped in shock, dropping the paper as if a scorpion had just crawled out of it. Was it my imagination or were those words bigger than the usual headline? While I wandered into the house, I attempted to read the story, however the words blurred and swam on the page like a school of minnows speeding from a shark. Where was this coming from? I couldn't believe Detective Rogers would call the media about my visit to his office. But if he didn't, who did?

"Look at this, Jesse." I pointed to the article when he came into the kitchen for breakfast. "Can you believe it?"

Jesse released a low whistle. He took the paper and lowered himself onto a chair at the table. I stood over his shoulder, deliberating on every word.

The basic facts were true. But mixed into the facts, a subtle slant made it sound as if the fingerprint on the murder weapon had definitely been matched to mine. The writer named me a person of interest in the death of Mary Wilson, never once using the word *alleged*. Speculation concerning my motive suggested a botched drug deal. Were they accusing me of selling drugs? A previous arrest on drug related violations rendered Mary's character questionable and me guilty by association.

I perused the article for the third time. "What in the world? Where are they getting this stuff? Don't they have an obligation to the public to verify stories before they go to press? Can I sue them for slander?"

Jesse finished reading without answering. Then he laid down the paper and turned to stare at me. "Sit down, Christine."

I slid into a chair beside him. "What?"

The way he continued to stare, I imagined all sorts of dreadful things he might be about to say. "Come on, Jesse. You're scaring me now."

He caressed my cheek. "Christine. This is serious. You're might need an attorney."

"An attorney? What for?" I laughed nervously. "You're kidding, right?"

He sighed deeply. "I wish I was. They can accuse you whether you are guilty or not and it sounds like they're revving up to do just that."

Did I hear him right? "Accuse me? Of what?"

"Murder."

Jesse had an odd sense of humor. I searched his eyes for a glimmer of laughter. Not finding one, I pushed away from the table and started to pace. "How could they? This is completely ludicrous. I had no reason to murder Mary. I just found her, that's all. What's my motive? Where's the proof?"

Jesse studied me with sad eyes.

I stepped to the table, feeling my face drain. "Detective Rogers said the paper printed lies. That's all this is. More lies. They're not seriously going to charge me." I planted both hands on the table to steady myself. "You aren't serious, are you?"

The gate buzzer sounded.

Jesse turned to look out the kitchen window. "Just on cue, the circus has come to town."

I followed his gaze.

News vans jammed the driveway outside our gate. Strange media people clamored at the fence, fat black microphones and video equipment poised.

Lines furrowed Jesse's handsome brow. "Welcome to your two seconds of fame, Christine."

❧

Another summons to the sheriff's office came that afternoon. This time Deputy Colter requested my presence. Ed and Zora Jane recommended an attorney, but when Jesse contacted the one they mentioned, a secretary informed us he was in court and couldn't accompany us to the appointment. According to instructions given by the secretary, I should answer exactly what Colter asked without volunteering any additional information. Better yet, I could refuse to answer at all until the attorney could accompany me.

Jesse grabbed my hand and bowed his head when he parked the Jeep at the sheriff's office. "Here we are, Lord," he prayed. "You know Christine didn't have anything to do with this murder. Protect her today. Don't let her say or do anything that would give them reason to continue investigating her. Give her your peace."

The fear that gripped my heart like a clenched fist didn't disappear when Jesse said *Amen*. I continued to be so frightened that I went numb again. However, infused with a quiet underlying strength after Jesse's prayer, I managed to walk into the same interview room where I'd sat only a day before with Detective Rogers. It helped to know God went with me.

Once more, I studied the grizzled walls and large black sheet of glass through which viewers could listen without being seen. Again, I experienced the coldness of the metal chair and table which seemed more unfriendly and unyielding than before. The single light dangled from the ceiling, waiting to shine on the guilty.

What was I doing here? *Dear God, is this all part of Your plan?* Was this happening because I put my trust in Him?

After nearly thirty minutes, during which I squirmed on the chair, paced a bit, and was finally reduced to counting holes in the ceiling tiles, Deputy Colter entered. He wore a sour disagreeable expression as if meeting with me had ruined his day. A young deputy I didn't recognize followed him closely. The stranger leaned against the doorposts popping his wad of gum while Colter heaved his neatly uniformed body into the other chair.

Deputy Colter squinted for a moment before reaching into his pocket to extract the tape recorder which he set up on the table. Before speaking to me, he pulled a large white handkerchief out to shine his star badge. An overpowering whiff of saccharine sweet cologne wafted toward me.

What odor was he trying to mask with that disgusting smell? Surely, with a nose the size of Texas he'd notice when he went overboard with his aftershave.

Deputy Colter repeated identifying information into the recorder after snapping it on. I stated my name at his request.

"You are here to explain your part in the death of Mary Wilson. Please start by explaining your relationship to the deceased."

I didn't mean to be uncooperative, but surely he could read the transcripts of yesterday's interview. "I already told that to Detective Rogers."

"Very well. Mary Wilson consorted with drug dealers. What is your part in that?"

Sitting straight and prim as a spinster schoolteacher, I stared him squarely in the eyes. "I had no part in that. I have never used drugs, don't know anything about drugs, and certainly wouldn't know where to purchase them. In other words, Deputy Colter, you will not be able to find one tiny bit of proof that I ever had anything to do with drugs."

He held my gaze, a triumphant smirk spreading over his face. "We already have."

In that instant, his words deflated my haughty bravado. "What?"

"Your 2003 Jeep Grand Cherokee is currently parked on department property. At such a time, it is subject to search according to our discretion. Acting on an anonymous tip, we searched your vehicle this afternoon and recovered a stash of methamphetamine from the back seat."

A sudden roar pulsed in my ears. I shook my head to clear my hearing. What kind of nightmare was I living? "What?" Certainly I hadn't heard him correctly.

With the maniacal grin of a mad scientist, he rocked back in his chair. "Now. Tell me about your part in this crime."

I thought I might be sick. "I… haven't a clue what you're talking about." I raised my leaden body to a stand so that I towered above him in case he questioned my authority to make this request. "However, I have nothing else to say without my attorney present."

As soon as I made that statement, the young deputy and Colter collected the recorder and exited the room without another word. I waited impatiently, pacing and fidgeting.

Two hours passed. During that time, I rapped on the door several times, but no one came. Even though I couldn't see anyone, I called out, "This is ridiculous! I'm being detained and you haven't told me why. That's got to be unconstitutional."

I checked my watch again. It didn't seem to be working. I shook it, then looked once more. Time dragged on.

Close to three hours after Colter left, the door flew open. In bustled a tall portly man stuffed in a black pinstripe suit followed by Deputy Colter gloating down his large nose.

The man extended his hand. "I'm your attorney, Jeff Goldburgh. Sorry to keep you waiting so long. I've been in court all day."

I shook his hand. A firm handshake denoted confidence. Confidence is a good characteristic for an attorney.

He banged a few folders onto the table and gestured for me to return to my uncomfortable metal seat. Beneath his serious expression, Mr. Goldburgh's brown eyes glowed with intelligence. "So, Mrs. Sterling. Do you know how the methamphetamine got into your vehicle?"

My neck felt stiff when I shook my head. "I have no idea what this is all about."

Colter pointed a finger into my face. "We've got you now, Mrs. Sterling."

Without taking his eyes off me, Mr. Goldburgh said, "Please excuse us for a moment, Deputy Colter. I'd like to confer with my client."

Colter strutted out, throwing back an ugly face just before he slammed the door.

Mr. Goldburgh searched my eyes. "You're quite pale. Are you feeling okay?"

"I just want to go home."

"Do you know anything that could explain these accusations?"

My headache increased when I shook my head.

"Well, let's see if we can get you out of here then."

He collected his folders, tapped the table with them, and hurried out the door.

Through the opaque glass window in the door, I watched shadowy shapes of Colter and Mr. Goldburgh. Judging by the arm gestures, they appeared to be engaged in an animated discussion. Soon after, the door opened and they reentered the room, Mr. Goldburgh first with Deputy Colter behind.

Colter bristled. "I'll be seeing you again soon. Don't leave town."

Mr. Goldburgh looked serious, but congenial. "It appears that they found evidence in your vehicle. However, you are not being arrested at this time." He gestured at the door. "You're free to leave. Please come to my office tomorrow morning at ten to discuss a strategy."

Without further discussion, Mr. Goldburgh guided me to the lobby where Jesse still waited. He left without even introducing himself to Jesse.

Bewildered, flabbergasted, speechless, I watched the door bang shut after Mr. Goldburgh left the station. The world seemed to be running in slow motion. This must be a bad dream. Maybe I should pinch myself.

"What is it?" Jesse threw a protective arm around my shoulders. "You've been in there for hours. What took you so long?"

"That's the attorney. He... I..." All sensation of reality drained away. Blackness closed in on me and I felt myself falling again.

Jesse grabbed me, shaking my shoulders. "The attorney. What's he doing here? What did he say?"

I blinked hard trying to focus on Jesse's dear familiar face. "Colter… drugs… in the Jeep."

Jesse frowned and turned his good ear toward me. "It sounded like you said, 'Drugs in the Jeep.'"

My head weighed a ton. With great effort, I nodded.

"What drugs? What Jeep?"

I finally focused on his eyes. They looked so concerned. "Ours, Jesse. He said they found methamphetamine in our Jeep."

"Impossible." Jesse shook his head. "There are no drugs in our Jeep."

I swayed and Jesse steadied me. If this wasn't a nightmare, when would someone explain what was going on?

❧

Jeff Goldburgh's office took up the second floor of a two-story building on Main Street in the old Victorian section of downtown Grass Valley. With trepidation, I climbed the steps with Jesse right behind me, our shoes clacking on the marble in time with my throbbing headache. We found his name and title, *Jeff Goldburgh, Attorney at Law*, painted on his office door in impressive gold lettering. The door opened to a miniscule waiting area. The middle-aged receptionist sported a bun on top of her head that looked like a cinnamon roll. She glanced up from her computer desk to greet us.

"We're here to see Mr. Goldburgh." Jesse's voice shook a tad.

Cinnamon Roll removed her reading glasses. "May I give him your name?"

Jesse cleared his throat. "We're the Sterlings."

"I'll tell him you're here." She glided around her desk and hurried into the office behind her.

I sat on the edge of one of the two overstuffed chairs in the waiting area. Jesse paced. In a minute, the receptionist returned with Mr. Goldburgh directly behind her.

"Please come in," he said with a welcoming gesture, shaking our hands when we passed by. Why couldn't I feel as calm as he acted? Let's hope our confidence in this man would prove well placed. Zora Jane had highly recommended him.

Jesse and I entered his bookcase-lined office and lowered our bodies stiffly into the two chairs he indicated.

Mr. Goldburgh seemed to sense my nervous state. "This must be a frightening time for both of you." He seated his corpulent body into an imposing black leather chair behind his oversized oak desk.

Jesse glanced at me, signaling that I should speak.

I gulped. "That's putting it mildly. I'm certainly way out of my comfort zone."

Mr. Goldburgh adjusted his spectacles and leafed through a pile of papers from a folder on his desk. "Well, let's see if we can get this over with before it goes any further."

I liked that idea a lot.

After reading several sections, he glanced up and removed his glasses. "The evidence against you is insubstantial and inconclusive."

I nodded dully. A slight consolation, but I'd rather not be here at all.

"Do you own a black fringed purse, Mrs. Sterling?"

Of all the questions I expected him to ask, that one would never have made it to the list. "Black fringed?"

"Do you know why a black fringed purse would be in your vehicle?"

Baffled, I shook my head, looking at Jesse for assistance.

Jesse leaned toward Mr. Goldburgh. "What's this about?"

"The drugs removed from your Jeep were concealed in a black fringed purse found under the back seat on the driver's side. Any idea how they got there?"

I laughed nervously. "We never sit in the back seat. Molly does sometimes. That's our dog. But she doesn't have a—"

Mr. Goldburgh's eyes met mine. He smiled. "Of course not."

"Mary," Jesse said, the light bulb above his head lighting up. "She sat in the back seat."

"Oh, my!" I suddenly remembered. "Mary Wilson carried a black purse with fringe on it." Hope trickled into my heart and I turned to Mr. Goldburgh for affirmation. "Well that explains it, doesn't it? The purse belonged to Mary."

He slipped his glasses off and rocked in his big chair, looking thoughtful. "When was Mary Wilson in the back seat?"

"The night before she died. That's when we took her out to the mill. She brought her purse that night. I remember she took it off the hook beside the front door at her house when we were leaving."

Mr. Goldburgh placed his glasses back on and consulted the paperwork again. "From the contents of the purse, I'd say it wouldn't be difficult to establish that this purse belonged to Miss Wilson. Red lipstick, black eye pencil, and eyeliner. Black finger nail polish. That's not likely the type of makeup you use, Mrs. Sterling, unless you have an alter ego." He peered over his glasses and smiled as if he'd made a joke. "We could have the lipstick tested for DNA." He nodded agreement with himself. "There's no substance to this evidence. It's really just a nuisance."

That sounded promising. "I'm off the hook then?"

"Well, actually no. The drugs are still a problem because they were found in your vehicle. It's a significant amount of methamphetamine. You can still be charged with possession of a controlled substance." He leafed through a few more papers. "Did you know Mary used drugs?"

I shook my head. "Actually I rather thought she didn't. Her former boyfriend does. They have a drug lab out at the mill. But I thought she condemned his drug use." I glanced at Jesse for confirmation.

Jesse nodded. "I think alcohol was her drug of choice."

Mr. Goldburgh rustled a few more pages. "The autopsy didn't note drugs in her system." He gazed at us. "Perhaps she possessed the drugs with intent to sell."

That would surprise me but this entire affair was a puzzle. "I don't know what to think anymore."

He closed the file and rocked a moment longer. "It seems strangely convenient that Mary's purse showed up packed with drugs at precisely the time you were being questioned at the sheriff's office."

Jesse leaned toward him. "I assure you, Mr. Goldburgh, we have no idea how those drugs got into our car unless Mary left them there."

He removed his glasses and chewed one end before speaking again. "My guess would be that someone planted them."

What an incredible idea! "Who would do a thing like that?" I stared into Jesse's eyes, seeing my bewilderment mirrored there.

Mr. Goldburgh watched our faces. "Probably someone from the sheriff's office. Is there anyone there who might want to get you out of the way?"

Colter came to mind. But why? What could make him risk his job and reputation to frame *me*?

18

CHAPTER EIGHTEEN

Thursday morning another news story proclaimed my guilt in scathing terms. Above the article, a second picture that was taken when I left the sheriff's office made my face look scary enough to frighten small children. Why didn't I notice someone taking it? Not that I would have posed so they could get a better shot. But good grief! How do news photographers manage to snap the worst possible angles? I winced while I read the incriminating article. Even if they didn't manage to convict me of murder, association and innuendo would forever sully my good reputation within Nevada County.

The media crowd outside our gate grew in number and strength; a few hearty news people ran alongside any vehicle that drove in or out of our driveway. I hid in the house whenever possible. Ed and Zora Jane brought groceries and casseroles along with encouraging words. For once I had no appetite, but it comforted me to know that my friends believed in my innocence and were praying for truth and justice.

At Mr. Goldburgh's suggestion, Jesse and I both submitted to drug testing which, of course, showed no drugs in our systems. We invited a crew of detectives to our house and watched them search with drug-detection dogs through every inch of our property. They made a huge mess that took hours to clean up, but didn't find a whiff of drugs or a single piece of drug paraphernalia.

Mr. Goldburgh also suggested I volunteer for a lie detector test, but Ed advised against it since such tests were often inconclusive. An inconclusive result might cast undue suspicion. Besides, lie detector results couldn't be considered evidence in court.

"I know this is a huge pain in the heinie," Ed said on Friday when they visited to encourage us. "But it'll pass, I promise. They've got nothing on you. They would've already arrested you if they have what they say they have. Trust me. This Colter fellow's trying to scare you off. Nothing more."

"But why?" I asked incredulously. What possible threat could I be to Deputy Colter?

Ed scratched his bald head. "I hate to say it. It feels like ratting on one of my own. However, from what you've told me, the conclusion I keep coming back to is…" He studied each of us in turn. "He's got to be involved. If he is, maybe you're getting close to something he doesn't want you to find."

A dirty cop? I'd never considered that. Could Colter be involved? For what reason? Puzzling things I'd wondered about clunked into place. Did Colter's agenda involve illegal activity?

After Ed and Zora Jane left, I stayed outside, rocking in the redwood slide. Our cats, Hoppy and his nearly identical brother, Roy, came to sit in my lap as if sensing my need for comfort. If Molly had been there, she would have been sitting at my feet where I could feel her hot breath against my leg. I could've buried my head in her soft fur and smelled her wonderful aroma. I missed her fiercely.

Caught up in the insanity of having to defend myself, I'd put finding Molly on the back burner. The Molly-sized hole in our house and my heart grew more depressing each day. One morning, I mentioned that to Jesse. "She has been gone over a week. We need to contact Detective Rogers. See what they found out at the compound."

Jesse shook his head. "Zora Jane and Ed already told us everything Rogers can divulge. He won't be able to share more until he's made an arrest. Maybe not even then if there's going to be a trial someday."

"Let's try, at least. If he says no, we'll know we have to take our questions somewhere else." I recited the phone number of the Nevada County Sheriff's Office which I still remembered after numerous calls during last year's Lila Payne investigation.

Jesse placed the call.

I paced, waiting for the dispatcher to pick up.

"Hello. I'd like to make an appointment with Detective Rogers." Jesse stared at me and shook his head. "When will he be in?" He raised his eyebrows. "Okay. We'll try back then."

After he hung up, Jesse turned to me. "He won't be in until tomorrow."

A stifling sense of urgency billowed around me like a hot air balloon. Not only did media people constantly surround us, but Jesse also hovered over me day and night as if he feared I might shatter under the pressure of these false allegations. I needed to get away from the house so I could look for the entrance to the mineshaft. How could I shake Jesse for a few hours? No more lies or cover-ups. Maybe I'd try the direct approach.

"Jesse, my darling." Stabbing with my fork, I picked at the salad Jesse had prepared. "You're so good to me. I'm just about smothered to death with all the wonderful attention you lavish on me. I know how concerned you are and I do appreciate you so much."

He glanced up from his plate. "But—"

"I need to get away by myself for a few hours."

He stopped chewing, his fork suspended in air. Worry crept into his eyes.

"Not for long." I patted his hand. "Just a couple hours."

"Where do you want to go?"

"I just need a little space, that's all." I bent toward him so I could rub his cheek. "I've been under a lot of strain lately. I feel kind of cooped up. Maybe it's cabin fever."

He wasn't buying it. His hand closed protectively over mine. "Okay. What's up?"

"Can't I just have a little time by myself without something being up?"

He laughed mirthlessly. "Sure. But I know you. You have something in mind. You're not planning to get in more trouble, are you?"

"Really, Jesse. Don't you think I've got enough trouble without going out to find more?"

His dubious look remained but I persisted, so he saw me off with a sigh and sadness in his eyes. He even allowed me to drive his Ford dualie since the Jeep had been impounded. A twinge of guilt condemned me while I sped past the media crowds, but I squashed it down before I could dwell on it.

I had to find Molly no matter what.

A sign announcing the entrance to the historic Empire Mine, part of California's state park system, stuck out through the trees. I hoped to find information at the Empire about the location of other mines in the area, particularly the Star Mine, which had been a smaller operation to begin with. Its wooden and tin buildings had long since collapsed leaving little to create a state park around. The Empire Mine, on the other hand, was the oldest, largest, and richest gold mine in California history, operating from 1850 all the way up to 1956. An enormous quantity of gold had been mined out of the 367 miles of underground shafts and tunnels during its operation. Experts estimated that the total extracted comprised only about twenty percent of the total gold in the region. The mine closed when mining costs became prohibitive, leaving the remaining gold untouched. The shafts and tunnels were abandoned; most of them had caved in or been flooded with water.

Many of the original Empire Mine buildings had been preserved and restored. The picturesque office and stone house of the owner, built in the early 1890s to resemble an English country estate, provided a popular tourist attraction. Docents dressed in period costumes conducted tours through the house on weekends. With its redwood interiors, leaded glass windows, and massive granite walls, the cottage held great charm. Trees and shrubs grouped in traditional Victorian style decorated the spacious grounds. We often brought guests to these gardens to see the local color and spend an engaging afternoon traveling back in time.

I bounced over the gravel drive into a small parking lot where I shaded my eyes against the sun's glare and considered the best place to start. The tour office seemed promising. A woman behind the ticket window looked up when I interrupted her concentration. "May I help you?"

My recent notoriety concerned me. I hung my head trying not to let her get a good look at me. But she showed no sign of recognizing me from my newspaper pictures. What a relief!

"I need information about the old mine shafts in the area. Not the Empire, but smaller mines. The Star in particular. Do you have a map that might show that one?"

She didn't question my need to know, just indicated the direction to the gift shop with a simple wave of her hand. "They have maps in there." Immediately she returned to her papers.

Wandering among the aisles in the gift shop, I came upon a rack of maps. Sure enough, one of them showed locations of other mines in the vicinity. The Star Mine was included.

After I made my purchase, I took the map to the Jeep where I spread it open on the steering wheel. According to what Mary had told us, the mineshaft leading to *Satori* would be somewhere near the main entrance to the Star Mine, marked with an *X* on this map.

Near the *X* a box with double lines contained a written warning: "Caution! This area closed to the public due to instability caused by miles of underground tunnels. Entrances to mine shafts are sealed."

Individual mine shafts within the box were not marked.

"Oh, no! This map is no help at all." However, it did show the location of the main entrance. If I got that far, I'd have a bit of exploring to do.

Finding the front entrance took some hunting. I drove down several long streets before getting close enough. The mountainous forested terrain all around me made me suddenly thankful I'd worn tennis shoes instead of the less comfortable but more stylish sandals I sometimes donned when the weather warmed.

I parked the car along a dirt road at the bottom of a hill where I finally found an old sign announcing the "Star Mine" ahead and climbed out of the Jeep. My watch read 2:25. I considered phoning Jesse, but the cell phone on the passenger seat beside me had been flashing "No service" after I left the Empire Mine. Mary said cell phones didn't work in certain places near these mines. Well, I still had an hour or so before Jesse would begin worrying. I locked the car and started up a dirt road.

About a third of the way up the mountain, I spotted the mine entrance. Nearby, the old powerhouse stood in ruins beneath massive wooden beams that had collapsed around mounds of rusting machinery. Broken tracks led out of the mine. Piles of boulders lined the sides. Metal ore boxes once stacked beside the tracks had fallen in a tall heap. A concrete barrier blocked the entrance to the mine.

I stared at the towering barrier and spoke aloud although no one was there to hear me. "If the other shaft has one of these, I'll have to figure out how to get over it." I raised my arms to estimate the height. A couple inches of rock spanned between the tips of my fingers and the top. "Could I climb over?" I studied it, walking along the side to find somewhere to see through the tiny gap between the barrier and the tunnel. "Somewhere between zilch and nada, that's what my chances of climbing over are. All these mine shafts probably have the same kind of barrier. I'll have to get a ladder." I imagined lugging a heavy ladder up the hill and wasn't sure I could accomplish that on my own.

Ignoring the "Keep Out" sign, I hiked to the right first, reasoning that since the caution box on the map had been placed to the right of the "X" which marked the main entrance, perhaps the accessible entrance would also be to the right.

A dirt path wound through stacks of corroded metal and weathered lumber. The trail circled the mountain by way of a little valley and then started up another hill.

I passed through piles of rusted machinery parts and found myself at the top of a knoll. An endless carpet of green forest spread out before me as far as I could see. I gasped at the pristine scenery, uncluttered by man's discarded waste. I turned in a circle, taking in the beauty. A little breeze ruffled through my hair; the air smelled clean and fresh.

Along the path, pine needles crunched under my feet. Around another bend, the walk became steeper. Judging by the time it took me to get this far, I figured I'd come between a half mile and a mile from the main entrance. I stopped again and squinted at the hillside ahead. Up the mountain, where the trees became sparser, a mine opening covered by another concrete barrier became visible.

I'd never be able to climb that mountain and then the concrete barrier, so I decided to return later with a ladder. Maybe I'd be able to drive all the way up to the main entrance. I studied the dirt road while I hiked back to the Jeep. That appeared to be a possibility. Here and there, I saw tire tracks in the dirt. Perhaps someone else had driven this far in the last few days.

Getting away from the clamoring media people cleared my head somewhat. Or maybe hiking in the mountain air did it. Conversations with Mary replayed in my mind. I wished I'd known her better, been able to protect her. I wished someone hadn't taken her away so soon. *Why didn't we just take her home with us that night?* We would have kept her safe. I brushed away a little tear. I'd better think about something else before I started to sob. *Was anyone arranging for Mary's funeral?*

Trudging toward the car, I remembered Colter's accusations. An odd feeling like I'd forgotten something important nagged my conscience. What was it?

The drugs in the purse? No, something about that purse. Mary had the purse in the back seat when we went to the mill. *Did she leave it in the car when we dropped her off?* I replayed the scene:

Early that morning, almost four, we returned to Mary's house. Jesse eased the Jeep into the wide space near Mary's front door. Mary looked as tired as I felt.

I reached back to squeeze her hand. "Thank you for trying to help us find Molly."

She hesitated. "She must be in the mine shaft. That's why we didn't see her. Frankie will take care of her. He loves dogs."

Jesse raised his eyebrows. "He does?"

She nodded. "Oh, sure. He's got a real mean streak where people are concerned, but he would collect every stray in town if he could. That German shepherd out there, that's his dog Brutus. He has others too. Probably a dozen or more. Strays mostly, that he found on the street, just like me. He's very fond of them. He won't let anyone hurt Molly."

I knew she wanted to give me hope. "Well then, we'll have to figure out how to get her out of there."

Jesse groaned.

The corners of Mary's mouth turned up just a bit. "Thank you for praying with me. I won't ever forget that."

"You could come to church with us," I said. "To learn more about Jesus."

She nodded. "That would be nice."

She opened the door and stepped into the darkness. We watched until the screen door flapped shut behind her.

Did she take her purse? Surely she wouldn't leave it in the back seat. I couldn't shake the impression that I'd seen that purse another time. Where?

Then it hit me. The black fringed purse lay on the floor underneath the overturned kitchen chair when I entered Mary's house for the last time. I was positive I'd seen it there. *How did it get into our Jeep?*

Someone put it there deliberately, probably even added the drugs, for the sole purpose of implicating me, just as Mr. Goldburgh had suggested. *Who would have done such a thing?*

I knew with one guess.

Empowered by anger bordering on rage, I pushed the door at the sheriff's office open with more force than necessary and demanded to see Deputy Colter.

The woman manning the front desk raised her eyebrows in surprise. "May I have your name?"

"Christine Sterling. He knows me."

Her expression told me she'd been instructed to stall while sizing up the mental state of crazy folks who make such demands. "I'm sorry. Deputy Colter is in a meeting. Perhaps one of the other officers could assist you?"

I planted both hands on her desk. "That won't do, my dear. I must see Colter. Now."

She moved from behind her desk and hurried through the door.

I paced several times across the rug, ignoring stares from the couple seated in the waiting area. Shortly, Deputy Colter marched in with the receptionist trailing right behind.

Outrage oozed from his every pore. "This better be important."

"Believe me, it is." I led the way toward the hall where interviews were held.

Colter gestured toward a cubicle where we could talk. I did not sit. After he closed the door, he turned to face me. "What is it now?"

"The purse." I panted while I described my sighting of it at Mary's house. "How do you suppose it got into our Jeep? Mary certainly couldn't have put it there. She was dead already. Who did then? It had to be you."

He flinched slightly. "You have no proof of that."

My heart and my head throbbed out of control. "I know

what I saw! Mary did not leave her purse in my Jeep. She left it in her house. Neither Jesse nor I put it in the Jeep. Who's been trying to keep me from the truth? Who threatened Jesse and me? Who had no interest in finding the black van? Who had time and opportunity to plant the purse in my Jeep?" I pointed my finger. "You, you, you! It's all adding up. That means you are involved in these deaths, Baxter's *and* Mary's. Why else would you try to get me out of your way?"

He pulled himself to full height, towering above me as if he could silence me by sheer size. "How dare you! Those are all preposterous accusations."

I placed my hands on my hips and glared.

He blinked. "It would come down to my word against yours, an esteemed officer of the law against a woman known to consort with druggies. Who do you think people would believe?"

I would not back down. "If you don't admit it, I'm going directly to your superiors. If they're not investigating you already, they will be by the time I finish."

Deputy Colter stared hard. His mouth opened, but words didn't tumble out. He closed his lips and plopped into a chair.

For a moment, he appeared to shrink. His brow furrowed deeply. When he spoke at last, he had to prop himself up to regain his professional demeanor. His voice stammered out, "You are clearly overwrought, Mrs. Sterling. Surely we can work this out without involving anyone else."

Too late for that. Adrenaline rushed through my veins, giving me strength. I didn't back down for an instant. "What'll it be? You tell me what's really going on or I start talking. I'll tell this story to everyone all the way up to the high sheriff himself. I'll even hold a press conference. I will not stop talking until they get the truth out of you."

He cleared his throat and pinched his bulbous nose while considering a moment longer. "I think I know what you want." He swiped his chin. "In reviewing the, uh, evidence against you in Mary Wilson's murder, I find that we have been a bit hasty in naming you a suspect."

I couldn't believe my ears. "What? Haven't you heard anything I said?"

He stood. That seemed to give him a confidence boost. When he continued, his voice had regained its usual pompous tenor. "We will immediately recommend that your name be removed from the list of suspects and issue a statement to that effect for the news media. That should be completely satisfactory. Now please allow me to show you out."

Before I could utter another word, he took my arm and maneuvered me through the offices to the reception area. He marched me all the way to my Jeep, then turned on his heel and walked away.

It wasn't what I wanted, but relief swept through my body anyway. I shook my head while I unlocked the Jeep. So many questions crowded my brain that I couldn't make sense of them. Certainly some of the answers involved Deputy Colter.

Exhaustion overwhelmed me. I felt alone and, oh, so very old. I had to regroup and process what had happened. For now, I'd have to let the questions go.

Just for now.

19

CHAPTER NINETEEN

An article on the front page of the Sunday morning newspaper announced that I'd been formally cleared of suspicion in Mary Wilson's murder. The news crews were gone before we left for church. A few people gawked at me when I entered church, then glanced away quickly. How long would it be before the sight of my face or the mention of my name didn't raise eyebrows in our small town?

We had picked up our newly released Jeep from the impound lot as soon as we could. Jesse suggested an outing to celebrate my freedom from pending prosecution. But when we turned off toward Nevada City, a row of strangers clad completely in black lined both sides of the freeway overpass. Pasty white faces without smiles turned to stare while we drove by.

The Channel 11 news van occupied the middle of Broad Street. Jesse swerved to miss it. "What's going on here? It's too early for Halloween. What costumed holiday falls in the spring?"

"I don't know." Hordes of somber kids milled through the narrow streets. "Nevada City will use any excuse for a celebration." Parades and festivals abounded in these foothill gold-boom towns, but I hadn't heard of anything planned for this Sunday.

Teens costumed in dark Goth clothing swarmed the entrance to the little market just off Broad Street. Streaks of bright purple, blue, or neon green decorated their hair regardless of gender. Body piercings protruded from eyebrows and noses and tattoos cluttered their skin.

For several years, these teens loitering in the vicinity of the downtown market had ignited controversy among adults who didn't understand their unorthodox taste in attire or lifestyle.

Jesse drove around the block a couple of times looking for a parking space. "This is kind of scary," he said on his third pass. "Maybe having lunch here wasn't such a great idea."

As we rounded the corner near the market, a dented blue Chevrolet pulled out of a space in front of us.

"Bingo." Jesse expertly parallel parked in the tiny gap.

When I set my foot on the sidewalk, the throbbing cadence from boom boxes pounded the air right out of my chest. The atmosphere hummed with tension. No one laughed or smiled. Fists waved. A cacophony of voices clamored. Scary grunge music blared like drumbeats of warring tribes; it was clearly not happy music, although I couldn't identify a single word.

Jesse joined me, tucking his hearing aid into his pocket. *Dare we leave the Jeep in the midst of this unstable crowd?*

I approached the nearest clump of bystanders. A thin, teenage girl turned her doleful white face toward us. Her eyes were heavily outlined in black. Fingertips of the black lace gloves on her hands had been hacked off revealing long black fingernails. An ornate metal crucifix dangled from a long beaded necklace that appeared to be rosary beads. The effect startled me. "What's going on?"

The steel toecap on one of her army surplus boots clinked the sidewalk when she stamped her foot defiantly. "The pigs are trying to pin that girl's murder on us."

My stomach lurched. "You mean Mary Wilson's murder?"

"Yeah." Her lips curled into an unattractive sneer. "They're saying a gang of us kids did it. Imitating some psycho I never heard of. It's insane!"

Beside her, a tall grim male glared down from beneath a halo of spiked hair. "It's a total frame, dude. They been tryin' to get us outta here for years." He stuck his clenched hand in the air as if shaking his fist at the heavens. The sun sparkled on the spikes imbedded in his black leather wristband. "Too bad. We're staying."

Just then, I spotted Leonard Pinzer, wielding his ever present microphone like a sword slashing through the mob on the sidewalk. His faithful cameraman shuffled close behind, jostled by the crowd. I nudged Jesse and pointed. "Let's see what he's up to."

Leonard threaded through, asking questions where he could. He had just lowered his microphone when he saw us. "Hey." His face brightened in recognition. "It's the former person of interest. What are you doing in this mess?"

"What's this all about?" I asked above the din.

"Looks like the animals are taking over the zoo." He chuckled while he extracted a large handkerchief from his pocket to wipe the sweat off his jowls. "The kids aren't going to take this lying down."

Jesse cupped one hand around his ear. "Take what?"

An expression of complete disbelief spread over Leonard's face.

I interpreted. "He wants to know what's happening."

Leonard stopped and stared at each of us in turn. "Don't you folks ever watch the news?"

Jesse leaned closer. "What did he say?"

"Your Deputy Colter arrested three boys this morning for the murder of Mary Wilson."

"Colter?" What was the man up to now?

Jesse looked at me. I shrugged.

"Yep." Ignoring Jesse's inability to hear, Leonard puffed himself to his full height as if the importance of his insider information had inflated him. "He's been working on this since before he brought you in for questioning. Apparently bringing you in was a ruse he orchestrated so he could concentrate on his real focus without getting these kids too riled up." He nodded at the crowd, smirking knowingly.

"A ruse?" I repeated. How dare Colter put me through such torture just to divert attention from his real target! Anger bubbled. I should send him the attorney's bill.

As if Leonard hadn't a clue about the injustice I'd suffered, he continued. "For weeks I've heard rumors that something big is about to go down. Looks like these three boys planned to do something at the school, like Columbine, but settled for offing that poor unfortunate girl. Old Colter's made the arrests."

He lowered his voice to a confidential tone. Jesse bent to hear him. "She was one of them… a street person originally. Lived out at Pioneer Park with that pack of runaways. Didn't move to Rough and Ready until a little while ago. Guess they recovered plenty of evidence in one of the boy's houses." He nodded, looking thrilled by the direction this investigation had taken. "She's been ratting on them to the authorities. It's all in the stuff they took from the houses. They've got weapons and tons of ammunition. However, these kids out here—" He gestured around us. "These kids say, 'No way.' So far, everyone's standing behind the boys. Everyone I've talked to anyway."

Jesse and I stared at each other in amazement. Would the craziness never end?

The commotion suddenly swelled to a roar. Leonard and his cameraman raced into the tumult like piranhas to a morsel of meat. The dense crowd stampeded as one unit. We lagged behind, craning our necks to see above the hubbub, jostled by hurrying bystanders. By the time we got to the edge of the onlookers, bodies were crushed so tightly together that nothing could be seen.

Jesse's head towered over everyone, one of the advantages of being tall. "Looks like a fight," he said, without taking his eyes off the action. He dodged and flinched while he watched. "I think there's a deputy in the middle of it."

"Oh, no! Is it anyone we know?"

Jesse didn't answer.

The backs of the kids in front of me blocked my view, so I tried to decipher words on the back of a black sweatshirt. Chunky block letters like those drawn by graffiti artists had been bleached into the fabric. *Skinny Puppy? What did that mean?* Other t-shirts had Japanese characters. For all I knew, they didn't say anything in English.

All of a sudden, a loud thud and the crash of breaking glass caused the crowd to shift left.

"What was that?"

"Ooh," Jesse exclaimed. "That must've hurt!"

I tugged on Jesse's shirtsleeve. "What?"

"Someone fell through the window in front of the Hat Shoppe. Looks like there's blood."

The dissonance swelled in reaction. I sighed, feeling quite left out.

"Here," Jesse said, looking down at me as if he'd just remembered my size handicap. "Climb on my shoulders."

I raised my eyebrows. "Do what? Are you kidding?"

"Come on, Chris." He made a little foothold by clasping both hands and bending toward me. "Remember how we did it when we saw the Queen Mum?"

We'd been in Windsor during the Queen Mother's ninetieth birthday celebration and lucked out with a royal sighting when she did a walkabout on the street outside the castle gates. That day the crowd pressed so tightly together I had to climb on Jesse's shoulders to take pictures. "You're talking twenty years ago!" I didn't want to remember how many pounds ago.

"Give it a shot." He grinned. "You can do it."

Jesse grunted and swayed when I put my weight into his hands, but managed to keep them together. I swung one leg over his shoulder, kicking the boy in front of me soundly when Jesse struggled to straighten.

"Hey!" The boy turned so quickly his chains rattled. "Watch it, lady."

Now in a rather precarious predicament, I decided since I'd made the commitment, I'd best just get on with it. "So sorry," I said from my sideways position, smiling as pleasantly as I could under the circumstances. We bumped several others near us while I tugged and pulled with all my might to heft my middle-aged body onto Jesse's shoulders. Additional glares and stares were hurled our way like daggers. One young man used unnecessarily rude language, but eventually I worked my way to a relatively comfortable position.

Once settled, I patted Jesse on the head. "Are you okay?"

He laughed. "We're not as young as—"

"You can say that again."

What I saw from my roost looked like a fight scene from a movie. *Was that why we watched like spectators without acting on behalf of justice, because it didn't look real?* I expressed my righteous disapproval with a loud *TSK*. Had our society become so jaded by what we viewed every day on our televisions or on the movie screens that we didn't react with outrage when faced with genuine evil?

At the center of the throng, several of the aggressors appeared to be beating the stuffing out of each other. A uniformed officer had apparently been caught in the middle. He didn't look familiar, although I only got an occasional glimpse of his face. His uniform was torn and bloodied just the same as the clothing of the three kids doing the majority of the punching. The officer defended himself remarkably well considering the odds against him. The horror of what I watched sunk in. This was the real thing.

"We should call 9-1-1—"

A blaring siren drowned out my words as a dozen vehicles surrounded the pandemonium. Officers jumped out with weapons drawn.

Jesse started to move away from the crowd. "It's time to get out of here."

"Let me down then." I patted Jesse's head again.

He stooped so I could climb off his shoulders. Gravity being what it is, unloading proved significantly easier than climbing up. I jumped to the ground with a grunt. When I straightened, I collided with a girl who was running away from approaching deputies. I recognized the pale-faced teen we had talked to earlier. "Careful now." I grabbed her arm to steady her.

"Thanks." She skidded to a stop. "You better hurry and get out of here."

"Why?"

Jesse bent to hear her answer.

"We ain't gonna take this." She glanced over her shoulder at the rapidly dispersing crowd. "We're gonna fight back. You could get hurt."

Jesse and I turned toward the advancing line of officers. *Dear, Lord. Please diffuse this situation quickly. Protect these people from injury.*

The girl started to run again, glancing back over her shoulder. When we didn't move, she returned to where we stood. "Come on, move! You don't want to be here when bullets start to fly, do you?"

Jesse frowned and grabbed my arm.

She hurried alongside us. Sandwiched between her and Jesse, I moved along with the mob. Her dark restless eyes darted through the throng. When we got to the car, she stopped and faced me. "Now get going."

I felt strangely drawn to this sad little person. Her mournful eyes broke my heart. Why did she stop to help us? "Can we drop you somewhere?"

She hesitated a moment, looking back at the mayhem. The injured officer had been rescued and a stretcher carried him away to a waiting ambulance. Deputies held back the throng of kids. Strident voices floated over the general clamor of the crowd.

"Um." She took a few seconds to think it over. "Sure, I could use a ride."

She scrambled into the backseat as if she'd ridden with us before and slammed the door. Jesse swung into the crowded street. During the several minutes it took to navigate through the multitude, she peered out the window, straining to see, but when we got onto Highway 49, she settled back in the seat. I watched her for another minute until she noticed my interest.

"Drop me at Kmart." She tugged her black hooded sweatshirt tighter around her. "If you don't mind."

I smiled and nodded.

"I live close to there."

Jesse's gaze darted to the rear view mirror and back to the road.

I gave her a smile. "What's your name?"

She didn't return the smile. "Amanda." Her sigh was long and deep as if she knew what our reaction would be. "Amanda Colter."

20

CHAPTER TWENTY

Jesse looked puzzled. "Colter?"

"Yeah," she said with a slight groan as if she knew what we'd say next.

Jesse studied her in the rear view mirror. "Any relation to Deputy Colter from the sheriff's office?"

Amanda's countenance wilted. Black hair fell forward, veiling her face. "He's not my real dad. I don't know my real dad. My mom married him when I was little. They got divorced last year." A monotone of information.

"Oh," I said. "I'm sorry."

"No." Silver chains dangling from her ears jingled when she shook her head. "That was a good thing."

"You don't like him then?"

She rearranged a clump of dyed black hair behind one ear. "He's a first-class jerk."

Jesse shot me an amused look. "You may be right."

I agreed with a nod. "We've certainly been disappointed in the way he's dealt with us."

Her look of surprise communicated how unusual it was to get agreement from grownups. "Really?"

"So you and your mother live by yourselves now?" I asked, making small talk.

"We moved in with my nana." She turned toward the window. "After the split."

"How's that working out?"

Amanda shrugged. "It's better than before. Not so much drama."

"Deputy Colter must be as difficult to live with as he is to work with," Jesse said.

"No argument there."

Her soft snicker reminded me of Mary. "Did you know Mary Wilson?"

"Mary." She looked out the window again. "She hung with us. Not exactly with me, but I knew her."

A sad knot formed in my throat. "She ran away from home."

Amanda shrugged. "I guess. All I know is she stayed at the park until she hooked up with that poser."

Jesse peered into the rear view mirror again. "You don't like Frankie?"

The force of her head shaking jingled the chains louder. "Too old."

I smiled. Frankie could be as old as forty, more likely only thirty-five. "You didn't like him because of his age?"

She met my eyes. "Not just that. He was way plastic, a pretender. I like living on the edge all right. A dude who's open to new ways to find happiness, whatever his age, that's cool with me, but that one…" Her voice trailed off in a jangle of chains when she shook her head. "He's not one of us. He's… messed up."

"Messed up?" I repeated. "In what way?"

"Totally into violence. Talks about killing and hurting people all the time." She shivered. "We're not like that."

That surprised me. From the negative music and ghoulish costumes, I had supposed these kids delved deeply into violence. "Really? It's the war talk you object to?"

Amanda twisted her rosary beads and tilted her head to study me as if curious about my honest interest in her world. "Hey. We're not violent. Terrorism, atomic bombs, military dominance... that stuff didn't come from my generation. We don't buy into the horrible squalor of life you people created. We hate war and we hate the materialism that drives people to war."

She sounded like every generation of teenagers. I remembered the hippies in my day making the same assessment of society's ills. "Make love, not war?"

"Exactly."

I didn't get a chance to point out that she had told us the teens were fighting back in Nevada City because just then Jesse pulled into the Kmart parking lot. "Here you go. Are you sure this is close enough to where you live? I don't mind taking you farther."

She'd already opened the door. "This is great."

"Hey, Amanda, wait." I leaned toward the window Jesse opened. She came back and stooped to listen. "Mary Wilson was my friend. I don't think those three kids killed her and I want to find out who did. If you hear anything on the streets that could help convict her murderer, please call me." I scribbled my name and phone number on a scrap of paper from my purse and handed the paper to her. "Thanks for helping us escape."

She took the paper and studied it a second, then raised a fist. "Stay out of the daylight!" She turned on her army boot heel and marched across the parking lot.

I watched her go, feeling strangely drawn. "What does that mean?"

Jesse shook his head when he rolled the window back up. "Haven't the foggiest."

❧

Monday morning Jesse allowed me to accompany Zora Jane into town. She wanted help, and moral support, I suspected, transporting boxes of Baxter's clothing and personal items to the Salvation Army. The trunk of Zora Jane's red Mustang convertible wouldn't hold all the boxes, so we took the Jeep. We planned to drop her boxes off, continue into town for a little shopping, and then indulge in lunch at The Bunnery, my favorite restaurant. It felt good to be doing something normal for a change despite the sadness surrounding the disposal of Baxter's belongings.

But we arrived in Grass Valley to find traffic clogging the streets, news vehicles lining them in droves. Reporters huddled on street corners. I pulled the Jeep into a long queue at the stoplight on Main Street. "Oh, oh. Looks like today's not a good day to come to town."

Zora Jane peered along the intersecting roadway. "Traffic has simply become unbearable here. Where are all these people coming from?"

Truly, an unusual amount of activity buzzed through town; however, anytime a line of cars waited for a stoplight in Grass Valley, longtime residents complained about the traffic. In reality, a few cars in one short line could hardly be considered traffic by Los Angeles standards. "You're talking like an old-timer."

She smiled.

I rapped the steering wheel a few times. "I told you about the crowd in Nevada City yesterday. Everyone's upset about the arrest of those kids. Honestly, Zora Jane, I don't think those kids killed Mary Wilson."

She searched my face. "Why not?"

Hard to distinguish the facts from the journalistic spin. Three full columns had reported the story in the morning newspaper. "Something's wrong. Why would Mary rat on her friends? She had nothing to gain. I think she got killed because those guys at *Satori* recognized her on the surveillance tape. Our visit to the compound and her death happened too close together to be a coincidence." I swiped at a tear. "It's all tied up with Baxter's murder. I'm sure of it."

Zora Jane's expression softened while she gazed at me. "Are you sure you're not imagining that, dear, because you so desperately want it to be true?"

I frowned. Hadn't I redeemed my reputation for wild imagining and jumping to preposterous conclusions? I started to comment when the light changed and my attention was drawn to a long, sleek black Cadillac. The limo pulled into the no parking zone in front of the Union Hotel and parked. When we drove by, Constance Boyd's entourage climbed out.

Zora Jane pointed. "Well, lookie who's back in town."

"What do you suppose she's up to now?"

"Why not pose that question to the lady herself?"

I parked the car four blocks down the street, the closest I could get. By the time we hoofed back, Constance Boyd and her groupies had disappeared. Her entrance had created quite a hubbub. We followed the crowds to a conference room at the back of the hotel. Assorted news people and common citizens swarmed the hallway, buzzing with excitement.

"What's Constance Boyd doing in the conference room?" I asked a cameraman who leaned against the wall.

He shrugged. "Got a meeting with someone."

Zora Jane leaned closer. "Do you know who?"

Looking bored, he shook his head. "Think it's those three freaky boys, the ones that offed that homeless girl."

His cavalier attitude and gross lack of compassion made my blood pressure rise instantly. I snapped at him. "You mean, *allegedly* killed that girl, don't you? And she wasn't homeless. For your information, no one has been convicted yet."

Zora Jane raised her eyebrows. The cameraman slunk away with a backward glance that communicated his belief that those three weren't the only freaky ones in town.

Zora Jane watched him go. "Well, you certainly let him have it."

In my impatience, I had already flown past that encounter and now I concentrated on how to get in to see Miss Boyd. "I don't want to wait around until she comes out, do you?"

"Well—" Zora Jane's wrinkled her nose and lifted her shoulders. I guess she'd rather wait than barge in.

I pulled her away from the crowd a few steps. "I think we should demand to see her. She hasn't had time to start the interview. Let's just open the door and go in."

"Christine—"

We had no time for her to object and I certainly didn't want her to stop and pray over whether we should go in or not. "Come on." I grabbed her arm and pushed her through the crowd ahead of me. "Excuse us. Pardon us. Oh, sorry. We need to get through."

When we got to the closed conference door, I opened it as if I possessed authority to do so. Pulling Zora Jane inside, I slammed the door quickly.

Constance posed on a chair at the end of a conference table. Three somber teenage boys slouched in their chairs across from her. Three women I took to be mothers of the boys huddled behind them with anxious expressions. The cameraman busily set up his equipment on the opposite end of the table and the spectacled assistant balanced on the edge of a chair near Constance's left. The drone of soft conversation ceased the moment we entered. All eyes turned toward us. The assistant rose halfway out of her chair.

"Miss Boyd." I bustled into the room. "We need to speak with you."

The assistant rushed toward us like a mother hen fending off a snake. "You cannot come in—"

Constance held up her hand. "Just a moment, Rebecca. I'll deal with them." She lowered her hand to the table and sat a moment, blinking her perfectly shaped eyes. "You have interrupted an important interview."

I hadn't thought how to approach her and, for an instant, words failed me.

Zora Jane came to the rescue. "We're sorry to bother you, Miss Boyd. I'm sure you are quite busy. Possibly we could make an appointment to speak with you later."

Constance glanced at her assistant. Rebecca shrugged. Looking as dumbfounded as I felt, she mouthed a few words that didn't get voiced.

"Very well." Constance frowned and consulted her expensive Swiss watch. "I will be available in three hours. Come back then."

"Oh, thank you so much." I focused on my cheapo Timex. "We won't take much of your time."

"No," Constance said with firmness. "You will not. I will give you fifteen minutes." She turned back to her interview while Rebecca showed us out the door.

Catherine Leggitt

21

CHAPTER TWENTY-ONE

"We've got two hours and forty-five minutes to kill," I said while we returned to the Jeep after delivering our load to the Salvation Army. "Do you want to see where I found the entrance to the Star Mine?"

Zora Jane raised her eyebrows. "Okay. But tell me again why you're so interested in that mine entrance."

"Well, for one thing, whoever took Molly must be keeping her in there."

"How do you know they're keeping her instead of...?"

I couldn't bring myself to voice the word either. Surely they wouldn't kill my sweet dog. "Because Frankie loves dogs, that's why. Mary said so. I'm positive he's keeping Molly with all the other strays he's collected. But that's not the only reason I want to go out there. That mine figures into Baxter's death somehow."

Of that fact I felt certain; I just didn't know how to connect the dots yet.

While we drove toward the mine, I reviewed my latest confrontation with Colter. "I got so angry with him, Zora Jane. But when I told Jesse, he could only see that the pending charges against me had been dropped."

"Well, that *is* something to praise God for! Aren't you relieved?"

"Sure. But I've been thinking about my conversation with Colter just before he decided to drop the charges. Something frightened him. He doesn't want me to tell my story about seeing that purse under the chair at Mary's house. Is he afraid I'll talk to his superiors or to the media?"

"Maybe both."

"I think so too, Zora Jane."

"Why would he be afraid of that?"

"Because he's involved with both Mary's murder and Baxter's."

"How is he involved?"

That was the big question. What *was* Deputy Colter's agenda? He was a dirty cop for sure. But what part had he played in the two murders? Zora Jane and I reviewed everything we'd learned so far. Discussing the clues while we drove brought certain things into focus.

I mentioned that Leonard Pinzer was the person who told me that Mary was rumored to be a snitch.

Zora Jane gazed out the window. "Leonard seems to attract confidential sources."

I turned onto the road where I'd found the entrance to the Star Mine. "I wonder how much Colter learns from listening to his stepdaughter talk about her friends. Maybe he bugged her phone."

Zora Jane shook her head. "Kids today don't tell grownups much, especially grownups they don't like. Plus, kids have cell phones nowadays. I never heard of anyone bugging a cell phone, although who knows. Maybe they can be intercepted. Anyway, I thought you said the Colters split up and Amanda moved in with her grandmother."

"Right, right, right." I shook my head to clear the cobwebs.

Zora Jane looked out the window while I steered the Jeep up the bumpy dirt road toward the Star Mine entrance. The tires kicked up tornadoes of red Nevada County dust. I clenched my teeth to keep from biting my tongue while we jiggled over rough terrain.

After dodging assorted rusty machinery, I parked as close to the front entrance as possible and we got out. I pointed. "I hiked in over there, through that pile of machinery, and up the hill. That's where I found the other entrance, about half a mile away, with a concrete barrier just like this one."

Zora Jane shielded her eyes to follow my finger pointing up the mountain to the right.

"Do you want to hike up to see it?"

She answered without a moment's hesitation. "Sure."

What a trooper! Always ready for adventure. I sized up her shoes; brown leather flats with pointy toes that didn't in the least resemble proper hiking shoes. "You're a good sport, my friend." I patted her arm when we started up the path, thankful that I'd once again worn my hiker friendly tennis shoes.

We marched along without speaking at first, Zora Jane setting the pace in front with long strides. My short legs had to keep moving at a fast clip to keep up.

After several yards, she stopped and turned to me. "Didn't you say Mary mentioned guards?"

I hauled up, panting and stared past her toward the hillside. "She did. She said they kept guards there all the time because of the valuables."

Zora Jane removed her brown and gold sweater, revealing the matching shell underneath, and tied the sweater neatly over her gold cinch belt. "Where do you think the guards would be on a day like today?"

"I didn't see anyone outside the entrance the other day. I'm guessing they wouldn't stand around where they could be seen. It's too hot outside anyway." I frowned when something else occurred to me. "Although if they're inside, I have no idea how they got in."

She studied me. "Perhaps we should ask God's protection before we proceed."

So she did.

When she finished, I quickened my pace and hurried ahead of her.

Before long, we'd arrived at the crumbling concrete barrier where we carefully inspected the impenetrable wall. The opening behind appeared narrower than the main entrance, just wide enough to accommodate tracks for the ore boxes to be hauled out.

Being half a foot taller than me, Zora Jane reached higher than I could to run her fingers across rows of scrapes along the top. "Maybe they get in by going over the wall. They could use a rope ladder or something to pull themselves to the top."

I stretched my arms as far up as they would go. "I couldn't do that. But I guess someone taller and in better physical shape could." Say, strapping young men.

I peeked in the overturned ore boxes near the concrete. "Maybe they store rope ladders near the entrance where they'll be handy." But the boxes contained only rusted metal parts, no rope.

Zora Jane crouched. "Did you see these footprints?"

When she mentioned it, I noticed sizable boot prints heading to the left. Up ahead, the boot prints marched straight for the concrete barrier. Zora Jane followed them and I followed her. "Good thinking there, Sherlock. I wasn't even looking for footprints."

She glanced up and smiled, then returned to tracking.

The trail of footprints led along the face of the mountain several yards. To my uneducated eye, they looked fresh.

Zora Jane stopped abruptly with her nose inches from a large boulder. "That's odd. The tracks stop right here."

I followed her line of sight. "You're right. They do. What do you think that means?"

She shook her head, looking quite puzzled.

We surveyed the boulder from top to bottom. Fully as wide as its height, the top reached just above my head. Zora Jane stepped toward the boulder again. Reaching in front with both hands, she pushed hard on the rock. I stepped up to help. The boulder didn't budge though we pushed until my muscles ached. We ran our hands over the rough granite surface, but felt nothing out of the ordinary.

"How could they move this big thing out of the way? There has to be something here." She bent sideways to peer behind the boulder. "Aha!"

My gaze followed her stare. Underneath the boulder, a scraped track ran toward the mountain.

I leaned on my knees to rest, frowning. "Okay. What does that mean?"

She pushed the boulder from the side where she found finger holes. "It means…" The boulder squealed when rock scraped across rock and the boulder inched sideways. "It means that this rock is actually a sliding door."

Bracing my feet, I pushed with all my might. The boulder moved slowly out of the way.

With great effort, we soon gained an opening of about ten inches. When we stopped, we panted as if we'd just finished a marathon. These two middle-aged ladies didn't move boulders often enough to develop sufficient muscles for such a strenuous endeavor.

"So." I gasped for air. "That's how they get in and out. Good work, Zora Jane. I never would have found that on my own, let alone been able to move the rock."

She beamed at me from upside down where she'd doubled over to recuperate.

"Be as quiet as possible," I whispered. "In case the guards are standing close to the entrance." I peeked into the space, but saw only darkness. Sliding through sideways, I crept forward a few feet and then paused to listen.

I waited several minutes for my eyes to adjust to the lack of light. But no adjustment of my pupils could bring in enough light to enable me to see. Stillness permeated the dank cavern as if the quiet itself had form. When I satisfied myself that I could neither see nor hear anything, I inched back out, thankful for the little line of light from outside to lead the way.

"Can't see a thing in there," I whispered to Zora Jane.

We pushed the rock back into place. Moving it back was much easier. Even so, the work exhausted us and we leaned against the boulder to rest.

"We need strong lanterns before we head in there again."

She raised an eyebrow. "What about the guards?"

"I haven't figured that out yet. I wish I had a light that would let me see without being seen."

She looked thoughtful. "I've heard of something like that. I think the army has night vision equipment, but I don't know where you'd buy it."

After resting a few minutes, we headed back down the path toward the front entrance where we'd left the car. A shiny spot just off the dirt trail caught my eye. Between the sun reflecting object and the path, a small puddle of mud suggested the presence of an underground spring. It didn't look threatening. But when I attempted to step over it, I misjudged the distance and my foot slid into the mire. In an instant, the sludge sucked my foot in, shoe and all.

I squealed like a lassoed calf.

Zora Jane turned when she saw my predicament. "What are you doing?" She tried to conceal her smile behind one hand.

I didn't see the humor. "My foot is stuck."

In just a few seconds, my leg sunk in up to my knee. I pulled with all my strength, but the mud held fast. "The mud sucked my leg in. I can't get it out."

She giggled.

"It's not funny, Zora Jane. I think it's trying to pull me under."

She stopped giggling. "Oh, my dear let me help you." She stepped easily over the mud and came up on my backside. Putting her arms around my waist, she pulled and I pulled. With a plop like suction releasing my foot popped out, minus the shoe and sock.

The sudden release landed us both on the ground. I wiggled my muddy toes. When she saw my bare foot, she broke into a fit of laughter.

"My shoe!" I moaned. "How will I find my shoe?"

While her giggling turned to gales of laughter, I gingerly stuck one hand into the mud. Feeling with my fingers, I couldn't locate my shoe. I pushed my arm in farther. Still no shoe. By now, my arm was up to its elbow in gooey Nevada County quicksand.

Zora Jane composed herself a little. "I'm sorry, Christine," she said with a small titter. "But that looks really funny."

I couldn't imagine what amused her about a single-shoed woman with mud dripping from one leg and one arm stuck in the ground. "This mud hole has eaten my shoe." With great effort, I extracted my arm and grabbed a tree branch lying nearby on the ground. I pushed the branch into the mud and stirred. Being longer than my arm, the branch went deeper, but didn't snag my shoe. In utter frustration, I lugged the branch out and plunked down hard on the ground.

Zora Jane stood beside me, one hand pressed against her mouth to keep the laughter from escaping. Such a thinly veiled attempt to disguise her amusement didn't work. I could still see mirth in her eyes.

Peering into the mud hole, I couldn't keep the whine out of my voice. "What should I do?"

She pressed her lips together and glanced away. "Are you sure you're looking in the right place?"

I gave a heavy sigh. "You're not helping me."

My arm and leg were now crusted with a thick mud pack. "I can just hear Jesse." I shook my head and mimicked his booming voice. "'This could only happen to you, Christine!'"

When Zora Jane caught my eye, we both burst into laughter. She sat down on the ground beside me and we howled until our sides hurt and tears ran down our faces.

After a few minutes, I composed myself. "Seriously now. How will I ever find my shoe?"

Zora Jane stopped chortling to pray. "Oh, Lord God, please release Christine's shoe from this mud."

Would God answer such a silly prayer? Just in case He would, I grasped my branch and stuck it into the hole once more. I wiggled the branch around the perimeter a few times, pulled it out and pushed it in a slightly different spot, with no success. My sock and shoe had gone to China. Maybe that's where all those single shoes stranded on highways come from. They've popped out of mud pits all over the world.

Nevertheless, I persevered until all hope of retrieving my wayward shoe had vanished. Zora Jane also tried, somehow managing to keep herself spotlessly clean. Eventually, we had to abandon the search.

Trudging back to the Jeep, great dollops of mud dripped off me with every step. I clomped along lopsided, wincing when my tender bare foot stepped on every pebble and sticker along the path. With nothing in the Jeep to wipe off the mess, I carefully eased my mud-encrusted body into the front seat. The mud on my jeans had already started to dry and flake off in places. My sweatshirt sleeve was wet and muddy to the elbow, my hand still covered in goop.

Zora Jane started to whoop again when she saw my face while I settled into the seat. "I'm so sorry, but I wish you could see how you look. How did you manage to get mud on your face?"

I glanced at the clock on the dash of the Jeep. In less than fifteen minutes, we were due at an appointment with a nationally syndicated newswoman and I was covered in mud and had only one shoe. Starting the Jeep, I planted my bare, mud-caked foot on the accelerator and zoomed away.

22

CHAPTER TWENTY-TWO

First, we stopped at the church where I borrowed a hose to wash off as much mud as possible. Of course that didn't solve the shoe problem, but I felt less like the Creature from the Black Lagoon. Zora Jane composed herself sufficiently so that she only chuckled softly now and then, mostly when she looked at me.

I turned the car heater up full blast, hoping to quickly dry my clothing, and away we flew to Kmart to buy another pair of shoes. I slogged into the store with one shoe off and one shoe on like "Diddle, diddle, dumpling, my son John" in the Mother Goose rhyme, dripping wet from one side and sweating like a pig from the heat in the car.

People stopped to stare. Of course, I had to buy a pair of socks first so I could try on shoes. Then I couldn't find a pair of shoes that fit. In the interest of time, I settled on flip-flops several sizes too large. By the time we located a parking space downtown and hurried up the hill to the hotel, we were a full half-hour late for our appointment.

Constance Boyd had not waited.

I stamped my flip-flopped foot. "Now what?"

Zora Jane searched the street. "Where would she go next?"

We asked a few people milling outside the hotel, but no one knew where she'd gone. I flopped inside and approached the front desk. A man with white hair curling over his ears peered over the top of his spectacles. "May I help you?"

"I'm looking for Constance Boyd," I said. "We had an appointment with her, but we were… unavoidably delayed. Do you know where I can her?"

He frowned. "Sorry, I am not authorized to disclose that sort of information."

I started to object, when the cameraman I'd offended earlier wandered by. I left the front desk to apologize. My conscience pricked me. "Listen." I stepped toward him. "I didn't mean to criticize you before. Please forgive me."

The cameraman stopped abruptly, shifting the large video equipment on his shoulder, and produced a blank stare. His gaze took in my wet clothing, wilted hair-do, and exposed toes. "Oh, you. From the hall." He nodded, his stare brightening. "You seem a tad wet. You still chasing Miss Boyd?"

Zora Jane stepped up from behind me. "Do you know where she went?"

"I heard mention she wanted to check in at that fancy bed and breakfast in Nevada City…what's its name? The one at the top of Broad Street."

"Morgan House?" Zora Jane suggested.

He nodded again. "That's it."

I pumped his hand, thanking him more profusely than necessary and we hurried out to the Jeep. On the way to the car, we passed an army surplus store.

"Look at this. I never noticed this store before." I peered in the window. "Maybe they've heard of those night vision things you mentioned."

A door chime tinkled when we entered. The place smelled musty. A scruffy man in army fatigue pants sauntered out from the back. But my eyes had already spotted a display featuring night vision goggles.

Intent on chewing his large wad of gum, the salesman didn't take note of my wet clothing. "Can I help you?"

I pointed to the goggles. "How do these work?"

His voice sounded robotic as if he'd repeated the same sales pitch many times. "By amplifying the lower portion of the infrared light spectrum, the goggles pick up light that normal vision can't see. Thermal imaging captures the upper portion of the infrared light spectrum which is emitted when heated by objects like warm bodies."

Not understanding a word he said, I nodded to look intelligent. "If I wanted to see people inside a mine shaft where there's no light, could I do that with these?"

"Yeah, sure." He popped his gum and picked up a pair of binoculars, displaying tattoos of serpents cavorting the length of his arm. "That's what thermal imaging does, picks up body heat. Doesn't matter how dark it is."

Zora Jane stood beside me without speaking. Her expression gave no clue to her thoughts.

"How much are they?"

He snapped his gum and crossed his arms. "Depends. Which model?"

How should I know? I raised my eyebrows and shook my head slightly.

From the sigh he heaved, I gathered that he considered my lack of sophistication regarding military equipment to be a huge nuisance. "They range anywhere from two hundred dollars to three thousand dollars."

"Oh, my." I glanced at Zora Jane. I didn't want to invest quite that much in this venture. "Well, could I get something good enough to see inside a cave for somewhere in the lower end of that range?"

"Scope, binoculars, or goggles?"

"What's the difference?"

He rolled his eyes. "Scopes are single lenses mounted on your weapon or held in your hand. Binoculars have two eyepieces, a single lens or stereo lenses, just like the old fashioned binoculars. Goggles are binoculars you wear on your head to free up your hands." He threw around model numbers and specifications to prove expertise in this field, which only served to confuse me further.

With my head spinning, I selected a pair of binoculars made in Taiwan. They had stereo lenses and a sturdy leather strap to hang around my neck. We left the store with our purchase, raced back to the car, and headed toward Nevada City. I didn't ask Zora Jane's opinion about whether I'd made a frivolous purchase or not.

But she came up with her own comment. "Christine, honey, we planned to drop off boxes, shop, and eat lunch. Who'd have thought we'd end up buying binoculars and oversized flip flops?" She giggled.

I tossed her a dark glance.

A few moments later we rolled up behind the black limo parked next to Morgan House. Too long to fit in the parking space, it blocked part of Broad Street. The Cadillac limo could comfortably hold seven passengers. This one held none.

I rang the impressive Victorian doorbell beside the door and stepped back to enjoy its sonorous tones.

In seconds, a tall woman wearing a long lace apron opened the door. "Yes?"

With an *Ahem*, I straightened. Maybe she wouldn't notice my disheveled state if I used good posture. "We have an appointment with Constance Boyd."

The tall woman frowned and hesitated.

"We made an appointment with Miss Boyd at the Union Hotel but we were detained and didn't get back at the proper time. This meeting concerns an important matter. We really must speak with her."

The woman made no attempt to conceal her appraisal of my unorthodox appearance. After looking me up and down, she moved to Zora Jane. Her expression softened. "Miss Boyd is not here." She managed at last. "Her assistant came to make arrangements."

Zora Jane stepped up. "May we please speak with the assistant then?"

The woman looked toward the end of the hallway and then made a face when she looked back at me. How bad could I look? I glanced down at my exposed toes. The two big ones had polish smeared with red clay.

"Please wait there."

The ornate door crashed shut.

I glanced at Zora Jane. She stood staring at her brown leather flats which were speckled with red Nevada County mud. "Perhaps we should have freshened up a tad before our appointment."

I smiled at her. Her curly reddish hair seemed a bit windblown. I could only imagine what mine must look like. I brushed a piece of dried mud off my face, wondering how much more I hadn't attended to.

After a few minutes, the door reopened to Constance Boyd's assistant, Rebecca. She didn't look happy to see us. "May I help you?"

"We had an appointment with Miss Boyd—" I started.

"But you did not show up."

My shoulders tensed. "Where is she?"

"Miss Boyd has many obligations. She simply cannot wait for people who are not punctual."

What could I say to that? "No. Of course not. She must be very busy."

Rebecca crossed her arms over her chest.

Zora Jane stepped forward. "We're sorry to bother you about this, but…"

Was she going to say it? "My friend got sucked into quicksand…"

"… we had a bit of an accident and were late for the appointment. Please tell us about Miss Boyd's return to our community. Is she here to continue research for her broadcast about Baxter Dunn?"

Rebecca's stern scrutiny switched to Zora Jane. "I'm not about to lay out our agenda for you. That is my business." *Not yours* was to be understood.

"Perhaps Miss Stuart is available. The producer?"

Rebecca shook her head. "I'm afraid not."

Zora Jane tilted her head. "We have information that may help her uncover the truth."

Rebecca paused a moment, blinking her eyes. Then she reached to grab the door. "I'll tell her you stopped by."

"No, please." I pushed in front of Zora Jane. "We need to speak with her."

The closing door halted. "If you wish to leave your name and number, I'll give her the message."

Lacking any better idea how to get an interview, I scribbled my name and phone number on the piece of paper the assistant provided.

❧

My spirits sank lower than the Lusitania while we drove home. I hadn't thought we'd have Miss Boyd to contend with again so soon. I felt as if I'd been chasing horses on a carousel, racing in circles without making the slightest progress toward finding truth, digging deeper into the mire and obscuring the facts instead of finding clarity. How fitting that I'd fallen into a mud pit.

I didn't express my brooding thoughts, but Zora Jane, being her natural compassionate self, tuned into my expression. "We'll find a way to speak to her, don't worry."

I nodded, eyes fixed on the road.

"God is still in control. He already knows how He's going to work this out." She reached over to pat my arm. "You mustn't get discouraged."

"What else can we do?" I met her eyes. "What if there isn't anything else we can do? What if we never find out what happened to Molly? What if Baxter's murder never gets solved? Or Mary's?"

She set her lips firmly and shook her head. "Then God has a reason for allowing that. We have to trust Him, Christine. His Word promises that He is good and that He is able to bring good out of bad."

"Bad things happen all the time. Bad people get away with doing evil and innocent people get hurt. What good comes out of it? Why does God allow it? Don't you ever question what God's up to?"

"I know Him." Her smile had an angelic quality. "I know He's trustworthy. He is always faithful. That's His nature. He can't be anything else."

I couldn't see the light of God's presence just then. I did consent to bowing my head when we got to her house while she prayed for encouragement, asking for help accepting God's will and that He would make a way for us to speak with Miss Boyd.

Since I'd already begun to feel like my night vision binocular purchase had been a bit impulsive, I asked Zora Jane to keep them so I wouldn't have to explain my stupidity to Jesse. I just didn't have the strength to listen to his reprimand. Zora Jane promised to store them in her trunk until I needed them.

Truth be told, I was simply exhausted. During the two months since Baxter's death, my safe little retirement routine had been completely obliterated. I didn't sleep much at night and lacked the energy to exercise. Unless you counted hiking hills, moving stones, extricating oneself from a mud pit, and running from soldiers with guns and dogs. We'd been so busy, we tended to eat on the run or catch a quick meal whenever we could so even my healthy eating habits had suffered. Not to mention the intense stress of losing Molly, Mary's death, and being falsely accused.

As I walked up the steps to my front door, I realized that my fatigue extended deeper than any tiredness I'd ever experienced before. I felt tired clear to my soul. Exhausted and totally discouraged.

Jesse stood beside the kitchen island, making a meatloaf sandwich. When he saw the bedraggled state of my appearance, he stopped in surprise. "What happened to you?"

I fell into his arms and released a torrent of pent-up tears.

With his strong arms around me, he let me cry until I stopped, rocking slightly. When my wailing subsided, he pulled back and pushed a few strands of hair out of my damp face. "Tell me what happened."

Haltingly, I recited the day's adventure. When I got to the part about losing my shoe in the mud, he started to chuckle.

I gave him my fiercest warning look.

"I'm sorry." He struggled to compose himself. "You didn't belong out at that old mine. I sent you to deliver clothes to the

Salvation Army this morning and—" He grinned and shook his head. "This could only happen to you, Christine."

"Oh, I knew you'd say that." With one hand, I wiped my nose. "Then I had no shoe so we had to find a way to get the mud off and buy a new pair and by the time we got back to see Constance Boyd, she was gone. Oh, Jesse, we're never going to get Molly back and we're never going to find out what really happened to Baxter or Mary, and that woman is going to tell a pack of lies to the whole world on public television and—"

"Shh." With surprising gentleness, he placed his finger on my mouth. "You're getting all worked up. You know what you need?"

I shook my head.

"You need a nice hot bath."

My shoulders slumped. To Jesse, all of life's problems could be solved with a hot bath and a good night's sleep.

"Seriously." He pulled me back an arm's length away. "I'll get the tub ready for milady." He wiggled his eyebrows. "Come into the bathroom in a few minutes. It'll make you feel better. Trust me."

When I reached the bathroom, my favorite aromatic candles glowed and scented the room. From the Bose CD player, Sarah Brightman and Andrea Bocelli filled the air with lilting strains of "Con Te Partiró." A fluffy oversized towel lay within easy reach of the tub. Jesse welcomed me in and gently helped me remove the mud stained clothing.

I lay in the perfectly heated water with soothing lavender bubbles folded around me and closed my eyes. He was right again. Weeks of tension melted away. I drifted between sleep and wakefulness, wrapped in blissful comfort. Nonsensical disjointed thoughts swirled around my head like visions of sugar plums, a single tennis shoe bobbing in a mud pit, muddy boot prints, a black fringed purse stuck in the mud, Baxter's patrol car dragged out of the mud.

My eyes blinked open and I gasped, sitting straight in the tub. Tracks. What about tire tracks? Baxter's assailants would have needed more than one car. Had the investigators made casts of *all* the tracks found in the area? Maybe the murderers left tracks in the mud at Rawlins Lake, tracks that could identify them.

Good clue. With a sigh, I slid back into the tub. I'd have to share this insight with Detective Rogers, just as soon as I finished my bath and got a good night's sleep.

23

CHAPTER TWENTY-THREE

Jesse allowed no more talk about the investigation until after I ate and had a long sleep. He was right about that, too. Tuesday morning I jumped out of my comfy bed ready to venture into the world again. First thing after breakfast, I called Detective Rogers.

The dispatcher put me on hold, but I barely started pacing before I heard the detective's even voice.

"It's Christine Sterling. I thought of something about the patrol car, the one they pulled out of Rawlins Lake."

"What about it?"

"Did they take impressions of the tire tracks they found out there? *All* the tracks? Because if someone dumped the patrol car, they would need a way to get out of there. There had to be another vehicle. So there should be other tire tracks. Maybe the tracks could be matched to the black van."

A moment's silence made me wonder if we'd been disconnected. Then he spoke. "That is a logical assumption."

"Did they find other tracks?"

Another lengthy silence followed before he spoke. "I appreciate your assistance."

He didn't seem the least bit interested in my insight. What else could I give him? "Also Constance Boyd's back in town digging up gossip. She's going to broadcast a bunch of lies about Baxter. Isn't there something you can do about that?

"Thank you. I'm in a meeting just now. I'll call you later today."

In a meeting? Why'd they even connect me? I hung up, feeling quite disgruntled. How much longer did Molly have? Unless some headway was made on these murders, I might never find her. I needed answers and wanted them now, not later today. Rogers said he would call, but what was I going to do in the meantime? Turn the mattress? Clean the lint filter on the dryer? Learn French? Nothing seemed important except having the murder investigations resolved and bringing Molly home.

I'd just started upstairs, with my cat trotting at my heels meowing for attention, when the phone rang again. I hurried to my office to pick up, hoping Detective Rogers had finished his meeting. "Hello."

The blaring background noise sounded disorderly. Machines clinking and banging, people's voices, boisterous music. No one spoke.

"Hello?" I said again louder.

A small muffled voice. "Mrs. Sterling?"

"Who is this?"

The muffled static got worse, as if the small-voiced person had put a hand over the mouthpiece and yelled at someone else before returning to the phone.

"Are you there?" I frowned. "Is this a crank call?"

"No, no. Please don't hang up."

"What do you want then?"

"It's Amanda. Amanda Colter. Do you remember me?"

Surprised, I plopped into my desk chair. "Amanda. Of

course, I remember. You rode back from Nevada City with us. What can I do for you?"

"You gave me your number. Said to call if—"

A strident noise drowned out the end of her sentence. She muffled the receiver again and yelled at someone. I couldn't understand the words. Roy jumped onto the desk and waltzed in front of me waiting to be petted.

After the disturbance died down, I asked, "Amanda? Do you need help, dear? I could meet you somewhere."

"Where?"

"Where are you now?"

The noise continued, but not as loud. The music could be coming from a jukebox. Maybe she was calling from a bar. But she wasn't old enough for that and besides bars weren't usually full of people at this hour. I didn't know where Grass Valley kids hung out. Maybe an arcade.

"Amanda?"

"The Laundromat behind Kmart. In an hour." She clicked off.

Roy waltzed across the desk again, tail pointed upward, purring like a motorboat. I ran my hand the length of his silken body. He nuzzled my face with his nose. "What do you suppose that was about, Roy? What does Amanda want to talk about? Do you think I should go alone?" I knew what Jesse would say. I let out a dramatic sigh. I'd have to tell him.

Jesse was working in the art studio above the garage, pieces of sculpting clay spread across his table. He bent over a sculpture of a lanky cowboy partly clad in chaps, but glanced up when the screen door shut behind me. "Who called just now?"

"Amanda Colter."

One eyebrow arched. "Oh?"

"She wants me to meet her at Kmart."

"Why?"

"Don't know. Guess she wants to talk. Do you mind if I go?"

He frowned and set his carving tool on the table. "She didn't say what she wants?"

I shook my head.

Jesse brushed clay crumbs off his lap. "I better go with you."

By the time we changed our clothes, grabbed a Diet Pepsi for Jesse out of the refrigerator, and drove into town, the better part of an hour had passed. Jesse parked the Jeep outside the rundown Laundromat north of Kmart, but since the morning chill hadn't dissipated, he left the engine running so we'd have heat while we waited. We peered through the windshield at the rows of washers and dryers inside. No sign of Amanda.

Jesse looked toward Kmart. "Are you sure she said to come here?"

I nodded. "Think so."

Jesse finished guzzling his Diet Pepsi and screwed the lid back on. "Well, she isn't here." He burst into song, drumming the steering wheel with the empty bottle to keep time.

> *Come and love your daddy,*
> *Come and love your daddy all night long.*
> *Come and see what you been missing.*
> *Oh, baby. ...*

The minute hand of the dashboard clock didn't seem to be moving.

Jesse stopped singing, but continued to drum the steering wheel, a nervous habit he commenced whenever he had to wait. It drove me nuts.

Five minutes passed. Five long minutes punctuated only by his incessant drumming of the plastic bottle on the steering wheel. I wanted to grab the bottle out of his hand and flatten it, but that wouldn't be nice.

"How long do you think we should—?"

Before he completed his question, we heard running feet and Amanda raced from the back of the building. Jumping in the back seat, she hunched on the floor as if hiding from someone. "Step on it."

Jesse shoved the gearshift into reverse and backed out. "I assume you'll let me know where to turn once I leave the parking lot." He glanced into the rear view mirror, but she'd scrunched so low I doubt if he could see her.

Her drama made me giggle. "Why are you doing that?"

She tilted her head to shoot me a long-suffering look. "I don't want anyone to see us together."

"Oh? Why not?"

"He has spies everywhere."

By that time, we had rolled to the edge of the parking lot. Jesse stopped the car and turned so he could see her. "Who?"

Her head jerked up and she peeked out the window. "Colter."

I scanned the parking lot. Cars came and went in an ordinary fashion all around us. No one paid the slightest attention to us as far as I could see.

Jesse returned to driving. "Where do you want to go?"

"Nevada City. The market." She ducked to the floor again.

Nodding, Jesse headed onto Highway 49, driving north three miles to Nevada City without further questions. Once we turned onto Broad Street, I tapped her shoulder. "We're off the freeway now. I haven't seen anyone behind us. Do you want to tell us why you called?"

She craned her head to peer out the back. Apparently satisfied that no one followed, she climbed onto the seat, sitting sideways so she could stretch her matchstick legs. "You said call if I heard anything about Mary Wilson's death."

Jesse and I exchanged a glance. Hearing Mary's name, a lump formed in my throat.

Jesse asked, "What did you hear?"

Amanda twisted the large metal crucifix hanging from her neck and glanced out the back window before continuing. "Word is, she had what *they* wanted."

"*They* who?" I asked.

"The cops, of course."

That made no sense. "What could she have that the cops wanted?"

She shrugged and her black lips tightened into a straight line. "That scumbag came over last night."

Jesse studied the rear view mirror. Since Amanda was sitting up, he would be able to see her now. "I assume you mean Deputy Colter?"

She nodded, clenching her fist until her black fingernails dug into her palm. "He came in all lovey-dovey as if we don't know what kind of creep he is. My mom is so stupid sometimes. She was actually glad to see him. I knew he was there for no good."

I leaned toward her. "So, what did he want?"

She sneered. "Can you believe my mom let him touch her?" She shook as if shivering. "What a jerk! Totally arcane! All he wants is money." She jiggled her head, tinkling the chains hanging from her ears. "He'll shake out every last penny she has."

"Did he say why? What's the money for?"

"Well, that's the weird part."

Jesse parked in front of the market in almost the exact spot we first met her.

Amanda squinted out the window. "This is perfect. Thanks."

Jesse turned to her. "What's the weird part?"

"While he's buttering her up to take her good jewelry, the only nice stuff she's got left, he promises her that his ship is about to come in and when it does he's going to pay her back with interest. He says he's working on something big. Something that's going to leave him rolling in lettuce."

"What would he be working on that would bring in a lot of money?"

Jesse shook his head.

Amanda's black lips curled into a mocking smile. "Well, you can just bet he's not getting a promotion at the sheriff's office."

Jesse's frown deepened. "What do you think this has to do with Mary?"

She'd been about to climb out of the car, but stopped with one army boot already planted on the ground and looked back at us. "Oh, sorry. Thought I already told you that part. He said, 'That little slut snooping around almost blew the deal.' Guess that's why he needs money." She raised her fist and trotted toward the market where a group of kids dressed in black and chains had already gathered.

She didn't make any sense. We sat a minute staring after her.

Jesse broke the silence first. "Do you think we just got used for a ride to Nevada City?"

"Could be." I shook my head to clear the fog. "But she did have a little news."

As we turned toward home, Jesse and I discussed Deputy Colter's anticipated windfall and what Mary could have possessed that would interest the authorities. Not a single brilliant conclusion occurred to us. Rather than becoming clearer, the circumstances swirling around this case kept getting more and more muddled and confused. What could it all mean?

❦

I'd promised Zora Jane I would accompany her to the ladies' meeting at church that evening. Jesse urged me to go even though I didn't really feel up to it. He was right, of course. As usual. We needed to get out and do something purely social. Get our minds off the tangled happenings unraveling around us. I think he hoped it might make me forget Molly for a while, but nothing could keep me from fretting over my dog. She filled my thoughts at all times, no matter what I did or how I tried to forget.

For the Hawaiian themed dinner and program at church, Zora Jane and I dressed in colorful outfits. Zora Jane, of course, wore authentic Hawaiian garb purchased on a trip to Maui several years earlier. A beautiful long sleeveless sheath with tropical blue, red, and yellow flowers cascading over a beige background. The dress featured a slit up the side which showed off one shapely leg. She even wore a fake flower lei to complement the dress, a yellow hibiscus in her hair, and a brown kukui nut bracelet. I wore a bright red dress with flowers and a shell necklace Zora Jane loaned me. I did my best to mimic her laidback island demeanor while we rode into town.

Just before we got to church, the long black Cadillac pulled out in front of us.

I glanced at Zora Jane. "Do you think she's in there?"

Zora Jane leaned forward to peer out the front. "Can't tell with the tinted windows."

I contemplated the clock on my dash. "We're a bit early. What say we follow her and see what she's up to? Maybe we'll get a chance to talk to her."

Zora Jane nodded so I passed the church driveway and continued following the Cadillac.

The long vehicle glided through town, winding around a few corners into Nevada City before coming to a stop in front of Morgan House on Broad Street.

I pulled into a parking spot down the street. "Bet she's turning in for the evening."

In silence, we watched the chauffeur hop out to open the back door. Out stepped Constance Boyd, still looking every bit the lady, even at the end of the day.

"What do you think?" I asked Zora Jane. "This looks like our chance. We may not get another."

She exhaled a long breath. "Guess so. Dear Lord, please guide us."

By the time we'd hurried through the white picket gate, Constance and her entourage had nearly made it to the front door of the Victorian bed and breakfast. She spun flawlessly on one heel when she heard us, her expression more stunned surprise than welcome. "Well. Don't you look festive?"

Babble bubbled. "We were on our way to a ladies' meeting. It's Hawaiian night and that's why we're dressed like this. But we saw your limo and it's very important for us to speak with you, so we followed you."

Zora Jane joined in. "Could you spare a few moments to hear us out? We won't be long."

Rebecca, the assistant, started to protest, but Constance held up one perfectly manicured hand. "I'm terribly sorry. It's been a long day. You understand, I'm sure. I need my rest." She turned to walk toward the door again.

I went after her, getting between her and the door when she mounted the porch steps. "Please, Miss Boyd. We're terribly sorry we missed our appointment with you. We, that is, *I*, had a mishap and got covered with mud. I fell in a mud pit and lost my shoe and then I had to buy other shoes. I couldn't think where to get shoes close by. You know Grass Valley really has no good shoe stores. I ended up at Kmart. Then I had to buy socks too, but could only find flip-flops that fit, so by the time we got back for our appointment, you had already left. We chased you all over town—"

Miss Boyd tittered. Her assistant stared at the ground. The chauffeur holding the front door fixed his eyes on the sky.

"What?" What was so funny about a shoe lost in the mud?

Miss Boyd shook her head. "That's the most original yet most pathetic excuse for being late I've ever heard."

I pleaded with puppy-dog eyes.

She reached for my arm to help her up the last step. "Oh, all right. Come in, won't you? You don't mind if I sit while you talk?"

Miss Boyd led the way with Zora Jane and me bringing up the rear.

Once inside, her flunkies bustled ahead, taking the load of files and papers she carried and bringing a tray of tall crystal glasses with disks of lemon stuck on top. A glass pitcher of iced tea and a plate of cookies rested on the tray. Rebecca poured iced tea in the glasses and passed them around with the plate of cookies. She motioned for us to sit in the front sitting room with silk embroidered pillows at our backs. Constance Boyd sat across from us, adjusting the pillows behind her. Her helpers toiled like worker bees for a few minutes while no one spoke. Then, as if someone had struck a gong, they all disappeared leaving us alone in the exquisite antique filled room.

After taking a sip of her beverage, Miss Boyd leaned on the pillows and folded her hands in the lap of her periwinkle skirt. "Okay, ladies, what can I do for you?"

I opened my mouth, but before words came out, Zora Jane spoke. "Miss Boyd, I've been praying for you every day since our first meeting. Do you remember that we talked about

Jesus that day? Have you thought about Him since then?"

My mouth stayed open while my eyes widened. I stared at Zora Jane in disbelief. Did I hear her correctly? Had she forgotten the reason for our visit?

Constance Boyd squirmed in her chair. "I… actually, I've thought a lot about what you said. These days not many people dare to speak to me like you did. I've been wondering… about spiritual things lately." She paused to look down at her long painted nails. "Not because I think you're right, mind you. We each have our own truth."

Zora Jane bent toward her and asked quietly, "What were you wondering?"

She spoke without looking at us. "I've come so far in my life. Accomplished everything I ever set out to do and more. I work hard and I attract success because I believe with all my heart that I will be successful. Yet once I attain my next goal, I always find it's never enough."

I studied Constance, amazed at the vulnerability this very public figure shared with us. What did it mean? Was she so exhausted that she'd let down her guard with strangers? My eyes swept back to Zora Jane. How would she respond?

Zora Jane nodded, eyes glued to Miss Boyd. "It's that way for all of us. Material things, things of this world, were never meant to satisfy our souls. Only God can satisfy that hunger."

Miss Boyd's perfectly modulated voice sounded almost wistful. "I do believe God is in all of us. I am a good person, no matter what you say. I give back more than anyone else I know."

Ball in Zora Jane's court. Would she continue?

She did. "*I* didn't say you're not good. That's what the Bible says. God's Word says no one is good enough by God's standards, no matter how we try. I quoted that verse from Romans 3:12. Paul goes on to say that we're all sinners in need of a savior. The one true God is completely good. Can you say that about yourself? Can you truly claim never to have told a lie or dishonored your parents? Never gossiped or held a grudge?"

Miss Boyd's elegant eyes met Zora Jane's. "What I really want to know is, how does God satisfy the soul's hunger?"

Zora Jane did not back down. "That's what Jesus came to do. He died a horrible death on the cross to give you this gift. When you come to Jesus humbly, admitting that you are a sinner in need of a savior and ask Jesus to take your sin and set you free, then you begin a personal relationship with God. That relationship will satisfy your soul."

A veil dropped over Constance Boyd's eyes. The professional barrier. She brushed her blue skirt as if she could oust that idea with a sweep of her hand. "I'm afraid I just don't believe all that Sunday school stuff. That truth may work for you, but not for me. I cannot believe God would allow His Son to suffer so horribly for only some of the people He created and let all the rest go to hell. No. What about people in other nations who never heard of Jesus?"

Zora Jane answered right away. "All we can say about that is that God will be just. He cannot be otherwise. But as for Truth, there can't be many truths. That would be like saying the earth is either flat or round depending on your belief. The Truth is unchangeable, regardless of what we choose to believe. God is Truth. He cannot lie. His character is unchangeable."

Constance Boyd shook her head as if trying to shake the words out of her ears. Then she stood, signaling our dismissal with her Ultra Brite smile. "Thank you for coming, but that's all the time I can spare just now."

Zora Jane started to reply, but Constance had already waltzed toward the door. "Rebecca?"

The studious assistant appeared almost at once. She must have been spying on us from the next room.

I stood firm. "But we didn't talk about the investigation yet."

"Please show these Hawaiian ladies out." Constance Boyd turned toward us. "I do appreciate your prayers, but please don't worry another second over the eternal state of my soul."

Rebecca nearly pushed us out the door, but Zora Jane managed to get in the last word. Just before we were shoved through the door, she turned toward Constance. "I will continue to pray for you, that God will satisfy your soul hunger through His Son Jesus."

24

CHAPTER TWENTY-FOUR

Wednesday morning brought rain, hard Nevada County rain that clattered on the rooftop like Santa's sleigh and reindeer. Jesse and I bundled on layers of warm clothing and drove through the torrent to the sheriff's office, where I'd been summoned for a ten o'clock appointment with Detective Rogers.

Phones rang and officers moved in and out. Some carried a file or a coffee cup. A few chattered on cell phones. One had a German shepherd on a leash which made me think of Molly. I still hadn't given up hope of finding her.

Jesse sat next to me, waiting. I put my arm through his and squeezed. His sleeve was wet probably because he'd held the umbrella more over me than himself. Water puddled off the folded umbrella next to me.

The clock in the waiting room showed ten o'clock. Sitting still was not in my nature. Just when I'd decided to go get one of the donuts from the pink box next to the coffee machine, Jesse stood and pulled me to my feet. "You're on, little lady."

He drew me to him for a quick hug and an encouraging smile.

Detective Rogers shook Jesse's hand, and then led me to the conference room.

Around the conference table sat the same Goth boys we'd seen with Miss Boyd at the Union Hotel, along with their mothers. Also a couple of fathers had come along this time. A serious man in a brown business suit studied a file on the table in front of him. I settled where Detective Rogers pointed at the other end of the table.

The detective seated himself in the middle between us and cleared his throat. "I really appreciate your coming this morning, Mrs. Sterling. These boys were arrested in connection with the death of Mary Wilson and have been questioned several times. They are now on bail. I would like you to hear their story."

I nodded.

He continued, "First, let me make introductions. On the far end are Josh Walker and his mother, Mrs. Susan Walker." He pointed to a lanky lad wearing green spiked hair, a ring in his lip, and a dark expression.

"Next to Josh are Matt Mazzerella and his parents, Gregory and Anna Mazzerella." Multiple silver rings pierced Matt's eyebrows, ears, and nose. Matt glared at me through the mass of rings. His father's face showed no emotion, but his mother managed a polite nod and slight smile. Matt's forearms rested on the mahogany table. A jumble of tattoos covered them. From my vantage point, they looked like Celtic symbols.

"Last we have Chris Callaway and his parents, Peter Finch and Tanya Blakely."

I dipped my head.

Chris presented the most normal appearance among the three, with close-cropped blond hair and wholesome good looks. His attitude, however, was pure Goth. Mrs. Blakely looked and acted as if she was sitting on tacks.

Detective Rogers concluded his introductions. "The boys are being represented by Mr. Kurt Benson, attorney-at-law."

I turned to the gentleman. Without a smile or greeting gesture, he extended his card as if I might need his phone number and would want to call him.

I took the card. "Pleased to meet you all."

Detective Rogers didn't have his tape recorder, just a big stack of file folders. He opened the top one and read to himself for a moment before leaning back in his chair. Then he glanced at the boys. "Perhaps we should begin by having you boys tell Mrs. Sterling what you know about Mary."

The three stared at each other. Josh spoke first. "Like we told the detective, life is bad. People hurt you. We gotta stick together for protection. Mary Wilson was Goth. Gothdom didn't approve her leaving us. First thing you know, she's arrested. When she gets out, she heads straight for the park."

Matt straightened in his chair. "We tell her get out while you can. She says her old man's gone but she wants to stay in his house. Says she's not afraid of him because she had 'insurance.'"

Now they had my attention. "Insurance? How much?"

Josh shook his head, making the ring in his lip quiver. "Not *life* insurance. Something important in case the psycho caused trouble. Insurance against him."

I regarded each one in turn. "She didn't say what this insurance was or where she kept it?"

Chains jingled when they shook their heads.

"That's all she told you—just that she had something she could use against the Kingfisher?"

They nodded agreement.

The expression on Detective Rogers's face read expectation.

I blinked at the boys, waiting for a brilliant moment of clarity that never came. So I turned to the detective. "And you have no idea what it could be?"

He shrugged. "Afraid not. Hoped you would. Or at least you'd know where to look."

I focused on the table, trying to recall a discussion with Mary about any kind of leverage she might have on the Kingfisher. When nothing came to mind, I shook my head.

Detective Rogers's chair tapped the floor when he leaned toward the boys. "Rumor has it you kids were planning a big shootout at the high school. Any truth to that?"

The three gaped wide-eyed for a moment as if the question hadn't been asked in English.

The attorney suddenly came alive. "I advise you not to answer that—"

"Hey, wait a minute," Matt said. "We gotta answer. It's a big lie. We got nothing planned."

Detective Rogers consulted his notes. "Do you have guns?"

The attorney held up his hand. "I caution you not to answer."

Josh shrugged. "They're not ours, but, yeah, we got guns."

The attorney made a disgusted sound in his throat.

Detective Rogers ignored him. "Who do they belong to?"

Attorney Benson held up one hand. "Again, I advise you not to say anything."

The boys bent their heads and whispered to each other before speaking aloud. "Look," Chris said. "What we were planning or not planning has nothing to do with this. We heard Mary got killed with a mining pick. *If* Goths were going to be violent, we'd use guns or knives, not mining picks. Who keeps a mining pick around anyway? What for?"

The others concurred with vigorous nods and murmurs of accord.

Mr. Benson fell back against his chair with a thud.

Detective Rogers had the boys retell their alibis, all of which amounted to no one being able to verify their whereabouts. He turned to me. "Do you have any other questions for these kids?"

I couldn't think of any so Detective Rogers dismissed the boys, their parents, and their attorney. When they'd cleared the room, he faced me.

"You don't really think those boys killed Mary?"

"Nah. I just hoped you'd think of something to help us while they talked. Besides, I thought you'd like to know what they said. Also, I wanted to thank you for your suggestion about the tire tracks." He nodded. "That was good solid thinking, Mrs. Sterling. CSI did take other tire impressions out at Rawlins Lake where they found the patrol car. Nobody thought to bring those out in report. I had to dig to find them."

"And?"

"They match the tires on the black van from *Satori*. The one you saw out there."

Good news at last. "I knew it! But how did you get the black van?"

He seemed pleased. "The lab explosion. By the time the fire department got there, the big barn with the vehicles inside was burning. Most of the vehicles were consumed before the firemen got the fire under control. The explosion caused quite a commotion. Firemen and sheriff's personnel rounded up all the soldiers they found and transported them into Grass Valley to get beds at the 'YMCA' before they were questioned. While they were looking through the woods, they found the black van and impounded it."

Wonder of wonders! "So you have it now in the impound lot?"

He grinned. "I thought you'd like that."

"Did you find anything inside, anything to prove who was in it the night Baxter died?"

Detective Rogers shook his head and laughed heartily. "I've told you too much already. Don't share this with the Callahan's. We haven't notified them yet. You'll have to wait a little longer for everything else we know."

❧

Despite my promise not to report to the Callahan's, I blabbed the news to Jesse while we rode home through in rain. "Oh, my goodness, Jesse. Do you know what this means?"

He shot me a blank look. "What?"

"They have the black van and they matched its tire tread to the tracks at Rawlins Lake. So someone from *Satori* was at Rawlins Lake."

"Yeah? There's a lot of guys out at *Satori*. How're they gonna prove who was in the van that night? How will they know if the van was there the same time?"

"Well, they'll… uh… maybe they have boot prints, or… DNA."

"You wish."

Rain cascaded in rivulets down the window while I replayed everything I could remember from the first day we heard about poor Baxter's death. "Wait a second, Jesse. You remember when I talked to Deputy Colter and those other officers that day at the Callahan's'? Just after Baxter died? Colter said Baxter died at midnight, impaled on a rusty spike. How did Colter already know what time Baxter died? Before the coroner even got there?"

Jesse glanced my way, eyebrow cocked. "How do you know the coroner hadn't been there yet when Colter was out there?"

I ignored his logic. I knew I was right, but I didn't actually know how. "Another thing, don't you think it's interesting that from the very beginning the news people reported that Baxter died at midnight on Friday the thirteenth, just like Colter said? Leonard Pinzer used the exact same language about Baxter being impaled on a rusty spike. Who had insider information to send the media on that wild goose chase about Baxter's drug use? Who tried to sabotage the investigation at every turn, even trying to point the finger at me by planting evidence? Who doesn't want his superiors or the media digging into what he's done?" I slapped the console between us. "The finger of guilt points to one person. By golly, I think we've got proof that good old Sam Colter has been leaking misleading information to the press from the get-go."

Jesse watched the road while the windshield wipers swished back and forth. "I don't know if that would constitute *proof,* but if you're right, where do *Satori* and the black van fit in?"

I shook my head. "They've got to be tied together, don't they?"

Jesse nodded.

"And the drug lab, and Mary's death, and Colter's need for money until his ship comes in, *and...*all of it." A strange overwhelmed feeling flooded me. There was nothing conclusive enough for prosecution, but we must be close. For certain, Colter was right in the middle of the whole mess.

But how could we tie it all together?

Catherine Leggitt

25

CHAPTER TWENTY-FIVE

The next day I rose early so I could shower, dress, and finish my morning chores while Jesse worked his black stallion, Ranger, in the arena. I left a note about going into town on errands, trying to keep it as vague as possible, worrying all the way into town about whether I had lied or not. Eventually, my conscience got the best of me and I had to concede that an intentional omission equaled an overt fib. And that was wrong. Rather than return to set it right, however, I focused my thoughts on Mary.

Between town and Mary Wilson's house in Rough and Ready, torrents of pent-up emotion washed over me. I wiped tears with tissues from the Kleenex box I'd stowed in the car for such emergencies. Tears erupted often these days and I never knew when I'd need a tissue.

Although I hadn't yet figured how to gain entrance to Mary's house, I had to try. I also hadn't planned where to look, assuming I got inside. Surely, the detectives had already searched Mary's house for her "insurance" against any injury at the hand of the Kingfisher. I just wanted to have a look of my own.

As usual, I parked the car in the flat area near the door and got out. After the long drive, I stretched my back, hands planted on my hips while I surveyed the property.

Yesterday's rain had washed the land and trees, but standing there I still felt the sadness I'd always sensed. The sun sent shimmering light through the pines and oaks. A slight breeze moved the air. It would be a lovely spring day except for the horrible wound Mary's murderer had inflicted on the property. The only visible sign of her passing, a ribbon of yellow crime scene tape, waved from a nearby tree as if to draw attention to the crime scene.

Where should I begin?

I shuffled to the house and pulled open the screen door. The solid front door was locked, same as always. I cast about for a hidden key, under the worn welcome mat, over the lintel. No flowerpot nearby to hide a key under. Then I moseyed around the house pushing on windows. This reminded me of Lila Payne. In just such a manner, I'd gained access to Lila's house the first time I visited.

Dear God, what am I doing here? Don't I ever learn from past mistakes?

Unlike my former experience at Lila's house, none of the windows moved when I pushed on them through the screens, even though I tried each one. Where I could see the interior, it appeared that the formerly messy house had been thoroughly trashed. Someone had rifled through every cupboard, drawer, and cubbyhole. Probably the detectives, although it could have been Frankie.

The back door didn't allow admittance either.

Now what?

When I returned to the front, I considered the car, still gathering dust in the yard.

Frankie's old car.

Perhaps she hid whatever she held over her former boyfriend in the immobilized car.

But when I approached the car, I could see that it had also been searched. Seats and doors had been ripped apart. The trunk gaped open a crack. I pulled it up all the way to peek inside. The trunk lining had been yanked out and the spare tire removed. I bent to examine the discarded tire on the ground underneath the back end.

Nothing. I straightened and stared at the car. "Might help if I knew what I was looking for." Not having the slightest idea, I shook my head.

As I studied the trunk, I tried to think like Mary. Where would you hide something, Mary? Someplace Frankie couldn't find it.

I keep my insurance cards in the glove compartment.

An obvious answer, so why not look there?

I edged toward the passenger side and opened the front door. The glove compartment had already been searched, of course, leaving the door ajar. The compartment looked empty. I leaned in and ran my hand over the surface. Nothing. Now what?

Images of Mary played through my mind: Mary hunched in the back seat of the Jeep; Mary's silhouette hiding next to me in the clump of trees at *Satori*; Mary sparkling in triumph after pilfering the uniform for Jesse; Mary picking tufts of stuffing from the overstuffed chair; me hugging Mary's little body in the woods after she gave her heart to Jesus. So small. Just a child. How I wished I'd never involved her in this mess. If only I could turn back time. I wiped away a tear and sniffled.

Through my blur of tears, a tiny speck sticking out of the lining of the glove compartment caught my eye. It reminded me of the way the stitching sometimes holds a hint of a label after I've ripped the rest off. But why would there be a label in a glove compartment?

I picked at it with my fingernail, but it stuck tight to the lining edge. I picked more vigorously until an edge gave way. Then I pulled on the lining. It tore away to reveal a photograph.

"Aha." I extracted a small picture.

The color photo pictured a group of men in front of the building with the surveillance camera at *Satori*. I recognized the Kingfisher and the curly-haired man who called himself Bodhi wearing their typical muumuu costumes. A silly turban sat atop Kingfisher's big head making it look larger than usual. The two men knelt in the foreground with the tall man I'd seen coming out of the office. Their hands rested atop stacks of wooden crates with stenciled labels. Behind them, two rows of men in army fatigues posed with rifles and belts stuffed with ammunition like the soldiers I saw in the compound.

Why would this picture be insurance for Mary? It appeared to be a perfectly ordinary snapshot of *Satori* leaders. Each sleeve had some kind of patch sewn on, hash marks denoting rank no doubt. I held the picture at arm's length trying to focus my old eyes on the faces. Something looked peculiar about one of them in the second row. I squinted.

My, what a big nose that soldier has! That nose could only belong to one person I knew. Beneath an army uniform hat, the face of Sam Colter stared back at me.

Faster than I usually drive, I flew to sheriff's headquarters and sprinted inside. This should be enough to nail Colter for his ties to *Satori*. Adrenaline powered my resolve to expose him once and for all. My heart pounded in my ears and I knew my blood pressure zoomed near the red zone. Nevertheless, I must persevere in my duty as a citizen.

Even if Colter hadn't personally killed Mary or Baxter, surely an officer sworn to uphold the law would be prosecuted for involvement with a militant organization practicing weird rituals. Especially since this organization manufactured and sold drugs to finance their operation, and, most damning of all, they had committed murder to protect their interests.

I patted the photo I'd stuck in the pocket of my jeans to ensure I had the evidence I'd need. I couldn't wait until Detective Rogers got sight of this picture.

The receptionist glanced up while I raced through the waiting area and grabbed the doorknob of the door to the dispatch area. I yanked on it, but the door was locked.

"Miss!" she yelled at my back. "You can't open that door!"

The receptionist hurried after me. I wheeled to face her. "Then you'd better get Detective Rogers out here fast."

"I'm sorry, but he's not available. Perhaps someone else can help you. What is this about?"

Every cell in my body shook. I took a few deep breaths trying to slow the tremors of rage. "I don't want to talk to anyone else. Get him on the phone and tell him that Christine Sterling has found conclusive proof against one of his officers. He will want to see me right away."

The receptionist eyed me warily before backing away a few steps as if I might still take off and charge through the locked door. "Will you please take a seat while I call him?" She gestured toward the waiting room seats. "Please. You'll be much more comfortable."

I couldn't sit. I paced a few times while she leaned over her desk to make the call. Keeping her eyes glued to my face, she spoke in hushed tones.

My brusque entrance must have created some kind of breach in protocol because only a few seconds passed before the door burst open and three burly officers with their hands on their holsters hurried out. They surrounded me, standing close enough that I could smell their mixture of aftershave fragrances.

My shoulders sagged. "I just want to speak with Detective Rogers. I guess I should have been a little calmer about my request." I raised my hands. "I have no weapon or any way to injure anyone. Could I please speak with him?"

One of the officers spoke. "About what?"

I took a deep breath. "It concerns the deaths of Baxter Dunn and Mary Wilson."

The deputy extended his hand. "May I examine your purse, Mrs. Sterling?"

"Sure, take it." I slid the strap off my shoulder. "I have no weapons, and as I said, this is an urgent matter."

The officer pawed through my purse and apparently didn't find anything more lethal than my fingernail file. Surprise, surprise. He handed it back with a nod to the other two and they shuffled out without another word. They must have been the committee to assess potential danger.

I glanced at the receptionist now seated behind her desk. "Will you call Detective Rogers now?"

She scratched her head. "I… I'm not sure what to do, to tell you the truth."

At that instant, the door popped open and Deputy Colter stomped through. His red face and angry expression left little doubt about his frame of mind. He reached me and grabbed my arm. Before I could get a word of protest out, he hauled me through the hall toward the conference cubicles where he shoved me inside and slammed the door.

He spun to confront me, beady eyes glowing like burning coal. "How dare you barge in here like that? Who do think you are?" His voice held the intensity of a scream without the volume.

Between my bout of rage and the race to the conference room, I'd started panting like a woman giving birth. I swallowed, trying to slow down.

Impatient with my gasping, Deputy Colter glared at me. "Well?"

"I wanted to speak with Detective Rogers, but… okay." I pulled the picture out of my jeans pocket. "Explain this."

His beady eyes narrowed. "Where did you get that?"

"Do you deny being affiliated with this band of desperados?"

He reached for the photo, but wasn't fast enough. I yanked it out of reach and stuffed it back into my pocket. "No, you don't. Let me hear your confession before I turn this over to your superiors. You killed Baxter and Mary, didn't you?"

Lips thinly fixed, he started toward me. "You will *not* take that to my superiors."

I sidestepped, but not fast enough.

Colter grabbed my arm in a vise grip and twisted it to my back. In this position, he propelled me from the room. My arm felt as if it had been broken. I could hardly get my breath and didn't know whether to scream or grab onto something to keep from being forced out in this manner. We moved so quickly that in mere seconds it made no difference.

As we passed through the dispatch area, he lifted his voice extra loud as if he wanted witnesses. "I warned you before, Mrs. Sterling. You must stop snooping into our investigation."

His actions took me completely by surprise. I sputtered. "But… no…" I tried to resist. But when people get older, their reaction time slows.

While we zipped through the area where his co-workers could see us, he placed his lips close to my ear and whispered, "Just keep moving and do not make a sound. I will not hesitate to shoot you if you resist."

Just before we rushed out of the reception area, he called over one shoulder. "Sorry for the intrusion. Mrs. Sterling needs to realize she cannot barge in here and make demands. I am going to escort her to her car."

By then we had reached the outer doors. I tried to grab the sides of the doorway to stop myself from being shoved through, but he was far too strong.

Not until we reached the outer doors shut did I find my voice. "Let go, you're hurting me. Let go or I will scream!"

He paid no attention but continued stomping through the parking lot, pushing me ahead. Only we didn't go to the Jeep. We raced directly to his squad car.

I should have screamed while someone could hear me, but the entire time from our exit to our arrival at the patrol car zipped by like a fast-forward movie. What was happening to me barely registered until it was too late to resist.

As we reached the car, he drew his pistol and pressed it into my back. "Get in and do not make a sound."

With unnecessary force, he shoved me into the front seat from the driver's side, sliding in next to me before releasing my arm.

As the door slammed shut, I finally found my voice.

I screamed loud enough to pop a blood vessel in my throat. But no one came to my rescue.

26

CHAPTER TWENTY-SIX

I struggled to shake off drowsiness. *Where am I?*

Heaviness in my brain seemed localized to my eyes. *Maybe I'm dreaming.* Rolling to the left, I hit a wall. Discomfort intensified with each movement. My shoulder and arm throbbed with pain. With the other hand I explored the barrier, fighting to focus on my surroundings. *Rough splintery wood, not well finished. A box?* The bottom seemed to be lined with fabric. I clutched at it. It wasn't attached.

The weighty darkness pressed in, or maybe my eyes weren't opened yet.

*This can't be happening, I must be dreamin*g. I stabbed a finger into one eye. "Ouch!" So my eyes *were* open. I stared at where my hand should have been, but couldn't see a hand there. Several times I blinked, but the thick darkness persisted.

When I attempted to sit, I bumped my head.

Dizzy, I lay down mumbling to myself. "Think, Christine. What's the last thing you remember?"

The dull ache in my head made memory difficult. However, when I concentrated, disjointed scenes from my abduction in the sheriff's office flashed into mind: Colter dragging me to his patrol car, a gun pointing at me, tires spinning out of the parking lot, trying to talk, begging Colter to let me out. I yelled, but he never even looked at me. Head facing forward, he raced toward Highway 20.

Just before he got there, he removed his cell phone from his pocket and punched in one of his programmed numbers. "I have the Sterling woman. All hell is about to break loose." I watched the road whizzing by while he listened to the person on the other end. I could hear a loud voice. The words sounded angry although I couldn't understand them. Someone was reprimanding Colter. Good.

"It could not be helped. She found the photo."

More yelling from the other person.

Colter bit into his lip. "Look. We can hash this over when I get there. I will take her to the chamber." He snapped the phone off.

That must be where I was, the chamber. Whatever that meant. After the fuzziness in my brain cleared, I recalled Colter sliding the boulder door open and guards dragging me into the darkness. Hushed voices echoed in the tunnel. Flashlights beamed light. After a time, we arrived at a place lit by lanterns. Then, this place. They must be keeping me inside the old Star Mine.

Why couldn't I remember more? They drugged me. I'd never experienced drugs before except during my colonoscopy. *What a strange sensation!* One minute I remember lying on the gurney talking to the doctor while the anesthesiologist inserted an IV into my arm. I closed my eyes for what seemed like a second. When I opened them again, someone was wheeling me out. I asked, "Aren't you going to do the test?"

The person said, "We already finished."

Maybe I just died and they laid me out in a coffin. I pushed on the roof. Hinged along one long side, the lid raised about an inch on the opposite side, letting in a slit of dim light. *Ha!* I braced my feet against the wood and pushed with all my might. *Now's the time longer legs would come in handy.*

The lighting, though not bright, allowed limited visibility. With the lid balanced on my feet, wood braces on the rock wall and ceiling became visible in the dim light. I listened, but couldn't hear voices or any other sound except intermittent barking.

Molly! That must be Molly barking. Hope filled my heart. Molly must be confined somewhere nearby. Another bark. This time it didn't sound like Molly. Too deep. There must be more than one dog. Mary said Frankie kept a couple cages of dogs. I strained to hear my dear Molly bark again.

Was it really Molly or my muddled thinking? Molly didn't usually bark.

Okay, Christine. How are you going to get out of here without making a lot of noise when you flop this lid open? I raised my body to look out, but my elbows couldn't sustain that position for long.

I let the lid down slowly and stretched out flat on my back, puffing from the exertion. All of a sudden, I understood the benefits of regular exercise. *Don't you wish you did sit-ups every day, old woman?*

When I shut out the light source, the darkness closed in again. *What am I going to do?*

If my legs could open the lid, then surely my back could too. With many grunts, groans, and a series of contortions, I managed to turn my body over until I rested on my stomach. Then I pushed myself into a doggy position. According to some law of physics I dimly remembered, the extra surface on my back made lifting the lid easier. I slid my arm out to grab hold of the opened lid.

In the dim light, a circular chamber came into view. The box I peered out of sat along one side. Five shafts radiated off the chamber like spokes on a wheel, indicating access from many directions. *Which one leads out?*

Thick candles on carved wooden stands circled the outer perimeter of the crypt. Besides my box, the only other furnishing in the space appeared to be a heavy table in the very center. An ornate chalice, along with several other items I couldn't distinguish, cluttered the table. The strong odor of sage wafted through the stale mine air. *What would they use sage for?*

The weight of the solid lid soon became too much for my hands and knees, the exertion causing my muscles to shake. I gripped the heavy top with both hands, lowering it to the other side without making a sound. I popped my head up for a real look around. Once liberated from the coffin, my thinking cleared and I felt much more like myself.

Then, I remembered the guards. *Where were they? And Colter?* I peered into the chamber. No sign of anyone.

Occasionally, I heard dogs barking. An opening in the wall directly across from my box must be a mine shaft. The barking emanated from that tunnel. With great care, I kneeled in the box and peeked over the side trying to figure out how I was going to climb out. No small feat for a woman with short legs and limited strength.

The box sat on a small platform with no handholds. I not only had to climb out, but then I had to lower myself down the side of the platform without falling on the rocky floor. The whole process took much grunting and more strength than I knew I possessed. I can't say my exit would appear ladylike to an observer, but thankfully, no one observed.

Once I descended the platform, I wanted to sit and rest a minute, but I knew I didn't have that luxury. On tiptoes,

I raced across the chamber. Curiosity forced me to pause in the center to examine the objects on the table. Made from a heavy metal, the chalice had shiny glass pieces on the outside. It was empty. An old leather-bound book rested next to the chalice with bundles of green leaves sitting on top. I sniffed the bundles. Sage, just as I thought.

I stopped again to peer down the tunnel for specs of light. Inky darkness stared back. Undeterred, I set off toward the barking. *Good thing my hearing is still good.* The darkness pressed against me when I entered the mine shaft. I groped the rock wall on the side to feel my way along. After my eyes became accustomed to the lack of light, a slight glow appeared ahead. The glow intensified and the barking became louder. Around a crook in the tunnel, I heard male voices. I ducked behind a large wooden crate to listen.

"Hey, you dogs. Stop that racket, will you?"

"They want out, that's what they want. How'd you like being cooped up in a cave all day?"

"We *are* cooped up in a cave all day, dork. Here dogs, take this!"

A staccato clanging like metal dragging across bars echoed through the mine shaft. The dogs howled in reply, setting off raucous laughter from the men. I peeked around the side of the crate. Wearing army fatigues, two guards sprawled on the floor next to two large metal dog runs. Even in the lantern light, I saw their faces; they looked much too young to be to soldiers. *They're just boys!* Crouching inside the cages, writhing clumps of fur vied for attention.

Dim light from two over-sized military lanterns filtered through the musty air. The lanterns sat atop one of many wooden crates stacked along the wall. They must be using this part of the mine for storage. Beyond the cages the shaft narrowed and turned again, impeding visibility. I strained, hoping to see Molly, but shadows in the cages made it impossible to distinguish one mass of fur from another. In the dimness, I couldn't even tell the colors of the dogs.

At any minute, my escape from the box might be discovered. With no time to delay, I must hurry closer without being seen by the guards. An opening of a few inches separated the wooden crate I hid behind from the one next to it. Similar crates formed a line along the side with spaces between. The guards could see me if I crawled between the boxes. I sat back on my feet to think. Nothing popped into my mind. I'd have to give it a try.

Scooting like a crab along the back of the crate, I closed my eyes and eased into the opening. The perimeters of the shaft were hidden in shadow. If the guards weren't looking, perhaps I could inch across the gap without being seen. I held my breath until I arrived safely behind the next crate. *Made it!*

I stopped to listen. The guards continued their conversation. "What time is it?"

"It's five minutes after you asked me last time."

He yawned. "I need a nap."

"Come on, be a man, moron. You know what Colonel Bodhi says about giving in to desire for comfort. This is war."

"Who you calling a moron?"

From the grunting and slapping, I guessed they engaged in a bit of wrestling to pass the time. The perfect Laurel and Hardy routine. *Thank you for the perfect opportunity to scoot behind another crate.* I accomplished the next leg of my precarious journey in short order, sliding behind the third, fourth, and fifth crates without any difficulty while the guards played slap and tackle. When I stopped to rest, the pounding in my chest sounded even louder in my ears than the wrestling of the guards.

Speaking of desire for comfort, I would have given twenty years of my life and my firstborn child just then to be curled up in my comfy bed at home. If I ever made it back, I might never leave again.

But as the guard aptly put it, this was war.

Only two more boxes between the cages and me.

Peeking behind the next one, I realized with a sinking feeling that the opening between the crate and the wall wasn't big enough to squeeze a leg through, let alone my entire body. I plopped to a sit. *How would I get to the cages without being seen?*

The grunting and slapping ceased abruptly.

"What time is it?"

Sigh. "It's five minutes after you asked last time."

"Yeah, but what time does that make it?"

The young soldier squealed as he sucked in air. "Holy socks! It's nearly 1900!"

From the sounds, the guards then scrambled to their feet. Maybe they wanted to appear as if they'd been guarding in the prescribed fashion rather than goofing off. While I counted on my fingers to convert military time to civilian time, I heard marching steps coming from the far end of the tunnel.

Seven o'clock. I'd been gone from the station for over three hours.

Must be time for new guards. I eased back in my hiding place, pulling arms and legs tight to my body to keep them hidden.

A deeper voice commanded, "Report, sir."

"Area secured, sir." From the tapping and shuffling, I imagined a traditional changing of the guard. They did not engage in small talk, only grunts, but before long two new guards replaced the old ones and marching feet retreated. Thick silence filled the tunnel.

In slow motion, I peeked out from my hiding place.

The two new guards checked the cages before pulling one of the lanterns off the crate to light their way while they marched toward the circular chamber.

My heart stopped beating for a moment when I realized that once they got to the chamber they would look in the box and discover my escape. I must move quickly. Like a racer on the starting block, I hunched and sprinted from behind the crate to the first cage. Several dogs barked when they saw me.

The wire door was easy to find. I whispered, "Molly! Are you in there?"

But I couldn't hear myself whispering over the din of the barking. I repeated her name a little louder, "Molly!"

She didn't come.

Around the cage I hurled, searching the interior of the next one while I scrambled.

"Molly! Can you hear me, girl?"

Dogs in the second cage paced at the sound of my voice, opening a space in the middle. At the back, a heap of black and white fur peeked between the legs of a large Doberman.

"Molly?"

The Doberman laid back his ears and barked, teeth barred. Molly stood to her feet and whimpered.

"Where's the stupid door?" Of course, it couldn't be right where I stood. I raced around the cage grasping each side and pulling until I located the door. The Doberman moved with me, shielding Molly. The Doberman looked as if he'd rather eat me than look at me. *If I opened the door and let all the dogs out, how would I keep him from killing me?*

I was running out of time. *Think, Christine! Dear God, please help me.*

Releasing the dogs would provide a diversion. They would know the way to the exit. But the noise would also alert the guards.

How could that work to my advantage? Only if I could somehow get out of this tunnel with Molly while the guards rounded up the other dogs. They would find out about my escape soon. Besides, as soon as they looked into the box, they'd know I was the one who let the dogs out. Maybe they'd already gotten to the box.

There seemed no other way.

Before I could talk myself out of it, I returned to the first cage, pulled the wire door open, and hid behind it. Dogs longing for freedom bounded out with glee, scattering toward the outside at top speed. As soon as the last one vaulted away, I returned to Molly's cage and repeated the procedure, using the door for a shield. Again, the caged animals raced out and headed outside.

All but the Doberman and Molly. As if he'd been ordered to protect her, the Doberman stood his ground. "Please doggie! Please come out and let me have my Molly."

The Doberman barked and lunged toward me. His teeth looked very sharp.

Molly whined.

"Nice doggie. Nice doggie. Come out." I pointed out the cage. Why didn't I have a nice juicy steak to tempt him? "Come!"

Saliva dripped off the Doberman's fangs when he growled again.

The pounding of my heart in my throat made my head spin, and a queasy feeling swirled in my stomach. I forced myself to focus. I'd heard that dogs sense fear. He surely must be sensing mine. I'd have to bluff. Taking a deep breath, I stepped out from behind the shield of the wire door and summoned my most authoritative voice. "Go!"

The Doberman hesitated a moment, looking confused, and then took off out the door following the pack. Molly hurried to my arms.

"No time for this now, old girl," I said while she licked my face. "We've got to get out of here."

But when I turned toward the dark tunnel where the guards had disappeared, I saw the light of their lantern bobbing toward us. The guards were running.

27

CHAPTER TWENTY-SEVEN

Well ahead of the guards, Molly and I raced around a bend in the tunnel. The mine shaft narrowed and the floor slanted upward. *Where were we? Better yet, where were we going to end up?* An occasional brush of fur against my leg and a quiet whimper sent darts of joy to my heart. If I thought about it too much, I'd need tissues.

We came to an entrance or exit, I didn't know which; the shaft changed significantly anyhow. Wooden braces and bare rock on the walls gave way to a smooth surface like plaster, a doorway. *Would we soon be running in the woods?*

I peeked out. The doorway opened into one of the old sawmill buildings.

The parking garage opened before me. Three charred walls still stood, blackened reminders of what had once been. A thick scorched smell hung in the air. Parts of the roof covered burned vehicles. I looked up at where the roof should have been. The setting sun sent pink and orange rays across the sky, the colors creating a stunning contrast between the blackened barn and its contents.

Face upward, I sent another prayer heavenward. *Please God, we need help.*

With Molly trotting at my heels, I picked my way over burned rafters and ashes, hurrying through rows of toasted cars and trucks.

Then I skidded to a stop.

The pack of escaped dogs crowded in the compound courtyard, barking wildly. Beyond them, dozens of soldiers waved their arms and yelled, trying to corral the dogs.

Molly stared up at me, waiting for instructions. I turned my head, searching for another way out.

I ran back to one of the vans we'd just passed. A line of soot blackened one side, but it had sustained minimal damage from the fire. The driver's side door gaped open, presenting the most available hiding place.

With no time to spare, I jumped in and pulled Molly after me. Water filled the interior, most likely spray from firefighters' hoses. Molly whined when I pushed her toward the back of the van, into the darkness. Sloshing in puddles, I crouched to listen.

My fingers tightened on her collar. I pulled her close. She licked the tears on my face. I didn't need tissues with her around.

Cross voices scolded the dogs, many voices. I imagined trying to round up a pack of caged animals that had just tasted a bit of freedom. That wouldn't be an easy task. It should keep the soldiers busy for a little while. But before long, I heard running from the other direction when the two guards returned from the chamber, probably to report my disappearance. *Now what?*

When I rearranged my legs in the darkness, I kicked something solid. My fingers explored the floor of the van, finding the item at last. In the dim light filtering through the tinted windows, I pulled the small object toward one eye to inspect it. A radio, the kind a sheriff might clip to his uniform with the clip still attached. I wiped the radio on my jacket. *Does it still work?* No time to check just now. I patted the floor around the place I'd found it, sending splashes of water onto my legs. Not finding anything else, I slid the radio into the front pocket of my jacket.

Meanwhile, the battle between soldiers and dogs continued.

Once they rounded up the dog pack, they would search for me in earnest. Likely my absence had already been reported. As soon as they concluded I'd run out through this particular mine shaft, which would be easy to deduce since the dogs had been freed, they'd start looking through the cars. I had to find another place to hide.

How in the world would I ever get out? Obviously, no one would come to rescue me. No one even knew where I'd gone. I gave myself a mental head thump, wishing I hadn't been quite so hasty in my zeal to have Rogers apprehend Colter. What *was* I thinking?

I closed my eyes to picture the layout of the compound from my previous visits. On the left side of the two-story barn, the office must be heavily guarded; it was the building with the surveillance camera and the German shepherd. I should stay away from there.

What was on the other side?

A shack. Not an important building, it was small and unmemorable. It might not even be in use. *How could I get there?*

I scooted to the front of the van and peered out the side window. The group of soldiers rounding up the dog pack had doubled in number. They would soon be victorious over the dogs.

With so many men facing this direction, I'd have to be careful climbing out. I couldn't chance sneaking out the way I got in. I grabbed Molly's fur and nuzzled my face into it, hoping to gather courage. We'd have to jump out the other side. Luckily, the van had tinted windows. I rolled down a window facing away from the doggie roundup, wiggled out, and jumped to the ground.

Oh my goodness! That stung my feet. Several pains throbbed in my legs and back. *I guess I am old after all, like everyone says.*

Molly stuck her head out the window and whimpered. I hobbled a few steps, wincing in agony until the pain dissipated. Then I reached back inside to pull her out.

Had I been noticed?

I stooped as low as I could, given the new crick in my back, and scooted down the back side of the row of charred vehicles. At the end of the row, I stopped a moment to consider escaping through the chamber. If only I knew where those four other tunnels led. *Which one would get me to the boulder-door exit?*

The barking died down. I watched while guards led several of the largest dogs away on leashes. The Doberman's head stuck out above the pack. The other dogs, mostly medium-sized, followed. For the moment, no one looked my way.

I took a deep breath and ran for cover at the far side of the building with Molly sprinting ahead of me.

"You there. Halt!" A voice ordered from behind. "Stop or I'll shoot."

These men practiced marksmanship. The voice sounded close. I couldn't discount that threat so I stopped cold.

Molly darted ahead, sliding effortlessly through a small gap between the charred boards. On the other side, she whirled to a stop, walked back a few steps and cocked her head.

"Go," I said. "Get help."

Molly whimpered and stepped closer.

I glanced back at the approaching guards. *Please God, make her go.* "Run, Molly!"

Molly let out one final whimper before veering away. The guards focused on me without noticing her black-and-white tail when she bolted away on the other side of the wall.

A burly guard grabbed my arm and spun me to face him. "Thought you'd get away, did you?"

My heart thundered in my chest and I panted so hard I couldn't speak.

A second guard caught up, seizing my other arm as if he considered my ability to get away a serious threat. Sandwiched between them, I didn't resist when they hauled me toward the office.

As we reached the building with the surveillance camera, the door flew open and out stepped the unholy threesome: Bodhi, Kingfisher, and Colter.

Colter surveyed the scene with distaste. "You are proving to be way too much trouble, Mrs. Sterling." He shook his head, disgust reflected in his expression. When he stepped down, he lowered his eyes to the ground as if considering the next course of action.

Bodhi came toward me, jerking his head like a bird on alert for predators. When he came closer, I wondered again about his erratic movements. He stepped so close that he invaded my personal space. *Was he trying to sniff my shoulder?* In reflex, I stepped back as far as I could while the guards still held my arms.

Kingfisher hesitated on the porch, watching the other two. When he marched down the steps, his striped muumuu flowed behind him. He stopped less than an inch from my nose. "You surprise me. You're an old lady. Why'd you let my dogs loose?" His eyes were lit with a scary light. "You'll have to pay for that."

Again with the old-lady comments. At that moment, I certainly felt like an old lady. Old and powerless. But definitely not invisible. They could see me just fine.

As I hung my head, I remembered the outrage these people perpetrated against my friends. I still had a little fight left in me so I drew a deep breath and straightened to face them. "You don't suppose I'd be stupid enough to visit Deputy Colter without anyone knowing where I'd gone, do you? The officers will be along soon."

If only that information were true.

Perhaps that possibility hadn't occurred to them. Kingfisher stepped back and glared at Colter. Deputy Colter's beady eyes flickered in surprise. He raised his eyebrows and looked down his nose at me.

Bodhi's face twitched. "Bad karma." Spasms contorted his face, but no one seemed to notice. Kingfisher stomped toward Colter. "I told you not to bring her here. What if this is a trap to lure us out into the open? What about her car? Where is it?"

Colter swiped his mouth with one hand. "It is still at the office, but I seriously doubt that she is part of a trap. She is not smart enough to pull that off."

Bodhi fidgeted, jiggling his hands as if to shake off water. He jerked them behind his back and held them together, perhaps to stop the wiggling. Then he paced between me and the other two, alternately staring into the darkening sky and the ground. All of a sudden, he braked and raised a finger. "Council consensus is required before administering punishment." His words sounded like he'd memorized the manual and recited it instead of talking. "Gather the war council."

28

CHAPTER TWENTY-EIGHT

Once again, I found myself inside the circular chamber. Only this time, they dragged me in fully awake. Why they thought subduing a fifty-something old woman required two muscular guards, I'll never know.

At the center of the chamber, the guards threw me on the rocky floor beside the table. Scratched elbows, scraped hands, bruised hip, and arm aching from being twisted. I felt as if I'd been beaten.

Bodhi, Kingfisher, and Colter followed us while the guards stood at attention near the wall.

Orders had been given to summon the full war council. Presumably, we'd wait in the chamber for the others to arrive. Whoever the *others* were. *Would we have to wait until midnight?*

Three somber faces glared at me.

I straightened my aching back and stared right into their eyes, feigning bravado.

Maybe I could get a little information out of them while I had their complete attention, just in case I managed to get out of this mess alive. "Is this where you brought Baxter?"

Surprised registered on Kingfisher's face. He deferred to Bodhi.

Bodhi's mouth twitched, turning a crooked smile into a grimace. "All war councils are conducted in the chamber." He yanked on his robe.

"Did you have a war council to decide Baxter's fate the night of his death? Is that what happened during the two-and-a-half hours no one can account for?"

Colter glanced at Kingfisher. Resignation showed in the rigid set of Kingfisher's face. A muscle pulsed at his jaw. "It was necessary to eliminate Deputy Dunn for the common good. His snooping threatened our entire operation."

All of a sudden, I knew what happened. "So you were in the black van, one of you or all of you. The van that Baxter radioed in about, the one with the stolen license plate. You ambushed him at the Night Owl and brought him here. Right?"

No one denied it so I kept talking. "You held a meeting just before midnight and decided to kill him, *eliminate* him. You drugged him, took him to the top of that ravine, and threw him onto the piles of metal. Then you sank his patrol car in Rawlins Lake, thinking no one would discover his body or car for a long time."

Still no denials.

"But you were wrong. Someone found him right away and also his car. You hadn't planned on that, had you?"

Kingfisher glared at Colter again. "*Someone* was supposed to have enough clout at headquarters to prevent a thorough investigation."

Colter scowled over the top of his glasses, the nostrils in his prodigious nose flaring.

My neck ached from staring up. I reached behind my head to rub it and give it a little support. "Then you had to kill poor little Mary because you saw her on your surveillance camera."

Kingfisher looked away. "Mary shouldn't have come here."

I shivered, remembering what I saw at Mary's house. "But you cared about her. How could you…kill her like that?"

Going from zero to a hundred, Kingfisher's eyes blazed when he screamed, "We are not talking about this anymore! Got it?"

I blinked and shrank back. Guess I'd better not push that button right now. "So, what's this soldier thing all about?" I glanced at each face in turn. "Do you make drugs to finance the war games? Or do you do war games to cover up making and selling drugs? What about the 'God-speaking-to-you' part?"

Bodhi's hands clenched and unclenched out of control. He clasped them together behind his back. "War is coming. We must prepare."

I wanted to ask more, but Kingfisher's eyes still flashed. "We need to search her. What if she's wearing a wire?"

A wire? Oh no. I couldn't let him search me. He'd find the radio and the picture in my pockets. "Don't be silly. I wouldn't know how to use a wire. I'm no good with technology. Ask anyone who knows me." I patted my jeans pocket but didn't feel the crunch of the picture inside. I reached in. The picture was gone! Colter must have taken it when he drugged me.

Colter's beady eyes narrowed, and then he shook his head. "She does not have a wire. She went through the office metal detector without setting anything off. We have had her here ever since."

I didn't know the office had a metal detector. But thank you, God, for that.

Kingfisher paced back and forth in a short space. "Okay. Too much talking. We must secure her until the others arrive."

Colter glanced around the chamber. "The sarcophagus."

The what? I followed his gaze to the wooden coffin I'd crawled out of a couple of hours earlier. Decorations on the front of the box stood out like ugly red scars. I guessed they were symbols, slash marks carved deep into the surface and painted red.

Together, the three men hauled me to my feet and dumped me into the box like a bag of laundry. The lid slammed down. Luckily, I had that layer of cloth in the bottom to cushion my fall, but I'm sure I sustained a few more bruises from their roughness. Kingfisher assigned an armed soldier to stand beside the box in case I tried to escape. The other guards were sent to watch the entrance to the mine shaft.

"Just shoot her if she crawls out," Kingfisher said loud enough for me to hear.

Something akin to relief at being left alone in the dark washed over me. At least for the moment, they wouldn't hurt me. When I'd settled on my back in the most comfortable position available, I found that I could still hear muffled voices from the center of the chamber, about twenty feet away. I lay as still as possible trying to understand the words.

Kingfisher's voice sounded grim. "No one leaves here until the meeting."

"I need to move her car and check the office," Colter said. "To see if they're onto us."

Kingfisher sounded unconvinced. "You got us into this predicament, bringing her out here. You'll risk more trouble going into town."

Bodhi's voice sounded as jerky as his movements. "The police scanner."

Kingfisher sounded incredulous. "You have a scanner in your patrol car?"

"Yes," Colter said. "But they must know my car is gone. If they suspect I took the Sterling woman, they would not risk my hearing their plans on the scanner."

In the pause that followed, I imagined Kingfisher pacing again while he appeared to consider Colter's request.

"Why should we trust you? What's to stop you from taking off and leaving us to suffer the consequences?"

Colter snorted a hollow laugh. "Where would I go? Do you doubt my loyalty to this cause? My best bet is here with the army. We have all the ammunition we need now."

Ammunition? They must be talking about the wooden crates in the tunnels. I remembered the wooden boxes with stenciled letters the leaders posed beside in the photo. Maybe that's what Mary had on Kingfisher. They were posing beside a new acquisition of ammunition. *Where did the crates come from?* I'd bet those guns and ammo were illegal.

My backache prompted an involuntary shift of position. The radio in my pocket clanked against the wood. I had forgotten all about it. *Did the radio still work?* I pulled it out and turned it in my hands. I couldn't see a thing. I held it right in front of my eyes, but still couldn't see it. I'd have to open the lid to let in a little light and hope no one noticed.

As I maneuvered my sore body in the box, every spot I touched the wood caused a stab of pain. A groan almost passed my lips and I gritted my teeth. I would not give up. Wiggling in short motions, I managed to turn over onto my stomach again and pressed my back into the lid like before.

Ever so slowly, I pushed up until a little slit not more than an inch wide let in enough light for me to see the radio lying beneath me. It looked like Jesse's walkie-talkie. I shifted weight onto my bent legs, balancing the lid in order to free my hands. By examining the dials and buttons I found the on/off apparatus. I turned it until I heard a click, but no green light. *How could I tell if it was on or off now? What if it squawked and they heard it?* I'd have to be careful. I hunted for the volume control. *Would turning it clockwise raise the volume or lower it?*

Why didn't I pay attention to these kinds of details? Why didn't I know more about technology?

Maybe the radio didn't work in this tunnel. Mary said phones didn't work in some places near mountains. *What if the radio had rusted from sitting in water?* Maybe it wouldn't work anywhere. I slipped the radio back in my pocket. My thigh muscles burned with the tension of holding the lid, so I let it slide down again.

The men continued arguing.

Colter's voice sounded as if he must be facing my direction. "So we are agreed. Someone must go into town."

Bodhi stuttered. "C-council will convene at twenty-four hundred. Authorization is r-required."

Colter persisted. "I will be there and back before midnight."

Kingfisher's voice held an edge. "Very well. But be forewarned. If you aren't back before the meeting, I'll hunt you down and kill you."

During the subsequent scuffling, I imagined Colter dashing off through the tunnel. Why didn't I watch him go so I'd know the way out? In case I got the chance to run.

An eerie silence filled the chamber after Colter left. I pressed my back into the wood until I'd lifted the lid enough to peek out. The guard had his back to me. His head was turned toward the tunnel to the left of the table from my vantage point. Maybe he'd been watching Colter shuffle off. I took note of that, just in case.

In the center of the chamber, Bodhi and Kingfisher stood on either side of the table facing each other, hands folded and heads bowed. Sage wafted through the air. A thin line of smoke trailed straight up from the leafy bundle burning upright in the chalice.

By then, my knees wobbled. They might give way at any moment. I let the lid down slowly, lying flat on my stomach to rest. My joints would never be the same after holding up such a weight. Trying to settle the rapid beating of my heart, I sucked in several deep breaths. The aroma of burning sage penetrated my box. I stifled a cough and forced my tense muscles to relax. *A massage would be great about now.*

My chances for rescue did not look good. *Could Molly get away from the compound without being caught? If she did, where would she go? Would Jesse hunt for me? Someone must have noticed my car in the parking lot by now. Why, oh, why didn't I tell someone my plans?*

Dear God, please send someone to rescue me.

I stewed in these thoughts without hearing another sound from the chamber. Apparently, Bodhi and Kingfisher felt no need to speak. Maybe they were meditating. How tired I felt. Must be way past my bedtime. I forced myself to inhale a few more deep breaths of soothing sage and felt the tension ease a little.

My eyelids slowly closed.

I don't know how long I slept. My body felt stiff and sore when I awakened; I might have slept in the same cramped position without moving for hours.

A commotion startled me. Confused over my whereabouts, I struggled. When I realized where I was, I focused on the yelling, trying to understand the confrontation that echoed through the chamber. However, the uproar had reached such a fevered pitch that I could make no sense of it whatsoever.

I pressed my aching back into the lid and lifted it to peek out the slit again.

A mob of soldiers in fatigues swarmed around Bodhi and Kingfisher. Considerable pushing and shoving took place while the rabble competed to be heard. Fear reigned. Harsh loud, grating voices echoed off the chamber walls making the complaints indecipherable. Kingfisher and Bodhi waved their arms, shouting from the center of the turmoil. Totally out of control, Kingfisher climbed onto the table with Bodhi clambering up next to him.

"Quiet!" Kingfisher held up both hands and yelled. "Quiet!"

I wasn't buying Kingfisher's authoritative stance. His eyes bulged with panic. Nevertheless, the discord settled to a murmur.

Kingfisher waved over the crowd as if either warding off mosquitoes or invoking an incantation. "You men have overstepped your boundaries."

Bodhi's head jerked and he stammered. "D-disciplinary measures m-must be instituted."

A man yelled out. "Maybe we don't accept your discipline anymore."

"Yeah," yelled someone else. Heads bobbed in agreement while a murmur swelled and died down.

"We followed you to fight the enemy," another said in a loud voice. "Not to waste time rounding up dogs and chasing little old ladies."

Kingfisher held up his hands. "This little old lady *is* the enemy."

I raised my eyebrows.

That statement brought a renewed burst of chaos.

I am the enemy? I could understand why the soldiers were upset. They certainly didn't need crates of weapons and ammo to get rid of me. Not to mention all the hours of marching, drilling, and target practice.

Imagining being pummeled to death by an angry soldier mob forced out a groan. A flash of fear flowed from my heart to my extremities, intensifying my aches and pains. My breath came in short gasps. I let the lid down to rest my muscles.

Out of the ruckus, one voice bellowed, "You owe us an explanation."

The din faded.

When Kingfisher spoke at last, his voice sounded stronger. "This is not a matter for your concern. Your duty is to follow orders and trust our guidance. We have kept our promises to you so far, haven't we?"

The crowd grumbled.

Bodhi's voice thundered in the chamber. "We will p-preserve this r-regiment and be v-victorious in our cause regardless of the c-cost involved. We p-p-pledge that to you."

More murmuring.

Kingfisher continued. "You must trust Colonel Bodhi."

"Why have you ordered the war council?"

Bodhi jerked his head side to side like a rooster. "Disciplinary measures must be invoked. That requires approval from the war council."

"What about Major Colter? Doesn't he have to be here for the war council?" someone yelled.

"Major Colter will return in time."

Another voice shouted. "It's almost midnight."

"Leave that to us." Kingfisher's booming voice echoed when he bellowed, "Men. Assume formation."

I hunched my tender back to open the slit so I could peek out. How would they react to the order?

Sure enough, with only a little fussing, the disorderly mob rearranged itself into military lines. Kingfisher and Bodhi saluted. The soldiers returned the salute.

Kingfisher bellowed. "Dismissed."

Rows of soldiers retreated the chamber without another word, leaving Kingfisher and Bodhi standing alone atop the table.

Soon, all the men had marched out of sight, even the one who guarded my box. Kingfisher and Bodhi stood at attention until the sound of marching boots could no longer be heard, then climbed off the table.

Kingfisher looked at his watch in the candlelight. "It's almost time. We must prepare the room."

They shuffled into the tunnel to the right of the table and brought back five large wooden throne-like chairs, one by one. Symbols like I'd seen on the box were also carved into the backs of the chairs and the seats appeared to be red velvet. From the care with which Kingfisher and Bodhi carried them, I guessed they must be ceremonially important.

They arranged the chairs in a circle, each in front of one of the tunnels, leaving a wide band of space around the table. Apparently satisfied with the placement, they moved toward my box. I let the lid down.

"Aha! So you've found a way to spy on us." Kingfisher flung the top off my casket and yanked me out by my bad arm.

Hurt, I cried out.

Bodhi started his fist clenching.

"Never mind," Kingfisher said with a wicked grin. "She won't make trouble much longer."

Candlelight reflected in dark eyes that sparked with hate. I shriveled.

29

CHAPTER TWENTY-NINE

Kingfisher reached into the sarcophagus and pulled out the folded material I'd been using to cushion my aching body. Moving in a reverent attitude bordering on the ceremonial, he smoothed the large piece and laid it across the back of the chair at the head of the table.

I stepped toward it. "What's that for?"

In an instant, Kingfisher and Bodhi reacted.

Kingfisher yelled, "Don't touch that."

Bodhi quivered. "Pagan hands."

I stared at the fabric. "Why? What's it for?"

Kingfisher planted himself between the chair and me. "The general."

Bodhi's face contorted with twitches. " No one can touch it. You would defile it."

Kingfisher motioned me to step back.

I moved where he pointed. "Don't be silly, I've been using that for a pillow. It's a good thing I had it too. Old bones and all."

They ignored me.

Could I sneak out while they concentrated on their arrangements? I didn't know, so I watched in silence. Without warning, Kingfisher grabbed my bad arm and dragged me toward the box.

I dug in my heels and pulled back as hard as I could which made my arm hurt all the more. "Please. I'd rather not go back in there. Now that you've removed my cushion it's going to be most uncomfortable."

Without a word, he pulled a rope out of a hidden compartment in the platform under the box and tied my hands behind my back. Then he pushed me to a sitting position on the rock floor with my back against the platform and looped the rope around my feet so I could barely move.

The candles in the tall stands around the room flickered, burning low. Kingfisher bustled off. Bodhi stood guard when Kingfisher left the chamber, but soon returned with more candles. While Bodhi hurried down a different tunnel, he threw a jerky backward glance.

"Frankie," I said when we were alone. "You know it's pointless to keep me. You're just making it worse for yourself. The police are coming. Right now, we can pin the kidnapping charge on Colter, especially if you help me get out of here. I came to get my dog because I can't imagine life without her. Being a dog lover, I'm sure you understand. Mary said you have a kind heart. This position is very uncomfortable for an old lady, especially the rock on my behind. I never did you any harm, did I?"

He stopped working to glare at me.

"Okay, just that dog thing. But you got all your dogs back, right? How would your mother feel all trussed up like this?"

"My mother was no prize."

"Oh, well, think of the mother you *should* have had then."

Kingfisher bent to stare directly into my eyes. "Look. I would have eliminated you already if it was up to me. But the general's in charge here. He ordered us to go by the manual. The manual calls for the war council to order punishment."

"So you said." I tilted to the other side, hoping to relieve the pressure on my tailbone. It didn't help much.

Kingfisher returned to bustling about the chamber.

I closed my eyes and lowered my head onto my knees. The General. Colter was their Major and Bodhi was their Colonel. Kingfisher spoke of this other person as the General so it obviously wasn't him.

The rank of General topped the pecking order. I remembered that much from Jesse's stint in the army. But I thought Bodhi and Kingfisher were the top dogs around here. They had set up five chairs. Kingfisher, Bodhi, and Colter would only use three. Who would sit in the other two? Could there be someone I hadn't seen yet who actually called the shots? Were these buffoons just pawns in someone else's scheme? Scary thought. Who could the other two people be?

I raised my head. "Frankie?"

He stopped and looked at me.

"Who's the general?"

Kingfisher consulted his watch. "You'll find out soon. Meanwhile, shut your—"

Before he finished speaking, scuffling feet and gruff voices announced someone hurrying toward the chamber through the same tunnel Colter used, the tunnel I assumed must lead to the boulder door and freedom.

Kingfisher turned in the direction of a spec of light bobbing toward us. Deputy Colter soon came in view, dragging someone behind him. Colter's gun was drawn and pointed directly at the other person's head. His victim, who wore expensive high-heel shoes, tripped and stumbled on the rocky floor.

I gasped.

Constance Boyd!

Kingfisher's expression mirrored my shock. "What have you done?"

Colter doubled over, panting.

Creases marred Constance Boyd's perfect dress where the rope had bunched the expensive black fabric. Smeared makeup streaked her face. Her coiffure looked like her hairdresser had gone on an extended vacation. A knotted scarf dangled around her neck, looking out of place with the rest of her outfit.

Colter pushed her to the floor where she landed in a most unladylike position. She glared up at him. "You will be very sorry, little man. You don't know who you're dealing with."

Kingfisher gaped in amazement. "You brought Constance Boyd to the chamber?" His voice squeaked like a frustrated schoolboy. "Constance Boyd? What were you thinking? Every cop in the country will be looking for her."

Colter swiped a hand across his mouth. "They're onto us. We need big leverage. I am not going to prison without a fight."

Kingfisher shoved Colter in the chest. "What do you mean they're on to us? Are you crazy? The general will never be able to get us out of this now."

Constance lifted her head and pushed back hair that had fallen in her face. "I told him that already. Heads are going to roll. Apparently your deputy has air where his brain should be."

Colter pointed the revolver at Constance. "Look, you. Shut up."

Then Colter aimed the pistol at Frankie. "As for you. You keep your dirty hands off me. Do you understand?"

Kingfisher backed up, lifting both hands. "Hey, you're the one running on fear. Pull yourself together. And put that thing down before you hurt somebody."

Constance hooted. "This is total insanity! Help me up and get me out of here."

Colter didn't lower the gun.

Kingfisher heaved a heavy sigh. "What do you plan to do with her?"

Sweat glistened on Colter's forehead and dripped down his big nose. "We need a hostage!" he yelled. "Do you understand that?"

"What about *her*?" Kingfisher nodded toward me.

Constance lifted her head to glance at me. Recognition dawned in her eyes.

"Not her." Colter shook his head. "We need someone big. Someone the authorities care about. Someone the media cares about."

Well, I never! Invisible again.

Kingfisher arched his eyebrow. "Did she see where you brought her?"

Colter looked insulted. "Of course not." He reached toward Constance and flicked the knotted scarf around her delicate neck. "I blindfolded her."

"At least you thought of that." Kingfisher plopped onto one of the chairs. He closed his eyes and rubbed his face. "You've sealed our fate, you know. We'll never get away now. This woman is known all over the world."

The gun wobbled. Colter looked flustered. "The general will know what to do."

Shuffling and spots of light in the tunnel on the right announced Bodhi's return. With him, a third man marched in. I recognized him as the man in the lab coat, the tall man with the shaved head. Now he wore army fatigues and a scowl. *The general?*

When they spotted Constance Boyd, they halted, speechless as a couple of mimes.

Colter quickly explained Miss Boyd's presence.

Bodhi bounced and fidgeted, jerking his head from one person to another. "Bad karma, very bad."

Kingfisher nodded in agreement, fists clenching and unclenching.

The tall man expelled a loud curse. "Of all the lame-brained schemes." Stepping toward Colter with a hand resting on his holster, he looked like a gunfighter in a spaghetti western. "As your superior officer, I order you to holster that weapon immediately, Major Colter."

Superior officer? Then this must be the general. Silver bars on his sleeves must denote his rank. *Didn't generals have stars though?* I wished I remembered.

That accounted for four of the war council. Who sat in the fifth chair?

Colter vacillated a moment before holstering his pistol.

I sensed a collective relief. Even Constance's demeanor softened.

Not having to witness bloodshed, my thoughts turned to escape. *How would guards be summoned to the chamber if needed?*

Bodhi lurched and bumped behind the chairs while the new man focused his attention on Constance Boyd.

She sat straight-backed as a proper lady. When she saw Colter put away his gun, she extended her hand to the general and barked an order of her own. "Help me up."

He reached for her hand and pulled her to her feet.

Constance smoothed the front of her wrinkled dress and unknotted the scarf before leveling a stare at the general. "I demand to be released."

"I'm sorry, ma'am." He put both hands behind his back and spread his feet apart in a military at-ease stance. "I don't have authority to do that. You don't belong here, but now that you're here, we wait for orders."

Constance wrinkled her flawless brow. "You're not in charge?"

Bodhi stopped pacing and jerked his head back and forth. Kingfisher lowered his eyes. Colter stepped back. The tall man I'd assumed to be the general started to speak, but closed his mouth again.

What was going on?

Tall Man bit his lip. "No, ma'am. I'm not in charge. But the general will arrive soon. Please allow me to make you comfortable until he decides what to do."

Who was the authority behind this operation?

Tall Man commanded Bodhi to fetch one of the chairs, then winced while he watched Bodhi's wretched movements. When Bodhi dragged over one of the red-cushioned chairs, Tall Man gestured for Constance to sit. "Make yourself comfortable, ma'am."

Constance crossed her arms and remained standing. "I demand that you let me out of here. Now."

Instead, he reached for her.

She wrenched her arm away.

He put his hands on her shoulders and pushed her onto the seat where she landed with a most unfeminine plop. Constance crossed her legs and arms, as if pouting would matter to this motley crew. I remembered her telling Zora Jane that for a long time no one had talked to her in the way Zora Jane did. Constance Boyd had been calling the shots for a very long time. The predicament she found herself in right now must frustrate her to the max.

Bodhi, Colter, Kingfisher, and Tall Man huddled around the chair. From their stern looks and hushed conversation, I guessed they were discussing what Colter discovered when he went to town or possible courses of action they might take since bringing Constance Boyd had complicated the situation even further.

From my position on the floor, I had a clear view past the huddled group into three of the tunnels across the chamber. I'd decided that the tunnel to the left must lead to the outside to the sliding boulder door Zora Jane and I found. Since I could no longer hear their conversation, I stared into that tunnel and prayed.

Please, God. Help Molly bring help. Show Jesse where to look.

As I prayed, a slight movement caught my eye. Only a flicker, but enough to be certain I'd seen motion.

Someone or something moved in the dark tunnel.

Desperate to see more, I strained into the inky blackness. Every bone and muscle in my body ached from sitting on the rocky floor in such a cramped position and from the other injuries inflicted on me. It must be nearly midnight and real fatigue had set in. But I ignored all that and held myself as still as a cat waiting beside a mouse hole.

Surely I didn't imagine it. I knew I'd seen something but I didn't dare blink in case I missed the next sight of whatever or whoever hid in the tunnel. I held my breath. When my lungs felt as if they would burst, I let the air out in one long rush. Then I gulped in another lungful.

Bodhi's head jerked in my direction at the sound of air being expelled. He looked concerned, eyebrows twitching. I shrugged, giving a sheepish look. He yanked his head back into the huddle.

Several more minutes passed.

Maybe I imagined I saw something because I wanted someone to be there.

I fixed my eyes harder on the darkness, trying to penetrate it with my stare. If only I had my night-vision binoculars.

There it was again. Only this time, the person moved close enough to the light for me to see a man in uniform crouched in the tunnel. He remained in the light for a fraction of a second before retreating into darkness. I couldn't see his face, but the glint of a raised pistol made my heart flip-flop in hopeful anticipation.

God heard my desperate plea.

Someone had come to my rescue.

30

CHAPTER THIRTY

I held my breath, glancing from the dark tunnel to the group circled around the chair. Considering the coming confrontation, my heart beat faster than a jackhammer. *When would the general arrive? Would he come with guards? Why didn't I wear a watch so I'd know when midnight came?* I must warn the man in the tunnel.

With all my willpower, I forced my eyes to remain on the center of the chamber without a peek in any other direction. I spoke loudly and clearly, "Frankie, this position is becoming quite uncomfortable. Would you untie these ropes please? Or at least loosen them. I'm not going anywhere. How could I when any minute you're expecting the general to arrive for your war council meeting? Isn't it almost midnight?"

Kingfisher's big head bobbed up. All eyes turned to stare at me. "You sure she isn't wearing a wire, Colter?"

Colter looked puzzled by my sudden outburst.

I laughed. "Don't be silly. I wouldn't know how to use anything that complicated—"

A bullhorn blasted the silence. "This is a raid. All hands in the air!"

With those words ringing in my ears, Detective Rogers rushed out of the tunnel, pistol pointed at the group. Behind him, Deputies Wright and Anderson with four other officers I didn't recognize fanned out to surround them.

Confounded expressions turned to disgust. Colter, Bodhi, Frank, and the tall man raised their hands high in the air.

Detective Rogers aimed his pistol directly at Colter. "Surrender your weapon!"

Colter unsnapped his holster. With two fingers, he extracted his service revolver.

Rogers grabbed it and stuffed it into the back of his belt. "Anyone else packing?"

The tall man gave up a black military pistol. Frankie and Bodhi shook their heads.

Constance Boyd swayed to her feet like a damsel who'd just been rescued from the dragon. She looked as if she might swoon at any moment. "It's about time you got here, Detective. This ordeal has been intolerable."

I rolled my eyes. Too melodramatic for my taste. *She* got to sit in a cushy chair the whole time. How'd she like being trussed up like a rotisserie chicken?

While Detective Rogers and two of the officers held the captives at gunpoint, Deputy Anderson snapped handcuffs on Frankie; Deputy Wright locked Colter's wrists behind his back. Two of the other officers put handcuffs on Bodhi and the tall man. That accomplished, Detective Rogers inclined his head, signaling to someone else in the mine shaft. I squinted into the darkness. Jesse jogged toward me with Ed and Zora Jane at his heels.

A gasp escaped. We all spoke at the same time.

"Are you all right?"

"How did you find me?"

Jesse kissed me before tugging at the rope. "Let's get this off you."

"Did they hurt you?"

"Where's Molly?"

Bending toward me, Zora Jane grinned. "I used the night scope to guide us through the tunnel so we wouldn't be seen. Thank God you left it in my car." For the first time, I noticed the Taiwanese night-scope binoculars hanging by their sturdy leather strap around Zora Jane's delicate neck. Talk about a perfect accessory!

I rubbed my chaffed wrists now freed from their bonds. "Yes. Thank God."

Jesse pulled me to my feet. I looked with relief into his loving eyes. He lifted me off the ground and swung me around. I never thought I'd be so glad to see him again. I threw my arms around his neck and squeezed hard, hoping I'd never have to let go. But I had so many questions. I pulled away after a moment. "Did you find Molly? How'd you know where to look for me?"

Zora Jane smoothed my hair. It must be a sight. "Jesse called Detective Rogers. They'd already found your Jeep in the parking lot and knew Colter had taken you."

Detective Rogers looked pleased. "Baxter uncovered Colter's involvement with *Satori*. He found out they were importing illegal weapons and ammunition. He knew about their drug manufacturing too. That's why they killed him. We've known that much for a long time. Just needed proof. Had to smoke them out into the open to see who else might be involved."

"I told them about the sliding boulder door at the Star Mine." Zora Jane smiled. "Luckily, I had the night scope in my car."

Detective Rogers's expression became stern. "We also got the oddest intermittent signal from Baxter's radio. Don't know how the battery could have lasted so long. That part's a puzzler."

I knew how. My fingers touched the radio in my pocket. I had turned it on. No green light, but they got the signal. That had to be God. Someday I'd have to explain this puzzle to Detective Rogers.

Right now, his reprimand was in full gear. "I told you to let us complete this investigation without your help. You have acted in a foolish manner and could have gotten yourself killed. I ought to charge you with something for your own safety. I doubt that your husband would object if I did."

I hung my head, trying to look contrite. He had a right to reprimand me. "I am sorry. I was wrong."

Jesse's expression mirrored the one on the detective's face. "Rest assured. This girl is hanging up her amateur sleuth hat. Permanently. Even if that means I have to put her under house arrest. Got any of those anklet things I could rent?" He grinned and tightened his grip on my shoulders. "You'll never have to worry about her again."

I stroked Jesse's dear face. "Locking me in the house won't be necessary. I'm retiring, once and for all. I can't imagine there would ever be another murder close to home for me to get involved in anyway. Two is all anyone should ever have to deal with."

To prove my good intentions, I told them about the photograph which I didn't have anymore. "I'm sure Colter took it when he brought me here."

Colter squirmed and grumbled. "I have the right to an attorney."

But Rogers emptied Colter's pockets right then and there. Out tumbled the crumpled photo. Then I had to explain how I found it.

Jesse frowned. But Detective Rogers inspected the words stenciled on the wooden crates, shining his stainless steel flashlight to illuminate the words. He let out a low whistle. "Yes, siree. These boxes came from South America. With those labels, we'll have no problem establishing the illegal sources. We have more than enough to prosecute these yahoos now."

Just then, I remembered the general. "Oh my goodness! We've got to get out of here. The general will be along any minute."

Detective Rogers threaded the rope Kingfisher used on me through the handcuffs of the four captives and handed the end to Deputy Anderson. One of the men pulled candles from the tall stands in the circular chamber to light our passage through the tunnel. Tugging their captives behind them, the officers trudged toward the exit.

Constance, no longer the center of attention, had been pacing and gesturing, looking quite impatient with our lengthy exchange. When we moved out of the chamber, she flounced to the head of the pack, muttering about no one taking her pain seriously. Detective Rogers dipped his head when she passed, turning to wink at us. Jesse, Ed, Zora Jane, and I trooped along at the rear, our feet following the light of Ed's flashlight. Jesse put his arm around my shoulders while we walked.

Lit by flickering candles, the mine shaft spread before us bit by bit.

"But what about Molly?" I repeated. "Did she find her way home?"

Jesse chuckled. "Amazing dog, that girl. Some man found her wandering out on Highway 20. He read her tags and phoned me. Good thing we put on those heavy-duty tags. I picked her up on my way to the sheriff's office."

Joy swept over me like a tsunami. My Molly was safe!

Jesse continued. "But why didn't you use your cell phone? You do have it, don't you?"

I looked away. "It's in my purse in the back of the Jeep. It's probably not charged anyway."

Jesse lifted my chin toward him so he could see my eyes. He shook his head and laughed. My lack of technological skills must frustrate him. It frustrated me too.

"Anyway," Jesse continued. "Molly's fine. How'd you get her out?"

I told the story of the dog cages, even though it meant enduring another lecture about my reckless choices.

By then, we'd navigated the length of the mineshaft and approached the boulder door which Detective Rogers had wisely left open in case a quick escape became necessary.

Detective Rogers drew his revolver again and moved to the doorway to peek into the dark night. Constance shoved him aside in her rush to be the first out.

Detective Rogers ordered, "No, Miss Boyd—" But before he could complete his sentence, hands from outside the tunnel grabbed her and pulled her roughly away.

Constance screamed.

In an instant, the line of officers drew back, weapons drawn, shoving the prisoners together against the wood braces of the mine walls.

A stern voice outside the entrance shouted, "We've got Miss Boyd! Send out your captives and we'll release her."

Detective Rogers boomed back. "No deal, General. We've got you surrounded. There are deputies down the hill waiting for you to make your move."

My eyes focused on Detective Rogers. *Please God, let that be true.* He had called the man "General." Did he already know about him?

Jesse backed me against the wall and moved in front to shield me. I peeked around his side to see what would happen next.

"You're bluffing," the stern voice called. "You've got seven, no more than ten, deputies inside. You couldn't get more without me hearing about it, not for a rescue of this magnitude. I've got a whole regiment with military weapons out here. Don't make me order them to storm this tunnel. There will be a lot of casualties. You don't want that." The voice sounded familiar. Could it be that *I* knew the General too?

Rogers answered without hesitation, "We called in reinforcements from Placer County. You know procedure. Didn't you notice we didn't leave a guard outside the entrance to the tunnel?"

Could there be a regiment of soldiers coming to our rescue? Did Rogers anticipate this last standoff with the general?

While I strained to hear the answer from outside, Rogers pulled his radio off his shoulder and spoke into it with authority. "We're at the entrance. Oliver has Constance Boyd. Proceed with caution."

I sucked in a deep breath. Oliver? *Did I hear that right?* Did he mean Deputy Oliver? I shook my head hard, hoping to clear the cobwebs. Couldn't be. Deputy Oliver and Baxter were long-time friends. But wait a minute; he said this guy knew procedure so he must be a deputy. *Now I'm really confused.*

Jesse and Ed murmured to each other.

A muffled undertone of grunts and groans continued outside as if Constance struggled against her assailants. Probably someone held a hand over her perfectly shaped mouth.

I pulled Jesse's shirt and whispered, "Is he saying that Deputy Oliver is the general?"

Jesse whispered back, "Did you say *General?*"

Outside in the darkness, a scuffle could be heard and then Constance Boyd screamed, "Let me go immediately, you brute!"

A slap preceded a thud as if someone had fallen hard to the ground. I winced.

Constance growled, "How dare you!"

The stern voice bellowed. "We'll kill her right here if that's what you want, Jerry."

Jerry? Jerry Rogers? The "G" on his name badge could stand for Gerald. *Could these two be acquainted?* Maybe it really was Deputy Oliver. Deputy Oliver, Baxter's friend. A wave of sadness washed over me.

Detective Rogers shouted, "What do you want?"

Wasn't an army of law enforcement personnel about to converge on Deputy Oliver and his soldiers? What difference did it make what Oliver wanted?

"What's he doing?" Jesse whispered as if he'd heard my thoughts.

"Stalling for time," Ed answered.

Oliver yelled. "Send out Bodhi, Colter, De la Peña, and Johnson. NOW. Before I lose patience with this woman."

Rogers yelled back. "How do we know you won't take the woman anyway?"

Constance objected. "You can't use me for a hostage. I will not go with you."

Oliver laughed. "I'd be doing all of us a favor to get rid of this tyrant. You'll have to trust me not to. Send my men out and be quick about it. I'm losing patience."

We all started talking at once.

Detective Rogers held up one hand. Without turning toward us, he whispered, "Stay down. Out of the way. The reinforcements should be in place by now. There may be gunfire."

"So there really *are* deputies waiting out there?" I whispered, but got no answer. What if Oliver's soldiers outnumbered them?

We strained to listen, but only heard nighttime noises.

I jerked in surprise when a hailstorm of gunshots broke the silence.

Jesse threw me to the ground and covered my body with his. His chest heaved with heavy breaths.

Bullets zinged into the boulders outside. I dug my fingers into Jesse's arm. He whispered, "Don't move."

The officers must have attacked Oliver *and* his soldiers if he'd brought any along.

Who's doing all that shooting? I couldn't tell whether Deputy Oliver and Constance had taken cover. Maybe they hadn't. *What if they'd been shot?*

As suddenly as the gunfire started, it stopped. For long seconds inside the mine, I couldn't hear anything but my heart tattooing my chest.

Suddenly, Deputy Oliver rushed the doorway, dragging Constance in front of him for a shield. One of his arms circled her neck with his gun protruding from behind one shoulder.

Constance shrieked, "Let me go!"

"Call them off," Deputy Oliver shouted. "Or I swear to you, I will shoot her."

Candlelight glittered off Oliver's pistol leveled at Miss Boyd's head. I heard the click when he cocked the gun.

Frozen by fear, I held my breath.

Out of the shadows, Zora Jane hurled herself into them with the force of a football tackle, knocking both to the floor. In that instant, Detective Rogers and the other officers sprang into action, grabbing Miss Boyd and shoving her out of harm's way. Ed helped her off the floor and led her a safe distance away from the fracas. Detective Rogers hauled the bewildered Deputy Oliver to his feet and none too gently relieved him of his firearm.

In an instant, order and quiet returned to the mine shaft. Dizziness spiraled in my head from trying to follow the action. I shook it away and stared at Zora Jane. I'd never seen her move so fast. Who'd have thought such a fashionable woman could be capable of speed like that. "What on earth possessed you to tackle them?"

She grinned from a doubled-over position where she'd bent to catch her breath. "Not bad for an old lady in high heels, eh?"

Ed slapped the leg of his plaid golf pants and howled with laughter. "Woman, you never cease to amaze me."

I turned to Detective Rogers. "How'd you know Oliver was involved?"

Detective Rogers smiled. "Something he said the day of the funeral. He said he was at the office about five when Baxter took the call about going to the bar. I was there at that time and Oliver was already gone. He couldn't have known about that call unless he'd actually made it himself."

In the entrance to the tunnel, a voice boomed, "Detective Rogers, have you secured the area?"

"Affirmative. I have Oliver and the others," Rogers answered. One of the officers handed him handcuffs which he clapped on the wrists of the handsome all-American Deputy Oliver who scowled and hung his head.

I regarded him with amazement. The general. He'd been behind this fiasco all along. How could that be? Snippets of his kind words at Baxter's funeral flashed to mind. How could he say those things and not really care? His duplicity ranked at the top, the very worst kind, betraying a friend. No wonder he didn't help me when I begged him to.

A Placer County deputy stuck his head into the entrance. His lantern flooded the mine shaft with light. "Guess you don't need our help then."

Detective Rogers grinned and yanked his captive toward the doorway. "Thanks for the assistance. Couldn't have done it without you."

The other officers led four disgruntled *Satori* leaders into the night to their awaiting fate.

Constance Boyd regarded Zora Jane with wide eyes. "I don't know how to thank you. You risked your own life to save me. You didn't have to do that. Not after the way I treated you." She shook her head slowly.

Zora Jane straightened. In the glowing light from the lantern, their eyes met and held. "You know what the Bible says, 'Greater love has no one than this, that he lay down his life for his friends.' That's in the book of John speaking of the sacrifice Jesus made because of His great love for us." She smiled. "I consider you my friend because God loves you."

Truly, love of God radiated from Zora Jane's countenance, melting my heart with its heat. I turned to see whether that love would penetrate the hard heart of our national television star as well.

Eyes glittering in the candlelight, Constance Boyd beamed her Ultra Brite smile and extended one perfectly manicured hand. "Please, my friend. Tell me more."

The day I decided to join the search for Baxter Dunn's murderers, I cooked a bubbling Swiss steak for dinner. This recipe came from my mother, an excellent cook.

MOM'S SWISS STEAK

1/2 C. all purpose flour
1/4 C. bell peppers, minced
1/2 tsp. salt
1-2 cloves garlic, minced
1/2 tsp. pepper
1 can diced tomatoes
1/2 to 1 tsp. garlic powder
Dash Worcestershire sauce
1 to 2 lb. round steak - 1 inch thick
1 bell pepper (seeded and cut in rings)
Enough oil to brown meat (olive or canola oil)
1 head onion (sliced in rings)
1/2 C. minced onion
1-7 oz. can (or 1 pkg. fresh) mushrooms, sliced

Trim fat off steak. Mix together flour, salt, and pepper. Sprinkle one side of meat with half the flour mixture and pound in using meat mallet. Turn meat and pound in remaining flour. Cut into serving pieces.

Heat the oil in a skillet and brown meat over medium heat, about 15 minutes. Add minced onion, minced bell pepper, and minced garlic the last few minutes of browning. Cover tightly and simmer 1 hour. (Add small amounts of water if needed to keep from sticking.)

Place onion rings, pepper rings, and sliced mushrooms on top of steak; mix Worcestershire sauce with canned tomatoes and pour over all. Cover tightly and simmer 30 minutes or until tender. Great served over egg noodles.

Catherine Leggitt

ACKNOWLEDGEMENTS

Support systems function well based on two criteria: the character of the individuals who fulfill the role and one's ability to lean on support when needed. This second book in the Christine Sterling Mystery series was written faster and easier because I learned when to ask for help and how to accept the assistance given. In his grace, God provided ministering angels along the way to assist and encourage just when they were needed. Without these angels, this book would remain unfinished.

To my husband Bob Leggitt, thank you for understanding the time needed to nurture my obsession with the written word. To my firstborn child, Jule Wright, how grateful I am for your unwavering faith that because God called me to write, He would provide. Thank you for reminding me often. Still loving my iMac. Thanks again, Jason and Angie Leggitt for providing this sturdy, efficient machine. To my Mom and Pop, Pill and Gene Rogers, I am indebted to you as heads of my cheering section. Also, thank you, Pop, for steering me through the complex waters of the sheriff's department. To my in-laws, Jane and Dale Harman, thanks for sticking to your high opinion of my potential as a writer even when no evidence existed. To my beautiful sisters, Florenza Krnich, Toni Deaville and Patty Little, I hope you already know how much I value your praise and support.

Janna Schumacher and sister-in-law Merrilee Leggitt left their imprint on this manuscript through their skill at editing. Thanks for being tactful where improvement was required.

I owe much gratitude to the critique group at the 2007 Mount Hermon Christian Writers' Conference. Thank you Renae Brumbaugh, Margaret Kroening, Michael Tough, Russell Nakamura, Germaine Bleile, David Bena, Leslie Lynch, Debbie Sho, Lynda Munfrada, Susanne Lakin, and our tactful leader Kathy Ide. You received my new ideas for The Dunn Deal with enthusiasm and insightful suggestions, igniting my excitement.

My dear friend, the incredible author/editor Susanne Lakin—winner of the 2009 Zondervan writing contest and expert proponent of the fairy tale—you'll never know how much your timely emails have meant. I am indebted for your insight, knowledge, creative assistance, editing, and right-on fixes to problem spots. Thanks for never allowing me to quit.

Agent Les Stobbe steered me clear of the dark side of occult spirituality, which never belonged in a cozy mystery in the first place. Thank you, Linda Nathan at Logos Word Designs, for discerning words about the inherent danger of the occult.

My dear friends at the Stockton Bible Study Fellowship Day Women's class, how can I thank you enough for years of intercessory prayer? Your affirmation and support has been my lifeline at times. Thank you Pam Regan for encouraging me to reach for the stars.

Special recognition must go to my excellent critique partner, Marcia Lahti, for her timely contribution. Thanks for dropping everything to read for days. You are a true pal.

Kudos to Scott Hanna for the last-minute rescue affected by his computer skill.

I greatly appreciate the input and guidance of Rochelle Carter and the Ellechor Publishing House team. What an awesome group of dedicated believers! Thank you, God, for connecting us.

Most of all to my Lord and Savior, Jesus Christ—The Blessed Word of God, Author and Finisher of my salvation—I humbly submit my offering of eternal thanks for filling my head with words to string together and a burning desire to speak for Truth.

DISCUSSION QUESTIONS

1. Constance Boyd is a good and generous person, providing for the needs of countless orphans. She sincerely believes that when she dies, she will go to heaven for her good deeds. Does the content of what you believe matter or is it only necessary that your faith be sincere?

2. Is there one Truth or many truths about life, death and God? What about people who say, "That may be right for you, but for me…?" Is Truth relative?

3. How does a person find Truth about God?

4. Zora Jane proclaims God's Truth with boldness. Is this an effective way to witness? Should the Truth always be delivered straight or should it sometimes be watered down?

5. Are all religions true? If not, how can you tell which ones speak for God?

6. What's the difference between belonging to a religion or denomination and being a Christian?

7. What about the Bible? Is it relevant and truthful for today? All of it or only parts of it? If you think you should obey only certain parts, how do you decide which parts to follow?

8. Jesse Sterling suffered from hearing loss that distorted sound. Often what he heard wasn't what was actually said. Does this have a spiritual application? If faith comes by hearing the Word of God, how do people sometimes filter Truth through wishful thinking? Or rationalization? Or intellectualization?

9. Did Christine Sterling learn any lessons in The Dunn Deal? What about her inclination to go against her husband's wishes? Who should be the head of the family according to the Bible? Why does God desire that?

10. Did you see yourself in any of the characters of this book? Which character did you identify with the most? The least? Why?

Parrish the Thought

A man in the ladies' room?

I slipped on a take-charge attitude and shoved through the mumbling huddle of waiting women. Past pointing fingers and impatient faces, I managed to enter the three-stall bathroom off the church foyer. Sure enough, scuffed boots with significant holes protruded toes up from under the handicap stall. I bent to inspect them and found one hiked up pant leg revealing a calf with dark coarse hair. Definitely male.

A neon alert blinked warning in my brain. I censored the unchristian exclamation that almost tumbled from my lips. Where else but California would you find a man sprawled on the ladies room floor?

Of all the nerve! He had also managed to track red Nevada County clay onto our clean shiny floor. A whiff of alcohol and cigarettes reached out to me like clawing fingers. I didn't try to disguise my disgust. "Excuse me, sir. Can I help you?"

The shoes didn't move.

By then, a pack of female onlookers had congregated behind me. At the sound of my voice, they all spoke at once like a flock of hens. I faced them, waving my hands and clearing my throat. Their chatter ceased as quickly as it had started. "I'll get help. Meanwhile, please use the restroom downstairs." I produced a smile and pointed in the general vicinity of the stairs.

Tilted heads and squinty eyes faced me, but after one or two women turned to leave, the rest followed—a few sending back questioning frowns. They weren't the only ones wondering who put me in charge. Why did I always do this? Must be Jesse's influence. Leave it to me to marry someone with a compulsion for fixing everyone else's problems.

Heaving a long sigh, I returned to my inspection. With the tip of my pointer finger, I inched the stall door open just far enough for a clear view.

The stranger lay on his back beside the commode, eyes closed, lips a thin bloodless line. Tousled gray-flecked hair jutted from his head like greasy straw. An angular jaw rendered a hard edge to his face. One arm lay beneath him with the other bent so his hand rested on his chest. Good thing he chose the handicap stall. The other tiny cubicles barely contained space to sit. Even so, how could he sleep on this hard floor?

When I released the stall door, it clapped shut and the sound echoed through the empty room. I stuck my head out the ladies room door. A few people glanced toward me. I ignored their puzzled expressions and focused on my husband across the foyer at the sanctuary doors. "Jesse!" I shouted over the chatter. "Come here!" When I motioned for him, my purse thumped the door. More heads turned toward me. Those who knew me smiled and waved before returning to their conversations.

Jesse arched both eyebrows and peered over his glasses, sending a nonverbal message to his fellow usher on the opposite side of the doorway. The other man nodded, slightly lifting his brows in reply. Jesse shrugged. I rolled my eyes. Is it any wonder men are no good with words? They can communicate just fine with looks and grunts.

Certain that Jesse would come eventually, I hurried back to the stall. Despite the clapping, clicking, and thumping—as well as other general commotion—the interloper hadn't moved. How could he sleep through all that noise? And how did this filthy person find his way into our pristine church in the first place? I hacked an exaggerated cough. "Sir? Do you know you're in the ladies room?"

The man still didn't budge. Must be sleeping off a binge.

What could be keeping Jesse? I stuck my head out the ladies room door again. Looking as if I'd never called, Jesse stood planted at his appointed station, passing out bulletins to Sunday morning stragglers. When I delivered a second—more insistent—summons, he threw me a scowl. I dashed out, intercepting a woman I didn't know as she headed toward the ladies room. After a quick point toward the downstairs restroom, I stomped across the foyer, two-inch heels banging the floor. Jesse would have to get the man out of there in a hurry or some unsuspecting woman would be in for a most unpleasant surprise.

"Jesse! Please. Come now. I need you." I yanked his sleeve to drag his six-foot frame down to my five-feet-one-and-a-half inches so I could whisper in his ear. "There's a man on the floor in the ladies room."

He lifted one eyebrow and stared blankly.

Even with his hearing aids in place, he had to read lips to know what I said. Drawing a deep breath, I faced him and spoke louder. "Help me. In the ladies room."

Jesse's hazel eyes sparkled with amusement. "You never needed my help in there before."

With one final tug on his sleeve, I pointed across the carpeted space. "Please!" Then I darted off to check on the interloper, hoping my speed would communicate the necessity for immediate action.

Pulling the stall door wider, I braced it with my hip. Then I bent as low as my Sunday clothes allowed and inspected the unfortunate creature. Beneath his eyelids, his discolored skin suggested either poor health or severely neglected hygiene. An old scar lined one cheek from ear to chin. A dingy leather glove fully a size too small stretched over the visible hand. Scraped knuckles peeked out through tattered holes. Indigent, probably a homeless person.

I nudged his shoe with my foot. "Hey. Wake up." Should I check his breathing? The mere thought of touching him wrinkled my nose. Why didn't I carry plastic gloves in my purse for emergencies? I dropped to one knee with my fanny sticking out the door. My hand hovered three inches above his chest like a helicopter with no place to land while I pondered how to check his heart through all those layers of clothing. Unable to decide, I gingerly lowered my head until one ear brushed his chest. I held my breath and listened. An involuntary shudder shivered over me as I envisioned lice relocating. In spite of my magnanimous sacrifice, I heard nothing.

Nor did I hear the tiny red drop that splashed into an expanding crimson puddle under the man's head. I gasped. Had he fallen? My brain connected the blood to an old Columbo TV show where the rumpled detective discovered a bleeding victim. If his heart could still pump blood, it meant he wasn't dead. Unconscious, maybe. But not dead. Colombo was never wrong.

I couldn't hold my breath forever. Grasping one side of the stall to steady myself, I teetered to a stand. When I did so, I inhaled a huge gulp of alcohol, stale tobacco, urine, body odor, and who knows what else—a cloying odor worse than sour milk left overnight on a sponge. I recoiled at the stench. Some primitive instinct made me push backwards until I'd lengthened the distance between my nose and the offensive smell. When I stopped, I landed on my most padded part. Not a dignified position for a middle-aged woman.

Get a grip, Christine. Much as I wanted to flee, that bleeding had to be stanched. His life might depend on it. That meant I'd have to touch him again. I probably shouldn't move him, though. Didn't want to risk compounding the condition.

Come on. You can do this. Concentrate. Mouth to mouth? Nausea. The room began to spin.

Jesse flung open the door and bellowed. "Any ladies in here?"

Relief brought clarity and annoyance. Ladies. Was he making a commentary on my position? "Only me." I replied with as much vigor as I could muster.

Jesse didn't so much as glance at the shoes under the stall or hunt for the man attached to them. He simply reached for my hand and pulled me off the floor. "Where's this man you're so worried about? And what're you doing down there? Did you see a mouse?"

Mouse? "Would I be on the floor if I'd seen a mouse?" I jabbed a finger at the stall.

Jesse's lips formed an "O" without sound escaping. He squared his shoulders and yanked open the door. While he conducted his examination, I took up a post inside the ladies room door, pacing like a caged tiger.

In less than a minute, Jesse backed out the handicap stall. "He's breathing. Barely." A few steps into the room, he stopped and fixed his gaze on the floor, expelling a long breath. The set of his jaw spoke volumes about his state of mind. After thirty-eight years as his wife, I knew that expression—he didn't know what to do either.

Giving the man a backward glance, Jesse pushed past me and raced out of the ladies room. He stepped briskly into the foyer, calling over his shoulder. "I'll get help. My cell phone's in the car, but there's a phone in the church office. Meanwhile, don't let anyone in here."

As if I would.

I couldn't remember where I'd left my cell phone. I never remembered to carry the stupid thing. If I had it in my purse, I wouldn't have remembered to charge it.

Minutes later, paramedics trooped through the front of the foyer. I left my guard post and sank onto a bench near the double doors, far enough from the action to be out of the way.

The opening strains of a hymn floated from the sanctuary. "They Will Know We Are Christians by Our Love."

My stomach gurgled while I watched the efficient comings and goings of the emergency team. Their frozen expressions radiated professionalism—just another day on the job. How did they cope with the constant parade of human misery they encountered on a daily basis? Take this particular man. How did he arrive at such a state anyway? Not the injury. That certainly could have been the result of an accidental fall. Maybe he slipped on a wet spot. What happened before? What catalyst made him give up striving for a productive life? I didn't understand that part.

Being liberated from prejudice, I cared about this stranger's welfare. Didn't I get Jesse to help him even though the man didn't belong here?

Muted sounds of rescue filtered through the closed ladies room door. Who was our stranger? Tilting my head, I blinked at the door. Maybe he'd once been an important person. Betrayal and financial reverses left him broken and hopeless. His family deserted him. In desperation, he turned to the bottle for consolation. I rested my chin on one hand, elbow in my lap, while visions of sad possibilities danced through my thoughts like rotten sugarplums.

After several minutes, I shook off the wanderings of my wild imagination. What did it matter anyway? Soon the interloper would be gone and I'd never see him again. No need to pursue his sorry situation one step further. Besides, after pursuing two murders in the past five years, I promised Jesse I'd give up what he called snooping. (I called it sleuthing.) I straightened, brushing a speck of lint from my skirt. None of my business.

"Yes, they will know we are Christians by our love," sang the congregation as paramedics wheeled the still unconscious man out of the ladies room.

Be merciful to him, Lord.

The squeak of gurney wheels echoed off the soaring ceiling and disappeared into reverent silence. Time to get busy. Afraid that my friends might use that restroom before someone got the mess cleaned up, I returned with rags and a broom. The puddle of blood would be disquieting, to say the least. That reminded me of contamination from "blood-born pathogens"—something I learned from my nurse daughter—so I rooted through the supply closet for plastic gloves. Finding a suitable pair at last, I snapped them on and grabbed the bleach to disinfect the area. A person couldn't be too careful.

Back in the rest room, I kicked off my heels and tackled the mess. On hands and knees scrubbing away dirt and blood, a sparkle caught my eye. There. Behind the toilet, a small object gleamed like Rudolph's nose. After slight hesitation, I bent to retrieve it—a lady's clip earring with a bright scarlet stone nestled in a gold-filigree setting.

I fished hot pink readers out of my pocket for a better look. Nobody did filigree work anymore. Too expensive. The clip looked old-fashioned too. Could be antique. Too red for a garnet, it might be a ruby. I turned it in my hand. That would be one huge ruby—at least four carats. I held it to the light. Very clear.

With a sigh, I dropped it into my jacket pocket and continued cleaning. I would deliver the earring to the church's lost-and-found after service. As I cleaned, questions circled my head like an annoying cloud of gnats. How did the earring get there? Did the homeless man bring it? How would a man like that come into possession of such a fine piece of real jewelry?

Within minutes, all trace of the unfortunate occurrence had been removed. Only my questions remained.